The Diary
from the
Cottage
by the
Loch

BOOKS BY KENNEDY KERR

LOCH CAMERON

The Cottage by the Loch
A Secret at the Cottage by the Loch

MAGPIE COVE

The House at Magpie Cove
Secrets of Magpie Cove
Daughters of Magpie Cove
Dreams of Magpie Cove

A Spell of Murder

Kennedy Kerr

The Diary
from the
Cottage
by the
Loch

bookouture

Published by Bookouture in 2023

An imprint of Storyfire Ltd.
Carmelite House
50 Victoria Embankment
London EC4Y 0DZ

www.bookouture.com

ISBN: 978-1-83790-423-5
eBook ISBN: 978-1-83790-422-8

For Beccy, with the bluest eyes

PROLOGUE

Carrie would always remember the song playing on the radio.

Turn it up, she'd said.

Her sister had refused. *The weather's terrible. I can't see through this rain.*

I don't know if anyone's ever told you, but your ears don't affect your ability to see, Carrie had replied, twisting the dial so that the music filled the car. How she regretted that flippancy now.

Smartass, her sister had snapped. *It affects my perception. We'll never get to this bloody wedding at this rate.*

And when you need me in the dead of night, she'd sung, turning to perform to her sister, as if she held a microphone, *I'm just a minute away... ooh, ooh.*

Carrie. Turn it off. I need to concentrate. Her sister had frowned, leaning forward to peer out of the rain-lashed windscreen. *The air con isn't working. The screen's fogging up.*

Don't be scared of the night... Carrie had sung along, making a face at Claire.

They were already dressed for their friends' wedding in Devon, though Claire was driving in her bare feet instead of the heels she'd brought to wear. It wasn't night-time, it was early afternoon, but the sky was black and the rain was torrential.

Lovely day for it, Carrie had said when she'd got into her sister's Mini that morning.

By the time they'd got to Devon, the roads had become narrower and narrower, and now they were on a single-width road with hedges on each side that totally hid the fields beyond them. The road twisted, on and on, with no crossroads or junctions.

Please stop singing. If someone comes the other way, I'd have to reverse for about a mile, Claire had grumbled, just before the road widened out. *Ah, thank god. More room to manoeuvre.*

And when you need me in the dead of night, ooh, ooh, Carrie had repeated. She was bored. It had been a long drive from London.

The rain lashed down, impervious to anything but itself.

Carrie, I'm serious.

Whatever. Carrie had rolled her eyes. It was hard to think about that now. All of it was excruciating to remember, but especially that moment. Because it had been the last thing she had ever said to her sister.

Claire had said something indecipherable, panic on her face, and swerved.

Carrie remembered the sound of squealing tyres, and then the impact.

There was a huge, ear-splitting crash. That was all that Carrie remembered, that and a sense of the car being spun around like a fairground ride.

Afterwards, she learnt that a local lad had been driving at fifty miles an hour without his lights on and gone straight into them. It was the kind of road that was often quiet and the locals knew it so well that they didn't think anything of bombing along it at speeds usually meant for A roads.

She woke up in hospital, alone. Her ribs were cracked and

she'd fractured her collarbone, but apart from that, she was all right.

Claire wasn't.

Carrie wasn't even fully conscious when Claire passed away. When she'd come to, pain slicing her in half, she'd asked for Claire, but it wasn't until later when a nurse administering her pain medication told her what had happened. *I'm sorry for your loss*, she'd said, her eyes sad. *Is there anyone we can contact? There wasn't anything we could see in your sister's things.*

No, it's just me. Carrie had looked out at the rain in shock, not knowing what to do or how to react. *There's no one else.*

The boy was charged, but the case would probably take forever to go to court. Carrie had felt for him: he was just eighteen. Just beginning life. Yes, he'd been stupid. But everyone was stupid at eighteen.

Despite that, he'd taken Claire's life with his stupidity. He'd probably get a prison sentence and by the time he'd completed it, still have his life ahead of him, but she wouldn't.

And when you need me in the dead of night, I'm just a minute away... ooh, ooh.

If she'd turned the radio down like Claire had asked, her sister might still be alive. She should have listened to Claire. She should have considered her feelings, but now, it was too late.

Carrie knew she hadn't been a good sister to Claire for years. It had been stupid of her – just as stupid as that eighteen-year-old boy in the car he'd probably owned for less than a year – to be holding a grudge against her sister: the one family member she had left.

Now, it would always be too late for Carrie and Claire to rebuild their relationship.

It would always be too late for Carrie to say, *I'm sorry.*

ONE

Let yourself in. Key's under the plant pot.

Carrie Anderson pulled the note off the blue-painted wooden door, carefully unsticking its tape from the paint so as not to damage it, and nudged the closest plant pot with her foot.

Sure enough, halfway under, there was a small plastic bag which, when she picked it up, contained two keys on a keyring for the whitewashed cottage that looked out over the still waters of Loch Cameron. When Carrie opened the bag, she found that the keyring's fob featured the logo of Loch Cameron Distillery, and a picture of a woman's face with the words OLD MAIDS superimposed on it.

She remembered the whisky distillery; lots of these small Scottish villages were home to them. She didn't know a huge amount about whisky, but she'd picked up some knowledge here and there, like everyone with a Scottish family had. Her dad, when he was alive, had drunk whisky. He'd drunk it every summer when they'd visited Great-Aunt Maud when she and Claire were little.

But that was a long time ago, and it had been a while since she'd visited the village.

Carrie let herself into the cottage, shaking rain from her waterproof jacket and stepping out of her boots on the welcome mat. It was October, so she'd come prepared for bad weather, packing plenty of thick jumpers, thick socks and sturdy trainers.

Her great-aunt had lived just five cottages away from this one. Sadly, when Maud died, the cottage had returned to the Laird, who owned it. Carrie remembered that he owned almost all the property here, most people renting their houses and cottages from him. For whatever reason, though, this little cottage on the same cracked mud walkway as Great-Aunt Maud's had been available to rent on a holiday website, and when she'd seen it, she'd booked it instantly.

Inside the cottage, Carrie was pleased to find that it was as cosy as Great-Aunt Maud's had been. Gretchen Ross's cottage on Queen's Point – the strip of land that ran alongside Loch Cameron, with a tongue-like promontory that reached over the loch, where Gretchen's cottage stood – had just one large bedroom, whereas Great-Aunt Maud's had had two. Even then, it had meant that Claire and Carrie had slept in Great-Aunt Maud's old-fashioned lounge, while their parents had taken the small second bedroom. Carrie and Claire had always loved staying there, not caring about their squeaky pull-out beds with their archaic metal frames, or the roll-out mattresses that made them sneeze. They had loved waking up on cold mornings and watching their breath make clouds in front of them, then waiting for their great-aunt to rouse herself and build up the log fire in the old fireplace and then make them hot chocolate.

Ideally, Carrie would have liked to go back to Great-Aunt Maud's old place, but Gretchen's cottage was a close second. It was a familiar-feeling place where she could hide away and not see anyone else, if she didn't feel like it; a place she could be alone and walk in nature without being disturbed.

A place she could grieve, and a place that reminded her of happier times.

Carrie dropped her bag inside the door and stood for a moment at the entrance to the small lounge, taking it in. There was always the risk that an old Scottish cottage might smell of mildew and be full of spiders, but this place seemed to have had some recent love and care, and a thorough dusting, which was a relief. Floral wallpaper covered the cosy sitting room. An authentic-looking fireplace with light green tiles patterned with pink roses acted as a centrepiece, and a comfy upholstered chair with a hydrangea pattern, a vintage pink chaise longue and a plain cream sofa took up the rest of the space. There was a brass standard lamp with a green velvet lampshade in the corner that Carrie flicked on, alleviating the slight gloom in the cottage from the rain outside.

Loch Cameron was difficult to get to by train, and by car it was at the end of a long, winding unlit road through vast hills covered in purple heather that it was unwise to take by night. It wasn't close to anywhere in particular, apart from similarly small villages, and often, when Carrie had mentioned it to people over the years, hardly anyone had heard of it. Yet it was the place where she had been happiest in her life, before illness had taken her mother when Carrie and Claire were just twelve years old.

After their mum had died, they hadn't come back to Loch Cameron. Great-Aunt Maud had stayed in touch, writing them letters at Christmas and on their birthdays, but Carrie and Claire's dad had refused to take them back to visit. Great-Aunt Maud was their mother's aunt, he'd said, and now that Mum was gone, he didn't have to pretend to like that mildewed old cottage and the even more mildewed old aunt.

The girls had gone back, once, when they were eighteen and their dad had said he couldn't stop them. But by the time they got there, Maud had already died: they hadn't known.

Carrie sighed as she remembered her and Claire driving all the way up from Manchester in Claire's old Mini – her first car.

She'd always loved them. When they'd got to Loch Cameron, they'd forgotten exactly where the cottage was, so they'd had to ask at the inn. A kindly woman in a twinset and a tweed skirt had directed them up to Queen's Point, where they'd discovered Maud's cottage empty.

In Gretchen's cottage kitchen, Carrie discovered a blue leather Chesterfield-style chair which faced a blackened fireplace. The armchair looked comfortable, despite the fact that it was losing some of its stuffing. A large wooden dresser stood at one end of the kitchen, showcasing a beautiful array of vintage crockery, and the large window overlooked a rainy and slightly overgrown cottage garden.

Carrie filled a copper kettle with water and placed it on the old range cooker, looking for an ignition button. She couldn't see one, but there was a box of matches next to the hob, so she turned on the gas and lit it. A row of mugs and a floral porcelain teapot sat on a shelf above the wooden kitchen worktop, and there was a chipped white tin marked 'tea' in block blue letters next to it that Carrie opened, letting out the aromatic tang of tea-leaves. She shook some into the teapot.

She needed to find a village shop of some kind, at least to get a pint of milk and a loaf of bread. She hadn't planned much further than getting here, but now Carrie realised that she would have to be at least vaguely organised and remember where to buy food. She dimly recalled some local shops and a high street, and walking down into the village with Great-Aunt Maud, who had seemed to know everyone.

She sat down in a floral easy chair next to the kitchen table and looked at her phone. There was a message on the holiday rental app from the owner of the cottage, Gretchen Ross, hoping that she had found the cottage and let herself in okay.

I've arrived, Carrie messaged back. *Just making tea in the kitchen.*

Wonderful, the woman replied quickly. *I've asked a neigh-*

*hour to pop by with some essentials for you, but you can get food
in the village and I've left the number for the milkman on the
table with other contact numbers, if you need them.*

You read my mind, Gretchen Ross, Carrie thought, tiredly.
She'd flown up to Edinburgh from London on an early flight
and hired a car from the airport, but it had still taken hours to
get there and she'd been exhausted even before setting out. The
grief made Carrie heavy, as if she were made of lead. She could
hardly get out of bed for weeks after the crash, and that wasn't
just because she'd fractured her collarbone. In fact, the hospital
had let her go home after just a few days, though she hadn't
wanted to. She'd wanted to stay, because the hospital was the
last place she'd seen Claire's face, and the last place that Claire
had ever been.

Claire's sudden absence in her life felt as though she'd lost
her legs in the accident, or her heart had been cut out, but she
was still, somehow, alive.

After, Carrie had had a recurring dream of Claire walking
around the hospital, looking for a way out. She was trapped
there, like a ghost looking for the light. In the dream, Carrie
always tried to reach out for Claire, but her sister seemed
unaware of her presence, despite Carrie screaming Claire's
name as loud as she could.

Once she got home, and after a week in bed feeling woozy
from the hospital-prescribed painkillers, Carrie had realised
that she couldn't stay there. She shared a house with two coun-
sellors, Patty and Marcus, who she'd met while on a meditation
course her friend Suzy had dragged her to. They'd been looking
for a flatmate at the same time Carrie's lease had run out on her
old place. They were both really sweet, but they had begun
therapising her as soon as she'd got home. Carrie knew they'd
meant well, but the pressure to share and talk was too much
for her.

Do you want to talk about it?

No.
We're here if you want to talk.
I don't.
It's not good to bottle up your emotions.
Just leave me alone.

All she wanted to do was hole up in her room and not come out. She survived on eating macaroni and cheese from a box – bright yellow comfort food – which she sneaked into the kitchen and made with milk in a saucepan at night after Patty and Marcus had gone to bed. She stockpiled energy bars, apples and chocolate in her room, and apart from using the bathroom, stayed in bed under the covers.

Two weeks after the accident, Carrie realised that not only did she not want to be in her flat anymore, but she also couldn't go back to work. She'd been temping at an accountancy firm for six months. It was okay, nothing special, but it paid the bills and Carrie liked the fact that she didn't think about the job when she wasn't there. But even after her sick leave had ended, and she could have at least started doing some work remotely, Carrie was completely unable to function. She could hardly lift her head from the pillow, let alone book in meetings in the online calendar, type up minutes or order in catering, all of which was usually in a day's work. It felt as though all life had been sucked out of her the moment Claire died.

Meanwhile, Patty and Marcus had fussed around her like concerned hens, trying to feed her soup and make her do guided visualisations, until she'd begged them to leave her alone. She'd gone online in a fit of desperation and messaged Gretchen Ross to see if her cottage was available for months at a time. Gretchen had replied that, yes, the cottage was currently free, and she was happy for it to be rented long-term.

Carrie had some savings that she could live off until she was ready to temp again, plus the cottage was less expensive than her London flatshare, and so she'd given Patty and Marcus her month's notice and moved out. She'd never owned much, and none of the furniture was hers, so it wasn't hard to pare everything she needed down to two bags and a few boxes, that she'd couriered up separately.

There was still Claire's flat and all of her belongings to sort out at some point, but Carrie wasn't ready for that yet. Not by a long way. The cottage would be home now, for a few months at least – until she felt like rejoining the human race.

TWO

'Oh. Excuse me.'

The man hadn't seen Carrie standing there: that was obvious. He'd charged into the small grocery store like the proverbial bull in a china shop and almost knocked over a pyramid of tinned peas as he entered, holding out a redundant hand to steady them.

If they want to fall, one manly hand isn't going to stop them, Carrie had thought as she bent over to choose a loaf of bread from the shelf. And, then, *wham!* He'd walked straight into her.

She'd caught the impact on her hip, mostly. It didn't hurt, but she was instantly irritated at the way the man apparently thought his time was more important than anyone else's, and at his boorish barging around in the small shop.

She stood up, frowning. 'I don't excuse you, actually,' she said. She was wearing her waterproof mac and boots, jeans and a Fair Isle jumper underneath. Her dyed red bob was probably messy – she'd battled the wind and rain in and out of the car, and she probably hadn't brushed her hair properly for a number of days. Most of the time, she just ran her fingers through it now and again. Pampering was Claire's habit, not hers. The thought

of her sister made her feel dizzy, and so she banished the
thought from her mind as quickly as it had come, and glared at
the man again.

'What?' The man frowned back at her. He had dark brown
hair, longish around the ears and onto his collar, and a short
beard. He was wearing jeans and a black jumper, and was probably about her age or a little older, judging from the lines
around his eyes.

'I said to look where you're going. This is a small shop,'
Carrie said, raising her voice. She didn't have the filter for
politeness right now. 'You almost had those tins over when you
came in, and there's elderly people around. Just pay attention to
your surroundings. Manners are free.'

'Oh. I didn't expect a lesson in manners today. Thank you
so much for the education,' the man snapped. He had an
English accent, like her, and not the broad Scots of the locals.
'Now, if you'll excuse me, I'm in a hurry. I need some fresh
parsley.'

'Seems like an essential purchase,' Carrie muttered to
herself, thinking how ridiculous this man was to come and make
such a fuss because of *parsley*. 'Heaven forbid your scrambled
eggs might go ungarnished.'

'What?' the man repeated, looking genuinely confused this
time. 'I'm sorry. Is there a problem I'm not aware of? I need
parsley. I don't see that it's any of your business.'

'Oh. It's not.' Carrie walked away, past the man. She heard
him mutter something under his breath, but ignored it. *Rude.*

After finding milk and a few other bits and pieces –
bananas, peanut butter, some biscuits to go with her tea and
some cheese and cold meats – she found the till and waited to
pay, noting that the man was now in front of her. He paid the
sales assistant and left, holding three large bunches of fresh
parsley. Carrie watched as he jogged away up the high street.

The sales assistant, a teenager wearing a blue tabard over a floral polyester dress, and a name tag stating she was DEBBIE, must have noticed Carrie watching the man with the parsley run up the street, or she was bored, because she said, 'Rory McCrae. He's a chef in the restaurant up on the hill.'

'Who? That guy?' Carrie narrowed her eyes at Rory's retreating form.

'Aye. Always runs in here about this time, lookin' fer somethin' he's run oot of. Yesterday it was carrots. Got to be the local ones, though, or he doesnae want 'em.'

'Oh, right. Hence the parsley.' Carrie carefully finished putting her groceries on the counter and got a shopping bag out of her pocket as Debbie started passing the items through the scanner.

Carrie still wore a sling when she was at home, but she'd taken it off to come to the shops, which she was regretting. It had been hard enough lining everything up carefully on the conveyor; now she had to pack it all in a bag.

'Aye. He's no' bad, really. When ye get tae know him.' Debbie watched Carrie as she fumbled with her shopping bag. 'D'ye want a hand?'

'No, I'm all right. Thanks. Well, I doubt I'll be getting to know the guy. But, thanks for the heads-up,' Carrie said, reaching for her purse. *She's a proud one,* her great-aunt's voice sounded in her memory. Carrie had never really considered herself *proud*: she'd just had little opportunity to depend on other people. Except Claire.

She paid, and headed back to her hire car. She also doubted she'd be trying out the restaurant on the hill anytime soon. She wasn't exactly in the right frame of mind for fine dining, or for being among other people for very long. A quick visit to the shops every couple of days would do her just fine; in between, she was happy to live on bread and cheese, with the occasional biscuit and cup of tea. That was as much contact as she wanted with the outside world right now. She certainly wasn't up for random meetings with the boorish local chef. *That's very much off the menu,* she thought, surprised that she'd inadvertently thought of a pun.

Carrie's grief at losing Claire was almost all-consuming, and, in all seriousness, she just didn't have the bandwidth for anything else. She returned to her car, slung her shopping on the passenger seat and sat down in the driver's seat. As soon as she closed the door, she burst into tears.

THREE

Carrie spent most of the next few days on the sofa under a snuggly blanket. All her limbs felt leaden, still, and she slept, on and off, for most of the daylight hours. The pain in her collar-bone woke her up in the night when the medication wore off; it was reasonable, in the day, as long as she took them on time. The pain seemed to eat up the pills as if it was a hungry monster from a child's book, consuming the tablets she swallowed dutifully with water every four hours and threatening her with its teeth in the night when it was allowed out of its medically controlled cage.

Once the pain woke her at night, she found it hard to go back to sleep. On the first night, she lay on the comfortable mattress atop the cast iron double bed and stared out of the little bedroom window, which, like the kitchen, looked over the garden. The overgrown space was a riot of flowers and shrubs. In the dark, of course, she couldn't see the colour of the dusky pink and yellow roses, the blue delphiniums, or the lilac and white lupins, but she remembered their vividness: it was almost shocking to her eyes, so used to city greys.

At night, the garden rustled with the movements of mice,

hedgehogs and, probably, other creatures looking for food.
Occasionally, there was a crying sound that had startled Carrie
until she remembered the cries of the foxes outside her London
flat. Like the foxes, she had become mostly nocturnal; it was
grief that had prompted her transformation to a creature of the
dark. Night in Loch Cameron was quieter than the day, and the
blackness and the quiet somehow brought her feelings even
closer to the surface.

Carrie could ignore her feelings in the daytime, and in the
evenings, she brought her laptop into bed and binged trashy TV
reality shows: dating, home renovations, makeovers. When her
brain couldn't take any more TV, she'd switch off the laptop and
stare blearily into the corner of the lamplit bedroom until she
fell asleep.

There was a reality show following the lives of five new
nurses which she watched with interest: as a child, she'd always
wanted to be a nurse. She had annoyed Claire for several years
by trying to play hospital in her little white nurse cap and dress
with the red cross on the front. Claire was generally an
unwilling patient, preferring to play outside, climb trees, collect
pebbles and come in muddy at the end of the day.

When the phase had ended, Carrie had moved on to books
and dolls, and then, when their mum had passed away, she had
stopped playing altogether. But she had always still liked the
idea of nursing: caring for others when they needed it and
making things all right felt useful. That idea, of making things
all right, fulfilled something in Carrie after her mum had died.
The nurses at the hospital had been so kind to her and Claire
when their mum was in hospital in those final days: walking
them to the vending machines and buying them sweets, playing
catch with them in the hospital corridors, trying to distract them
from what was happening and from their father, weeping at
their mum's bedside. The idea that she could do that for
someone else in the future had made her feel slightly better.

The cottage bedroom was cute, like the rest of the place. The white-painted cast iron bedstead suited the cottage vibe, and the plain wood floors were stained with varnish. A rose-pink rug stretched under the bed and out of both sides, giving Carrie somewhere warm to stand when she occasionally hauled herself from under the thick hand-stitched quilts. In the corner, another brass standard lamp stood, and a built-in cupboard in the corner opened into a surprisingly large recess where Carrie had thrown her bags when she'd arrived. She hadn't unpacked any of her clothes, even though there was plenty of cupboard space, and a rail with hangers too. She just didn't have the energy.

The cottage was so quiet that Carrie jumped at the slightest sound – the cries of the foxes outside, foraging for the apples that had fallen from the tree, the rustling of the hedgehogs in the fallen leaves, or an occasional dog walker passing. It wasn't spooky, per se, but she wasn't used to how quiet it was out here. Sharing her flat in London with Patty and Marcus hadn't been anywhere near as... still.

But that was what she'd wanted. Somewhere peaceful, where she could fall apart unnoticed after losing Claire. Because Claire had always been the one she would go to when anything was wrong, even if they had grown apart in the past few years. Claire was the one that made it *all right*, who knew her better than anyone else in the world.

They'd been bound tightly ever since their mother died. Their dad had been there, but he was like a ghost most of the time. Carrie understood. He wasn't a bad father, particularly, though he drank too much, and more or less ignored them after their mum's death. He was just dealing with loss the best way he knew how – which was to retreat into his private world of pain.

Because of this the girls had started to learn to look after themselves: cooking, cleaning, shopping for what they needed.

When they got older, they took the bus to their secondary school and back every day, made their dinner and breakfast. There were no lifts to school from a kind father, no picking them up from their friends' houses after parties, or helping them revise for their exams. Their dad still loved them – probably – but he couldn't show it anymore. The girls knew it and, without ever discussing it, they learned to rely on each other. They were each other's support system, from braiding each other's hair before school every day to checking each other's homework, doing their laundry and cooking their meals. Carrie was there for Claire, and Claire was there for Carrie, and that was just how it was.

Until it wasn't.

I wish I could talk to you, Carrie thought, as she stared into the corner of the room. *You're the person I talked to about everything. Even when we weren't talking, you would have been there if I needed you.*

She picked at a hole in the sweatshirt she'd been wearing for the past three days. 'I never told you I was sorry about being distant. But I was. I am. And I wish you could hear me now,' she said, out loud this time. She knew Claire wasn't there. But, somehow, saying the words helped her feel that, in some way, perhaps Claire would hear.

'I'm not talking about the crash. Though I am sorry for that too. Of course, I am.' Carrie felt the emotion catch in her throat, and she struggled to keep her voice steady. 'I was a brat. I should have turned the music down. I should have listened to you.'

She took a deep breath, then continued. 'But I mean the other thing. You know what. I'm sorry.' She sighed, and two tears rolled down her cheeks. She hadn't washed her face or cleaned her teeth for days. She was a mess, but she didn't care. Nothing mattered anymore. 'Please. I wish you could forgive me. If I could go back and change it, I would. I'd change so much. But I can't.'

She started to sob, and the tears racked her body so that it shook. Carrie felt as though she might be sick; there was so much grief in her that she felt as though it would never all come out.

She hadn't cried at the funeral. She'd just about been able to stand through it, two weeks after the accident, and maybe the pain had distracted her from her feelings then. Or maybe it had been shock. Everyone talked about the stages of grief, but she didn't know if shock was one of them, or whether it was just part of a person's brain trying and failing to take in the enormity of losing someone so close to them.

At Claire's funeral, she'd felt a strange sense of unreality, as if she'd look up any minute and Claire would be standing on the opposite side of the grave, casting a flower into the hole in front of her, and it would be someone else's funeral. Someone else that had been lost forever.

The thing that was torturing Carrie the most, though, was the thought that the accident had been her fault. And that she could have saved her sister.

She had failed Claire twice, and she would never forgive herself.

FOUR

After four days under the covers, Carrie made herself leave the cottage.

You need fresh air, she berated herself, wrapping up in jeans, boots, a thick sweatshirt and her coat on top. She ran her hand through her hair and looked at herself despairingly in the mirror. She needed to get her colour re-done, and a cut wouldn't hurt either. But it felt like ages since she'd thought about anything like that.

Doesn't matter, she thought, grimly. *Doesn't matter what you look like. Hairstyles don't matter. Or clothes.* Nothing mattered anymore, without Claire.

The only reason she was leaving the cottage was because she had run out of food, and she hadn't been able to sleep at all the night before. Being up all night and then being exhausted and in pain all day wasn't great. At least if she got out for a while, the air and a walk might make sleep come easier. That was all she wanted. At least if she was asleep, she could forget Claire for a while.

Well, here goes nothing, she thought, pulling the cottage door closed behind her and making her way up the little path through the cottage garden that wrapped around the house. It was full of wildflowers, planted seemingly at random, and rose bushes that bordered the edge of the property alongside other shrubs and bushes: Carrie had no idea what they were, but she could recognise roses, even if they weren't in bloom. Roses had been her great-aunt's favourite flower.

Carrie remembered her Great-Aunt Maud letting Carrie and Claire use her special secateurs in the garden, showing them how to cut the tough rose stems and avoid the thorns. She had arranged vases of beautiful roses around the house in the summertime when her cottage garden was in full bloom: Carrie still couldn't smell roses without missing her. She'd taken such good care of the rose bushes, cutting them back every autumn, feeding them special mulch and covering them over when there was a frost.

As Carrie walked along, taking in deep breaths of the sharp, cold air, she tried to steady her nerves. Her heart was hammering and her palms were sweaty. Just the act of leaving the cottage had put her into a state of panic: grieving had made her into a hermit. In her normal life, Carrie would have thought nothing of going for a walk through a rural village. It wasn't exactly anything to get nervous about, but, nonetheless, she was having to take deep breaths and clench her hands into fists to try to stay calm.

It's one of those October mornings you saw in magazines, Carrie thought. The trees on the other side of the loch displayed a profusion of oranges, reds and yellows among the deep green pines and other evergreens that were so common in the area. The autumn trees were so deeply colourful that they almost seemed artificial: as if they had been created scrupulously by a team of painters in some kind of rogue art project.

She walked past the cottage next to hers and nodded to the man in its front garden, a tall, craggy-looking man with his face half-covered by a thick greyish-ginger beard. He was standing next to a large tree that dominated his front garden and was hung with a number of bird feeders. Carrie thought he looked like a Viking who had found his way to Scotland and decided to retire there.

'Morning,' she said, shyly.

'Mornin'.' He nodded. 'You rentin' the Ross cottage?'

'Yes. For a while. I'm Carrie Anderson.' She attempted a smile.

'Ah. Angus McKinnon.' He tapped his barrel-like chest. 'We're neighbours, then. How long you here?'

'I'm not sure. Gretchen Ross said I could see how it went.'

'Ah. No' a holiday then?' The man gave her a sharp look, but continued filling his bird feeders with seed.

'Not really.' She looked away. 'Anyway, I'm just going down into the village to get some food, get some fresh air, you know.' She shrugged, keen to be on her way and avoid a difficult conversation about what had brought her here. 'Can I get you anything while I'm there?'

She didn't really want to run errands for this Viking neighbour, who didn't exactly seem infirm or vulnerable – Carrie was sure that he was entirely capable of getting his own supplies – but she wanted to be polite.

'Ach. No, but thanks fer the offer.' He nodded again, not smiling, but with a kind look in his eye. 'Listen. I dinnae bite, so if we're goin' tae be neighbours a while, come in an' have a cuppa with me sometime. I could do with the company, and so could ye, by the look o' ye.' He gave her another shrewd look. 'An' if ye need anythin', just knock. If I dinnae answer, I'll be in ma workshop out the back. Just walk around.'

'Your workshop?' Carrie asked.

'Aye. I repair things. Clocks, furniture, whatever people need.' He shrugged. 'Keeps me outta trouble, now I'm retired. An' if ye hear me singin', dinnae call the police' – now he chuckled, a deep, sonorous laugh that made Carrie smile instinctively – 'I'm practisin' for my choir's show.'

'There's a choir in Loch Cameron?' Carrie asked with interest. She had always enjoyed singing as a child, and she'd even sung some solos in her secondary school end of year show. Not that her dad had bothered to come – but Claire had helped her practise, and watched proudly from the back row of the auditorium. Carrie felt herself tense up at the memory of her sister, and clenched her hands again to try to regain control over the surge of grief that rose up in her.

'Aye. Come along, if ye want. We're always lookin' for new members.' Angus closed up the big bag of birdseed and placed it on the grass by his feet.

'Oh. Maybe,' Carrie said, noncommittally. She might have once enjoyed singing, but the idea of joining a choir and singing with strangers right now was terrifying.

'Aye, well. Ye know where tae find me.' Angus whistled a little bird call to a nearby Finch. 'I'll let ye get on.'

'Okay. It was nice to meet you, Angus.' She gave him a little wave.

'And you, Carrie,' he called after her.

That wasn't so bad, she thought, as she walked along. *Human contact. It was okay. I didn't fall apart.* In fact, it was reassuring to know that Angus was next door. Not that anything ever happened in Loch Cameron – she remembered that from being here as a child. Great-Aunt Maud would often say, *it's more likely to rain frogs than a crime happen in Loch Cameron, my sweet little bairn*, and it had seemed true at the time. No one had ever locked their doors or been afraid of burglars, or worse. Carrie didn't know if the village was still the same, but she appreciated the fact that all six feet-whatever of Angus was next door.

A few cottages along, though, Carrie came to a stop and gazed at the place she remembered so well. She'd been avoiding it thus far, not feeling up to seeing the cottage where she'd spent so many happy times as a child. Not because there were any bad memories – it was the opposite. She knew that as soon as she saw Great-Aunt Maud's cottage again, she would be unable not to think of Claire.

The whitewashed cottage was similar to the rest along the row. Carrie was pleased to see that whoever lived in it now kept the garden neat, though they had repainted the door and the window frames from the cheery green that Carrie remembered, to white. However, there were children's pictures of rainbows in the windows, and Carrie could see a washing line in the back, stretched across the garden, and a swing set and slide. Clearly, a family lived here, and that made her feel a little better.

Still, seeing Great-Aunt Maud's cottage again was a jolt. Despite the changes, the familiarity of the place meant that Carrie could immediately see herself and Claire playing on the lawn, helping their great-aunt pick raspberries from the bushes in the back garden and bringing them inside in huge baskets to make into jam. Carrie stood there, feeling tears prick her eyes, as she remembered every detail: she and Claire being in charge of carefully placing the hot, sterilised jam jars on a clean tea towel on Maud's peeling linoleum kitchen table, making sure to wear Maud's huge floral oven mitts to avoid burning their hands. Great-Aunt Maud would stir the bubbling jam and, when it got close to being set, would test it on the back of a spoon. If the sticky pink jam cooled on the silver spoon and formed a skin, then it was ready, and Maud would ladle the hot jam into the jars that the girls had laid out. Then, she'd place on sterilised lids, though not screwing them down too tight. The best part was that there was always a little jam left in the pan, and when it had cooled down enough, Maud would produce some freshly baked bread or a couple of homemade scones, and the girls would be allowed to spread the jam on the baked treats and devour them in front of the ancient television.

She and Claire had loved jam day. It was a highlight of their summer. Sometimes Mum had helped, though Dad never did. But, often, Mum would go for a walk and Dad would go to the pub, and leave them with Maud. She and Claire had never minded.

But, now, Maud and Claire and her mum were gone, and her dad might as well have been dead for all that she heard from him. Not even Claire's funeral had prompted him to be a better father. He'd come, watched Claire's coffin be lowered into the ground, and then left again. He hadn't even come to the wake.

Carrie zipped up her coat against the sharp autumn wind, and put up her hood to disguise the fact that she had started to cry. She had wanted to come back to Loch Cameron for comfort. And it *was* comforting, in a way. But it was also tough to walk in the footsteps of her memories. Would she ever be able to get over losing Claire? She didn't think so. Carrie couldn't imagine a day where she would wake up and not think of her sister straight away.

She didn't know if it made losing Claire better or worse, staying in the cottage so close to the one that held so many memories. But something in her wanted to be here. And, even though it was hard to remember, it was also good to go back to those times. Because they had been good. A long time ago, life had been sweet.

FIVE

'Hello, dear. What'll it be?'

The man behind the bar gave her a kindly smile as he looked up from polishing a glass. He was perhaps in his late sixties and had a short white beard and a shaved head. He wore a thick, cream-coloured cable knit jumper and jeans, with a dark blue apron over the top, monogrammed with the name of the Loch Cameron Inn.

'Oh. Coffee, if you do it? And I wondered about lunch?' Carrie said shyly, as she unzipped her parka.

'We do indeed, aye. Ye can hang yer coat up on the stand, if ye like.' The barman nodded towards an old-fashioned wooden coat stand in the corner. 'Lunch is soup or sandwiches, or both. Vegetarian or ham.'

'What's the soup?' Carrie asked as she hung her coat on the hook and went back to her stool at the bar. The Loch Cameron Inn was quiet, with just one family in the next room where there was a TV mounted on the wall.

'Vegetable. Made fresh today. I recommend it.' He smiled at her. 'Hearty.'

'Well, in that case, I'll have some of your hearty soup,'

Carrie agreed. 'Can I have some bread with it?'

'Of course. Comes as standard. Cappuccino, filter coffee, flat white?' He raised a grey eyebrow.

'Flat white, please.' Carrie watched him as he retreated into a little kitchen behind the bar to operate a surprisingly shiny and modern-looking coffee machine. He returned with the coffee in a white cup and saucer on a tray, along with a wide ceramic bowl filled with a very hearty-looking, aromatic soup and placed them both on the bar in front of her.

'Oh. Bread and butter.' He clicked his tongue, went back to the kitchen and returned with a plate of two thick slices of soft white bread spread with yellow butter. 'Here y'are, lassie.'

Carrie smiled at the term. She didn't get called *lassie* at home, but it reminded her of her childhood holidays here in Loch Cameron. She thought she might have come to the inn then, but some memories were hazy; what she remembered most was Great-Aunt Maud, the cottage, the garden and the way she and Claire were allowed to run free on the headland to play, just being called in for mealtimes. A freedom she didn't think she'd felt since that time, in fact.

'Thank you.' Carrie sipped the hot coffee gratefully, sitting carefully so that she didn't put pressure on her collarbone.

It had taken some courage to stay out of the cottage this long, and to decide to find somewhere to eat lunch out, and not retreat to the safety of the cottage's thick stone walls. In fact, it had taken some courage to walk into the inn at all, on her own, but she had, and now she was glad.

'Hello, hello! Welcome, dear. Is Eric makin' ye welcome?' A smart older lady with a sharp silver bob, blue tweed slacks and a white blouse with a thistle-shaped pin at her neck walked into the bar.

'Yes, very.' Carrie returned the woman's smile. 'Thank you.'

'I dinnae think I've seen ye before? I'm Dotty. I run this

place with ma husband, who I see ye've already met,' the woman continued, breezily.

'No, I don't think so.' Carrie wiped her hands on the napkin Eric had provided. 'I'm just staying in the village for a while. Up in Gretchen Ross's cottage,' she added, since everyone seemed to know everyone else in Loch Cameron, and as soon as she mentioned the cottage, everyone always said *Ahhhh, yes,* like the name admitted Carrie into a secret village society of some kind.

'Ah, Gretchen's place, aye.' Dotty nodded sagely, just as Carrie had expected. 'Stayin' long?'

'I'm not sure,' Carrie admitted. 'Playing it by ear.'

'I see, I see.' Dotty gave her a long, though not unfriendly, look. 'Ye know, lassie, ye do look a little familiar, if ye dinnae mind me sayin,' she said, frowning a little. 'What did ye say yer name was?'

'I didn't, but it's Carrie Anderson,' she replied.

'Hmmm. Carrie?' Dotty tilted her head, staring into Carrie's eyes. 'That rings a bell. Have ye been to Loch Cameron before?'

'Yes. I used to come as a child, with my parents and my... sister.' Carrie cleared her throat, not wanting to say the word. Not wanting to talk about Claire at all. 'My great-aunt, Maud, lived up on Queen's Point.'

'Maud. Maud *McKinley*? I knew ye looked familiar!' Dotty stabbed the air in front of Carrie's face with her outstretched finger, triumphantly. 'I remember now. Ye and yer sister'd come every year. Then ye stopped comin'. Almost broke poor Maud's heart, that did, now I recall. Aye. She missed ye. What was it – move away, did ye?'

'No. My mother passed away. My dad didn't want to bring us back up here, I guess.' Carrie shrugged, not wanting to get into it.

'Aww, no. I'm so sorry. Ye poor bairn.' Dotty gripped

Carrie's hand, and Carrie was taken aback at the contact. She pulled her hand away, not used to touch, and certainly not from strangers.

Dotty pursed her lips, but Carrie could see that it wasn't meanness; it was a kind of sympathetic expression. Part of her was grateful for it.

'Well, I'm just taking some quiet time for myself,' Carrie explained. 'The thing is...' She exhaled, realising she had to explain about Claire, but not wanting to. 'My sister, Claire, also just died. It was a car accident. We were in the car together. I survived. She didn't.'

Dotty took in a deep breath; Carrie saw that Eric, behind the bar, exchanged a look with his wife.

'Oh, my goodness me,' Dotty breathed. 'Are ye tellin' me that lovely wee lassie passed away too? She always had her hair in bunches, aye. An' ye always had plaits. I remember that.'

Carrie nodded, unable to speak.

'Ach, no,' Dotty said, and without warning, she gathered Carrie to her in a firm embrace. 'I cannae believe it. I'm glad yer poor mother's in her grave, and yer great-aunt too. Isnae a thing any mother should have tae experience. But ye still had tae, an' that's a great shame.'

Carrie didn't have the energy to resist Dotty's hug and, she realised, she didn't want to. Instead, she let herself rest her head on Dotty's warm, firm shoulder. She might have stayed there longer, breathing in Dotty's comforting lavender smell, but the door to the inn opened and Dotty released her gently with a pat on the back, as if to say, *Let's preserve your dignity, dear*.

And Carrie was grateful that she did, because when she looked up, surreptitiously wiping a tear from her eye, she saw that the person who had entered the bar was Rory McCrae.

SIX

'Oh, hello, Rory,' Dotty trilled, adjusting the frilly white cuffs on her blouse and acting for all the world like she hadn't just been hugging Carrie, a more or less perfect stranger. 'How's tricks, dear?'

Rory nodded politely to Carrie, clearly not remembering her from their run-in at the village shop a few days ago. 'Hi, Dotty. All right, thanks. Just wondered if I could put one of these on your noticeboard.' He handed Dotty a paper sign, and placed the rest of the small stack of them in his hand on the bar. 'Eric, I'll take a flat white, if you have a minute.'

'Aye, nae bother.' Eric nodded, and headed back out to the kitchenette.

Carrie cast an eye over the sheaf of papers Rory had put on the bar.

WANTED

KITCHEN ASSISTANT, THE FAT HEN

20 HOURS PER WEEK/NEGOTIABLE

EXPERIENCE PREFERRED BUT NOT ESSENTIAL

START IMMEDIATELY

Rory's name and a phone number followed at the end of the page.

'Aye, I'll put one up for ye, of course. I was just headin' back out to the desk for a bit anyway, to do some admin, so I'll pin it up for ye.' Dotty took the sign and looked at it. 'Oh. Need a hand in the kitchen?'

'Yes. It's harder than you'd think, finding anyone who wants to do it.' He sighed, and sat down next to Carrie at the bar. He turned to her. 'You're not looking for a part-time job, I suppose? Preparing vegetables, washing up, that kind of thing?'

'I don't think so,' Carrie demurred, and looked away. She wasn't overly keen on engaging with the guy who had been rude to her in the shop.

'Oh. Well, tell your friends,' he said, taking the coffee that Eric placed on the bar in front of him. 'Thanks, Eric.'

'I don't have any here,' Carrie found herself replying. She hadn't meant to, and she felt herself blushing. Why had she said anything at all?

'Sorry?' He looked up, sipping his coffee.

'Forget it.' She looked away.

'You don't have any friends?' he repeated part of what she'd said, frowning.

'No, I said, I don't have any *here*.' Carrie looked down at her soup. 'There's a difference.'

'Sorry for the misunderstanding. You'll have to forgive me. I'm half deaf in one ear.' Rory smiled surprisingly warmly, turning to her. 'I was going to say, I'd be very surprised if someone like you didn't have any friends.'

'Someone like me?' Carrie frowned, looking up. 'What does that mean?'

'Well. You're very pretty,' he said, a playful expression lurking around the edge of his mouth. 'And you clearly love soup. Never underestimate that.'

'Underestimate... the power of soup?' Carrie's eyebrows knitted together.

'Never. That's my advice.' He grinned suddenly, and Carrie was struck by how different this Rory was to the distracted, sarcastic man she'd run into at the village shop. This Rory had a smile like a beam of sunlight which lit up his handsome face.

And he was definitely handsome, Carrie had to admit that.

Before, when they'd met, Carrie had noticed his longish dark brown hair and short beard. He wasn't that much taller than her, but Carrie had observed in the shop that day that he was powerfully built. Today, now that she had more time to look at his face, Carrie noticed other things. Rory had deep brown eyes with long, thick lashes: the kind of lashes that women envied and which lent a softness to his eyes she hadn't noticed before. There were a few laughter lines around his eyes – she estimated he was probably in his early forties – and today his beard wasn't as thick as before; she guessed he'd trimmed it. It meant that she could see the shape of his chin underneath, and a strong, square jaw. He wore jeans and hiking boots, but no jacket: instead, just a light blue jumper with a slightly loose collar that led her eyes to the bottom of his neck, where a suggestion of dark hair sat atop what looked like a very toned chest.

There was something in his expression that made her feel self-conscious, so she looked away again. Plus, he'd called her pretty, and she didn't know how to respond to that apart from either laugh in his face or blush, and neither was a great response. It had been a long time since Carrie had even thought about trying to look pretty. Pretty wasn't exactly top of her agenda right now. Was he flirting with her? If so, it had been so long since that had happened that Carrie didn't know what to say in return. She certainly didn't feel pretty with her hair all windblown, wearing no makeup and clothes she'd chosen for warmth rather than style. At least she'd taken off her parka, she supposed.

'Ummm. Thanks,' she muttered, and ate some soup to avoid having to say anything more.

'Anytime.' He drained the rest of his coffee and stood up. 'Listen. If you change your mind about wanting a job, my number's on there. Or if you want to call me for any other reason,' he added, with a wry smile.

Before Carrie could think of a response, Rory had waved a goodbye to Eric, left some money on the counter for his coffee, and had bounded energetically out to the front desk where Carrie could hear him talking to Dotty.

'Ye dinnae need tae mind Rory.' Eric came over to pick up the money Rory had left behind. 'Though, I hafta say, I've not seen him flirt with a lassie before. Usually, he keeps himself to himself. Bit of a cold fish.'

'Oh. I don't think he was flirting.' Carrie blushed, instantly embarrassed.

'Hmm. Well, I'm a man, and though I'm well past ma flirtin' days, I recognise it when I see it,' Eric chuckled. 'And why wouldn't he, eh? Lovely lassie like you.'

'I really don't think he was,' Carrie insisted.

'All right, have it yer way.' Eric raised an eyebrow and opened a box of crisps, stuffing the individual packs into a cubbyhole under the bar.

Despite the fact that Carrie had avoided talking to him as much as possible, there *was* something about Rory McCrae that she'd felt herself respond to: something in his wry smile and the twinkle in his eye. He was an attractive man, but it was more than that. There was a certain energy around Rory that she liked.

But what point was there in getting interested in someone in a little village you only intended to hide away from the outside world in?

Still, as she finished her soup, Carrie folded up the leaflet with the job details that Rory had left behind, and slipped it into her pocket. Possibly, it wasn't the worst idea in the world to earn a little money if she was going to stay in Loch Cameron for any amount of time: she only had a certain amount of savings, and they would dwindle quickly without a job.

It seemed highly unlikely that Rory McCrae had been flirting with her – she looked an absolute state and she hadn't exactly been nice to the man. Perhaps he was desperate for someone to take the job. She could probably do it and just ignore him; get on with peeling potatoes and washing up, or whatever else a kitchen assistant job entailed. If she was honest, she could probably do with a mindless something to keep her hands occupied, at least for some of the week, or there was a distinct possibility that she might never come out of the cottage again. She'd realised, being out today, that she needed to get out more. It was scary, but it wasn't as scary as she'd expected.

Be brave, she told herself. *At least think about applying for the job.*

Claire would have told her to do it. And Great-Aunt Maud would have positively encouraged it, being such a keen cook herself.

Who knows? You might enjoy it, Claire's voice said in her head, suddenly. It wasn't the first time that Carrie had imagined her sister's voice since she'd died, but it was possibly the first time that Claire's voice had come to her, unbidden, as if her sister had been standing next to her.

Fine. I'll think about it, Carrie thought, as if replying to Claire. And even the sense that there *was* still someone to reply to – even though she knew there wasn't – gave Carrie a brief sense of peace.

SEVEN

Carrie was passing the community centre, on her way back to the cottage from the shops, when she heard the sound of singing. She stopped on the high street outside the squat little building and listened for a moment, realising that she knew the song – an old one from a musical she liked. Carrie hummed along under her breath, smiling.

As she stood there, taking a break from walking for a moment and letting her collarbone have a rest, the singing stopped, and Angus, her tall, bearded Viking-like neighbour, emerged from the porch entrance of the centre, taking out his phone and peering at it.

He looked up and caught her eye. 'Ah, Carrie! Hello!' he called out, waving. He walked over to where she was standing by the black cast iron railings that surrounded the community centre. 'Angus. Yer neighbour,' he reminded her, though she hardly needed it – they'd met a matter of hours ago. 'I'm just on a wee break from *Les Misérables*. Choir practice,' he added. 'Remember I mentioned it? We meet every week.'

'Hi, Angus. Yes, I remember.' She smiled up at her neighbour, who must have been at least six foot five or more. Carrie doubted Angus would ever hurt a fly, but if she hadn't already met him and seen him walking along the street with a frown on his craggy face, she would have probably thought he was the local tough guy.

'Just tryin' tae get ma local odd-jobs woman tae come an' have a look at a plumbin' issue I cannae sort out at home. How was your trip intae town? Get what ye wanted from the shops?' He looked inquisitively at her empty hands. She hadn't been to the shop yet; hunger had overtaken her first.

'Not bad,' Carrie said, evasively. 'I just had some lunch at the inn, then I was going to pop into the shops.'

'Were ye wantin' tae come in? Yer more than welcome.' Angus indicated the little brick building behind him. 'They're just havin' a cuppa right now, and then we'll get back tae it. Yer welcome tae come an' have a bit o' a sing song. Nae pressure tae join.'

'Oh, I couldn't,' Carrie said, on instinct.

'The supermarket can probably wait, unless ye've got a lot on fer the rest o' the day.' Angus raised an eyebrow at her comfy grey joggers and cat sweatshirt.

'Well, no, not exactly...' She'd been intending to go home and get back into bed.

'Well, yer welcome, if ye want a bit o' company.' Angus gave her a warm smile, and then frowned at his phone. 'Ah. I've got tae get this. Might see ye inside, then.' He turned away a little and answered the call. 'Ach, hello, Bess. Thanks fer callin' me back.'

Carrie looked at the entrance to the community centre. In fact, it had been days since she'd had any company, and she was desperately lonely.

Perhaps just a cup of tea, she thought. *Then if I hate it, I can go back home and get into bed just like I planned.*

She pushed open the heavy wooden door to the centre, on which someone had stuck a piece of yellow A4 paper with a handwritten sign that said: CHOIR PRACTICE, THURSDAY 1PM–3PM, ALL WELCOME.

Inside the centre's small hall, a group of about twelve people were milling around, talking and laughing. To one side of the hall there was a no-frills stand-up wooden piano, and on the other, a wooden trestle table half covered with a floral sprigged tablecloth. On the table were a variety of mismatched mugs, a large teapot covered in a knitted cosy, an open carton of milk and two Tupperware containers – one full of what looked like large handmade oatmeal and raisin cookies, the other one full of thick, walnut-studded brownies. Carrie's stomach grumbled, despite the fact that she'd just had lunch.

At the back of the hall, rows of plastic chairs were stacked against the wall, and a number of children's paintings were displayed proudly around the windows. Many of them depicted flowers, huge yellow suns and the wide expanse of the loch as a simple blue line at the bottom; some of them had included the castle, opposite, daubed in grey or brown or with stick people painted with thick brush strokes.

Carrie smiled as she looked at the pictures, a warm feeling in her heart.

'Hello.' An elderly black woman with bright eyes and grey hair approached her. 'Here for the choir, dear?'

'Ummm. I don't know. Maybe? Angus said it was okay to come in.' Carrie felt a little self-conscious among this group of people who all clearly knew each other very well.

'Of course, of course! I'm June. Unofficially, I run the choir, mostly because I'm the only one that can play the piano,' the woman explained, smiling kindly. 'And you are—?'

'Carrie Anderson. I'm just staying in the village a while. I'm renting Gretchen Ross's cottage.'

'Ah, I see. You're Angus's neighbour, then?' June's bright eyes were inquisitive but kind; Carrie could tell she was being assessed, but found that she didn't mind that much.

'Yes. For a while, anyway.'

'And how long is a while?' June asked.

'I'm not sure,' Carrie confessed, but she held back on the full story. June didn't need to know that, right now. Or indeed ever, probably.

'I see. I've lived here forever, so I'm always interested in a new face. I was the local district nurse for most of my career, so I pretty much knew everyone,' June continued.

'Oh, a nurse? That was what I wanted to be when I was a kid.' Carrie smiled, thinking of all the times Claire had let her bandage her leg or her arm; of the hours she'd spent making her own little pretend boxes of medicine and adding them to her play medical bag. Her heart tugged, thinking of her sister. *Not now,* she reprimanded herself, and with an effort pushed the feeling back down inside her.

'Really? You should do it, then. The profession needs a lot more nurses.' June gave her another speculative look over, as if she was imagining Carrie in a nurse's tunic and trousers.

'Oh, well. I don't know. I've never thought about doing it, seriously. I just... always liked the idea of helping people, I suppose.' Carrie was aware that her answer sounded like a cop-out.

'Think about it seriously, then,' June replied, crisply. 'It's not the easiest of jobs, but it's rewarding, and sometimes you get to be the person that can make the worst day of someone's life into the best one, or at least, not the last one they'll ever know. Nursing's hard, but you'll also experience things no one else can because you'll be in intimate situations with people that are outside of the everyday. People trust you, and they need you.' June nodded. 'I was a nurse for forty-five years. Don't regret a day.'

'That's... inspiring, June.'

'It's just the truth, dear. If you ever want to talk more about it, I'm here every week. Always glad to share my wisdom, such as it is. I could even take you around my old hospital, if you liked. To get a feel for it.'

'That's incredibly generous of you.' Carrie was touched. 'I'm nowhere near giving it any kind of serious thought, but perhaps I will, then.'

'Hm. You should.' June looked serious for a moment, then smiled. 'Now, as far as the choir's concerned, we're an informal gang, so you're very welcome to join us, as and when you like, really. We rehearse every Thursday and there's always cake. Do help yourself, by the way,' she said, pointing to the trestle table. 'Have you ever sung before? I mean, in a choir, in a band, that kind of thing?'

'I sang in the choir at school. Always really enjoyed it. Not since then, though.'

'Ah, wonderful. A professional!' June trilled, and Carrie smiled, despite her nervousness. 'Right, then. Get a quick cuppa and a cake or a cookie, and we'll get back to it.' June rubbed her hands together and tapped a tall woman with a long black plait draped over one shoulder, on the arm. 'Zelda! Say hello to Carrie. She's joining us today, and she's staying up at Gretchen's old place, just like you did.'

'Oh, hi, Carrie! Great to meet you!' The woman turned around and grinned. If Carrie hadn't already felt mortifyingly under-dressed in her joggers and sweatshirt, then she certainly did now: Zelda, as well as being perfectly made up, was wearing tight, high-waisted jeans with knee-length heeled boots over the top, and a loose T-shirt that, Carrie thought, probably would have looked like a sack of potatoes on her, but on Zelda looked casual and elegant in a way that could only be achieved with expensive clothes and a tiny figure.

'Oh, you're American,' Carrie replied, and then corrected herself. 'Sorry. What I meant to say was, hello! Nice to meet to you too.' She held out her hand.

Zelda shook it. 'That's okay. Yes, I am, so I know I'm

kinda the odd one out, right?' Zelda laughed. 'So what d'you think of Loch Cameron? Cute, isn't it? I came here for the first time, like, a year and a half ago. Stayed in Gretchen's cottage, like Junie says. It still blows my mind places like this exist.'

'Oh, how strange! You stayed at the cottage too! Yes. It's very beautiful here,' Carrie agreed, reaching for a brownie and putting it on a plate. 'Actually, I used to come on holiday here as a kid. My great-aunt lived in one of the cottages next to Gretchen's.'

'No kidding? Small world. Crazy small, in Loch Cameron,' Zelda laughed. 'That's insane. So, your great-aunt was friends with Gretch?'

'A bit. I'm not sure they were best friends, but they definitely knew each other, yes.' Carrie bit into the brownie, which filled her mouth with the perfect sweet sludginess combined with chunks of walnut. 'Oh, my god. This brownie is so good!' she exclaimed.

'Right? Nothing in Loch Cameron is ever knowingly under-catered, I find,' Zelda chuckled. 'Every time I visit, I put on, like, at least six pounds.'

'So, you don't live here?' Carrie poured some tea from the cute jacketed teapot into a spare clean mug and added a splash of milk.

'No. I live in New York but I'm seeing someone here, so we kinda go back and forth right now,' Zelda explained. 'I mean, in the future, maybe. It's his family home and he's always gonna want to end up here. I guess we're just taking it slow and we'll see what happens.'

'Sounds nice, though. New York and Loch Cameron. The big smoke and the rural idyll.'

'Yeah, it's a nice position to be in. I'm not complaining. I do wish I could see more of Hal, but we don't do too badly.'

'We're just about to start, just to let you know.' June tapped

Carrie on the shoulder. 'Ah. Is Zelda telling you all about how she caught the most eligible man in Scotland?' She laughed.

Zelda blushed. 'June! I didn't *catch* him. He's not a salmon.'

'No, he's a wealthy landowner with a castle, a salmon farm and various other businesses.' June raised her eyebrow playfully. 'And he's pretty easy on the eye, too,' she added, for Carrie's benefit.

'June!' Zelda protested, grinning.

'Oh, are you saying that Hal isn't attractive?' June teased Zelda.

'Of course not. He's gorgeous,' Zelda sighed and patted her heart. 'I'm very lucky.'

'Not at all, hen. He's the lucky one,' June chuckled. 'I'm just teasing Zelda. She's made our Laird very happy, and long may that continue.'

'You're seeing the Laird?' Carrie turned to Zelda, sipping her tea. 'I'm impressed. Though I always think of lairds as paunchy old men with red noses.'

'Oh, no. He's our age. And he's hot,' Zelda laughed.

'Good for you!' Carrie finished the brownie in two large bites.

'Thanks. Are you seeing anyone?' Zelda asked.

Carrie shook her head. 'Not right now,' she said, making it sound like she dated all the time.

In fact, she'd never really had a boyfriend. She'd dated a little, but it never seemed to come to anything. Without realising, over the years, she'd given up trying. She'd assumed that she and Claire would probably grow old together and share a house again at some point. It wasn't that she didn't want a boyfriend, or someone to love. It was more the fact that she and Claire were so close, she'd never really let anyone else in. That, and she'd never really had much confidence with men.

Then Claire had started seeing Graham, and he'd come between them. Carrie could admit that she'd resented Graham and Claire for falling in love. *When you know, you know*, Claire had said, all starry-eyed. But Carrie hadn't understood. She'd been mean. She'd said things she shouldn't have. She regretted being stand-offish and cold about it now.

Carrie hadn't spoken to Graham since the crash. He'd called her, but despite the fact that Carrie knew he was a good man and he'd loved Claire, she wasn't ready to talk to him.

Claire had sometimes joked that she was Carrie's emotional support pillow, and Carrie was hers. Now that Claire was gone, where did that leave Carrie? Without her sister, Carrie had no one, and she was lonely. But the idea of finding a man – even someone as wonderful as Zelda's Laird sounded – felt impossible.

No, it was far more likely that she'd end up like Great-Aunt Maud, alone in a cottage somewhere, making jam and sleeping alone with just the sound of the birds for company. Carrie sighed, and put her cup and plate back on the table. She didn't especially feel like singing now, but it would be rude to back out after eating a brownie and talking to June and Zelda. They'd been so kind.

Plus, it was possible she might actually enjoy it.

EIGHT

'Any experience?' Rory looked up from Carrie's one-page resumé. 'In kitchens, I mean. I can see you've temped a lot. Unfortunately, this job doesn't require you to do mail merges or...' he cast his eye back over the paper, '... Excel spreadsheets. To be honest, I'm not sure what one of those is, either.'

They were sitting at one of the tables in Rory's restaurant, The Fat Hen. It was a small place with about ten tables, with white-painted brick walls displaying modern paintings. Overall, the look was clean and sophisticated, which had surprised Carrie when she'd walked in.

'I worked in a restaurant at university. Part time,' Carrie said. 'It was a while back, though. General washing up, clearing tables, taking orders. But it wasn't anywhere fancy.'

She'd decided to apply for the job after she'd seen one of Rory's flyers at the community centre after choir. Rather than ending up embarrassing herself with what she thought was probably some not very tuneful singing, Carrie had actually walked out of the community centre with a spring in her step for the first time since the accident.

Singing along with the group had felt good. No, actually, it had felt great. She'd experienced a kind of release while singing that was like crying; it was a way to vent her emotions a little, and after they'd finished going through the medley from *Les Misérables*, the act of singing had made her feel more focused and less sad.

She'd called Rory's number as she'd walked home, and he'd asked her to come in the next day for an interview.

'Hmm. Can you cook? I mean, do you cook at home?' Rory rolled back his sleeves, putting her resumé down.

Carrie couldn't help but notice not only his brown muscular forearms, but also the tattoo of a rather sexy 1950s-style lady straddling a cannon on one arm, and one on the other forearm that looked like some kind of military crest.

'A little. Not chef standard, but okay,' Carrie admitted. Her days making jam and other things – pies, puddings, roasts – at Great-Aunt Maud's elbow hadn't been wasted. 'We taught ourselves a lot after our mum passed away.'

She instantly regretted saying "we", but it was second nature to talk about herself in relation to Claire. They'd been a team for so long; it was going to take an equally long time to get out of the habit.

Rory didn't pick her up on it. 'Okay. And you're around for how long?' He sat back in his chair and gave her an appraising look. 'There's no point me training you up and then you just disappearing after a month.'

'I don't know, honestly. But a few months, I guess. And then, I don't know,' Carrie said, truthfully. 'I might stay for longer. I don't really know what I'm doing with my life right now, if I'm honest.'

'Can I ask why?' Rory folded his arms over his chest, but his expression was kind. 'And, if you think I'm being nosy... well, I guess I am. But I know how that feels. When I left the navy, I was at a loss. You come back to civilian life... it takes a lot of getting used to, let's just say that.'

'You were in the navy?' Carrie leaned forward. Today she'd made a little more of an effort with her outfit and washed and styled her hair. She'd even put a bit of makeup on – she was applying for a job, after all. When she'd called Rory the day before to ask for more details about the job, he'd told her to come in to the restaurant to chat. She knew she had to look at least vaguely presentable, so she'd worn a light blue knitted dress that she knew looked nice with her reddish hair, and lace-up knee boots which were practical, but also not as clunky as her wellies. With her newly mended collarbone, she was slightly cautious about such a manual job that required her to be on her feet all day, but on the other hand, she thought it would be good to keep busy.

'Yeah. Fifteen years. When I got out, I had to retrain, so I went to catering college. I always liked food, and it was something practical I could do. I couldn't stand the thought of being stuck at a desk or something, and I like the discipline of running the kitchen. Everyone has a job, everything has a process. It's like the navy in that way.'

'I can understand that.' Carrie watched him curiously. His previous flirtatiousness was absent; today Rory was all business. She didn't know which Rory she preferred: the offhand guy from the bar at the Loch Cameron Inn who had seemed to ask her out, or the handsome, in control chef sitting opposite her.

'You didn't answer my question.' He reached for the daisy that sat in its small vase by the menus on the table, and rolled its delicate stem between his fingers before replacing it carefully. 'Why don't you know what you're doing with your life?'

'I'd rather not talk about it, if you don't mind,' Carrie replied, carefully. 'I lost someone. That's all I really want to say. I'm here to get some peace and quiet.'

'Hmm. You'll certainly get that.' Rory let out a breath. 'I get it. I don't mean to upset you. I just need to know if you'll be here for a while, or if you're planning to disappear. I guess you're here for as long as it takes, then.'

'Yes. But I need a job. And I'll do a good job for you, I promise.' Carrie looked around at the cosy restaurant. She could see herself working here. And, although her rent at Gretchen Ross's cottage was quite low, it would still eat up her savings pretty quickly without any more money coming in. Carrie had started to realise that, now that the mental fog of grief had started to lift and she was faced with the realities of life once again.

Rory tapped his fingers on the table and gave her an appraising look again. 'Okay. Let's give it a try. It's twenty hours a week, so that's Tuesday to Saturday, six till ten p.m. We're closed Sunday and Monday. Suit you?'

'I guess so.' Carrie was taken aback. 'So... that's it? I got the job?'

'You got the job.' Rory gave her a weary smile. 'To be honest, I only had two people apply. And the other one... let's just say I had concerns about his personal hygiene. You, at least, seem to have washed this week.'

'Wow. I'm so happy to have passed your high standard of recruitment,' she chuckled.

'Indeed. And I need someone as of yesterday, so time is of the essence. My previous assistant quit weeks ago and I've been short-handed ever since.' Rory frowned. 'Okay. No time like the present! Come on, I'll show you the kitchen.'

Carrie followed him through a set of double doors into a spotless room with stainless steel worktops, trying not to notice his muscular behind and his wide, powerful shoulders. She could well imagine that he had seen active service in the navy with that physique, and she wondered what he'd done. Where he'd been. She'd always had a bit of a thing for uniforms, and for a brief second Carrie imagined Rory in a white navy dress uniform, clean shaven, his hair shorter. A shiver passed through her.

What are you thinking? Carrie berated herself. *This is no time to be fantasising about your new boss. It's completely inappropriate! And you're not exactly in a place to be thinking about this kind of thing. You're grieving, remember?*

She could hardly forget. Her injuries from the accident were still healing, and her heart was still in pieces. She had heard that some people, when they were grieving, got incredibly horny. Maybe that was what this was. A kind of life-triumphs-over-death thing. An instinct, unexpected and unwelcome, but just her body reminding her that she was still alive. *It's just the grief,* she thought as Rory started showing her around the kitchen. *It's not you, and it's not him. Just forget about it.* If Claire had been here, she would have probably laughed herself silly at Carrie's ridiculous lust and made faces behind Rory's back. And it probably would have helped.

But she wasn't there, and today, Claire's voice in Carrie's head was silent. Carrie nodded, trying to look interested in the dishwasher that Rory was demonstrating. She swallowed down her feelings. She needed this job, so she needed to pay attention and repay Rory's faith in her.

You probably would have felt this way around any youngish, reasonably attractive guy, she told herself. *Don't be too hard on yourself. Just focus. Your heart's hurting, and you need a hug. That's all.*

But it was hard, when the tsunami of feelings inside her was making her feel so unbalanced. *Come on, Carrie. You got this,* she told herself, but she really wasn't sure that she did. And the only thing that stopped her walking out of the restaurant kitchen altogether was the feeling that Claire would have wanted her to stay.

NINE

'That's Gretchen Ross.' The care-home nurse pointed across a wide lawn at an elderly woman with a straight back and her grey hair in a bun; she wore a colourful, loose dress with a daisy pattern and a long yellow cardigan over the top of it, with loops of beaded necklaces. 'Just go over and say hi. She's expecting you.'

'Thanks.' Carrie walked over the grass, stepping around two ladies and a man who were playing a lively game of croquet, and past a number of benches and tables and chairs, many of which were occupied with care-home residents enjoying the sunny day, some with blankets tucked over their knees and cups of tea.

'Hi, Gretchen? I'm Carrie Anderson.' Carrie had driven over to the care home after Gretchen had messaged her and asked her over for tea. The message had been quite brief, but Gretchen had explained that although the cottage belonged to the Laird, since she'd lived in it for so long, she liked to meet each cottage guest at least once and make sure they had everything they needed.

The drive itself had been stressful. Though she'd made

herself get in cars since she'd lost Claire and been injured herself, every time Carrie got in one her heart started racing. She knew it must be a kind of PTSD from the accident, but knowing something in your mind and understanding it in your body were two very different things. Carrie's mind knew why she was nervous in cars, but it didn't stop her body from panicking.

Therefore, when she arrived at the care home, even though the journey had been uneventful, it took Carrie ten minutes to calm down, sitting in the car park and taking deep breaths until she stopped sweating. By the time she walked up to Gretchen, though, she felt reasonably normal again.

'Ah, Carrie, dear! So lovely to meet you!' Gretchen turned to her with a beaming smile. 'Isn't it a delightful day? I've just been watching the squirrels in the trees. Look!' She pointed at a flash of grey fur as two squirrels circled the trunk of a nearby oak at lightning speed. 'Scatty little varmints, they are. But most entertaining.'

'They're cute.' Carrie watched the squirrels with interest.

Gretchen shook her hand and gave her an appraising look. 'So. Settling in at the cottage okay? Thanks for coming out to see me. I like to meet my old cottage's tenants at least once during their stay. Of course, technically, it isn't my cottage – it belongs to the Laird, but he hasn't got the time to do all the admin to rent it out, so I do that for him.' Gretchen lowered her voice conspiratorially. 'Confidentially, the Laird is to the internet what I am to calisthenics. Not terribly enthusiastic.'

'And you're online a lot, then?' Carrie smiled. She liked Gretchen's bright eyes and clipped way of speaking; she didn't have a Scottish accent but rather one of those old-fashioned voices that sounded rather like she was a lady detective in a book. Carrie could tell immediately that Gretchen was very sharp, despite her age. She doubted Gretchen missed much.

'Oh, yes. Not much else to do, except the endless bridge and canasta tournaments, of course. And I do like to have my hair done, get a manicure, pedicure, that kind of thing. You might as well take advantage of being held hostage in a place like this.' She rolled her eyes theatrically and Carrie snorted a laugh. 'Otherwise, I like to be on social media. Stay up to date with what people are talking about. Follow various celebrity animal accounts, read the news, see what all the publishers are spending their money on these days. I'm even on TikTok. Young people are endlessly inventive, you know.'

'Goodness. It sounds like you're far more involved online than I am.' Carrie smiled. 'Shall we sit? I could get us some tea.'

'Yes, why not? There's a sunny spot there.' Gretchen pointed to a free table and chairs on a sunny patio that was getting the best of the autumn sun, even though it was October. 'Can you get me a cappuccino, dear? And some pastries, perhaps. I'll go and bag the table, and then we can have a cosy chat.'

'Will do.' Carrie made her way back inside to the self-service cafeteria and selected some pastries and muffins, and poured two coffees from a machine. She took them back to Gretchen on a tray.

'Now, then.' Gretchen stretched her arms in a catlike way which made her various bracelets jangle. 'Tell me about yourself, Carrie. Why you're here.'

'Oh, just getting away from it all for a while,' Carrie said, evasively. Though she liked Gretchen, she had no desire to disclose everything that had happened to bring her to Loch Cameron. 'You know.'

'I do.' Gretchen sipped her coffee and stared out at the lawn, which was surrounded by woodland. 'You know, you're the third young woman to come and stay in that cottage since I left. I had to come and live here because I had a fall, living on my own. The doctor thought it was best.' She raised an eyebrow and met Carrie's gaze. 'Oh, I don't mind it. It's nice enough here. But I do miss the cottage. I grew up there, you know.'

'I didn't know. It's a lovely old place.' Carrie picked at a muffin. 'Very cosy. I—' She broke off, not sure whether to mention anything about coming to Loch Cameron as a child. If Gretchen Ross had lived in that cottage all her life, then she would probably have been there when Carrie and Claire visited.

'Yes, dear?' Gretchen took a bite of a Danish pastry. 'Hmm. Apple.' She frowned, but took another bite anyway.

'Nothing, really. I was just going to say...' Carrie sighed. She didn't want to talk about what had happened to Claire, but she found that she still wanted to talk to someone. And, she liked Gretchen. There was something unshockable about her. Perhaps it was her age, but Carrie could feel something else about her too. A kind of trustworthiness. For some reason, the idea of talking to Gretchen, who she had only just met, wasn't as terrible as talking to her father or her friends.

'What?' Gretchen's eyes were sharp. 'If you've got something on your mind, I can be trusted. Don't worry.'

'No, it's just... my great-aunt was one of your neighbours, up on Queen's Point. Maud McKinley,' Carrie said. 'Me and my sister, and our parents, we'd come up every summer until I was about twelve.'

'Oh, what a small world!' Gretchen exclaimed. 'How old are you? In your thirties, somewhere? So about twenty years or so?' She frowned. 'Yes, I lived in the cottage then. I grew up there and then moved away to Edinburgh to work for many years. My daughter and I lived there for a while when she was older, but mostly it was just me by the time you would have visited... Of course, when I was young, there were two bedrooms. I merged them into one when my daughter left home; the rooms were unimaginably small, before... Maud's great-nieces? I do remember you, of course! You were the apple of her eye!' Gretchen laughed and banged the table vigorously. 'Who would have thought?'

'I don't remember you.' Carrie tried to think of a time when they had ever really visited any of Maud's neighbours, but her memory failed her. 'I don't think we ever did much apart from play outside or down on the loch. Maud used to take me and my sister into the village, but we mostly helped her cook or played in the garden.'

'No, she wasn't that sociable.' Gretchen nodded. 'We had a friendship, because we were of an age, but she was quite a quiet person. But when we did speak, she always talked about you. It was nice for her, having you all there. She never had that kind of family experience for herself.'

'That's nice to know.' Carrie thought about Maud: about her comfortable cardigans and the fact she always seemed to be wearing an apron. 'We stopped coming up when I was twelve.' She didn't explain why. She'd blurted it all out to Dotty the other day, and that felt like enough for now.

'Oh, I know. I remember that.' Gretchen frowned. 'She wasn't happy with your father. He kept you away, didn't he? Of course, he was a bit of a one, according to Maud. She never liked him, that I do remember.'

'Didn't she?' Carrie frowned. She had known that, to some extent, Maud and her father weren't close. Maud was her mother's aunt. But she hadn't known that they specifically hadn't got on at all.

'Oh, no. Didn't approve of his drinking,' Gretchen tutted. 'Your poor mother, putting up with it. She was a saint.' Gretchen paused, and frowned. 'She passed away, didn't she? I do remember now. I'm sorry, I'd forgotten. It's been a long time since Maud passed, so I haven't been in the headspace to remember your family for a while.'

'Yes, she did. That's all right.' Carrie leaned forwards. 'His drinking?'

'Oh, yes. He was a drinker, that one. Every time you all visited, Maud had to get rid of all the drink in the house – not that she ever had much around, just a bit of brandy in the cupboard for cooking and a bottle of whisky for cold nights. Even so, he'd just go straight down into the village and bring back some bottles as soon as you all got here. I remember that because Maud started emptying them in the night, and then there was a huge row when he found out. He stormed out, went to stay at the inn for a few days,' Gretchen chuckled. 'Of course, Dotty overcharged him for everything until he came back, his tail between his legs.'

'I had no idea,' Carrie said, thinking about her father. She'd known that he drank, and she'd assumed for a long time that it was part of the way he dealt with the grief of losing her mum. She didn't remember him being drunk when she was younger, but, on the other hand, she also remembered the fact that her mum and dad had argued a lot. She'd just thought it was normal.

'Ah, well. It's not for children's eyes.' Gretchen shrugged. 'Still. You turned out all right, I can see. And I'm sure your sister did too. What is her name again?'

'Claire,' Carrie said, quietly.

Gretchen gave her a look. 'What happened?' she asked, gently. 'I can tell by that tone of voice something's wrong. Is she ill?'

'No. Claire...' Carrie choked on the tears that suddenly welled up in her throat. 'Claire... we were involved in a c-car crash. And Claire...' She trailed off, unable to say the words. *Claire died. And it was all my fault.*

Carrie started to cry, unable to stop herself.

Gretchen sighed deeply, stood up, and enveloped Carrie in her be-cardiganed arms. 'Oh, darling,' she murmured, holding Carrie to her shoulder. 'You poor girl.'

TEN

It was a while before Carrie could stop crying. Finally, she reached the hiccupping stage and was able to breathe a little more easily. She took some deep breaths. 'I'm so sorry, Gretchen,' she managed to gasp, her voice like a husk. 'Claire was... it's pretty recent, that's all.'

'And she was your sister,' Gretchen finished for her. 'You were close, I bet.'

'Very.' Carrie sniffed, and took the paper napkin Gretchen handed her. 'Thanks.'

'I was an only child myself, and I always wanted a sister,' Gretchen mused. 'Maybe that was why I didn't think anything of being a single parent for my daughter. I was used to that kind of one-on-one attention, I must say, when my parents were around. Especially with my dear old dad.' She smiled ruefully. 'I still miss him. Cantankerous old so-and-so, he was, but a heart of gold. He always supported my career, even when it meant leaving home. Mother didn't want me to go to Edinburgh to live and work, but Dad said, *The girl has an education – you might as well let her do something with it, Daphne.*' Gretchen imitated a deep, paternal voice.

'Daphne was your mum?' Carrie blew her nose in the napkin.

'Yes, that's right. She was more of the traditional Scottish stock. My dad had been in the air force, so he'd travelled the world by the time he met her. Daphne was born and bred here, in Loch Cameron.'

'Why didn't she want you to leave? If you had a good job offer, surely she would have seen it was a positive thing?'

'She thought Edinburgh was a den of iniquity.' Gretchen raised an eyebrow. 'You have to remember that life was different then. She'd lived in a small village all her life. She didn't approve of a daughter of hers going off to be around sex, drugs and rock 'n' roll.'

'And was it like that?' Carrie asked.

'No, of course not. I mean, yes, it was the sixties with all that entailed. But I was just a good Christian girl, living in a boarding house for unmarried women run by a very strict widow, Mrs Carstairs. We weren't allowed gentleman callers, drinking or smoking indoors and she used to measure the length of our skirts before we left for work in the morning. With a tape measure.' Gretchen met Carrie's gaze with an indulgent smile.

'That seems unnecessary,' Carrie said, grateful to be distracted from the subject of Claire for a moment.

Grateful to be distracted from me? Charming, Claire's voice said in her mind.

'Yes, it was, but at the time I think she thought she was protecting us from the evils of the sexual revolution.' Gretchen shrugged. 'My mother wouldn't let me go to Edinburgh unless I stayed with Mrs Carstairs when I got there. Some old connection of hers... I don't know. Anyway, I went, I stayed there a couple of years and then I managed to move into a shared house with some other girls and I went on from there. No more skirt-measuring, and the seventies arrived. I spent those years working my way up into an editorial role. Very slowly, I might add.'

'Did you always work in... publishing, was it?' Carrie sipped her coffee, which had gone cold.

'Yes. But, listen to me, gabbing on about me. Tell me about your sister. I remember her a little, but if I'm honest all I remember of the both of you is a couple of little redheads with plaits, running around in Maud's garden, making daisy chains.'

'Well, I was enjoying hearing about you,' Carrie protested, but Gretchen waved her hand impatiently.

'No. More important.'

'I don't know where to start.' Carrie thought for a moment about Claire. How could she describe her to someone who had never known her? 'She was... we were... very similar in a lot of ways, of course. She was only a year older than me. We had the same sense of humour, more or less. We had a lot of shared references, you know. I'd know what she was thinking a lot of the time. She could read me. She knew if I was lying or sad or uncomfortable.' Carrie took a deep breath.

Gretchen nodded encouragingly. 'Go on, dear.'

'I kind of hated parties but she loved them. She was more outgoing than me. But she could tell if I was getting over-whelmed with people – that happens, sometimes – and she'd give me an out. She'd say something like, "Carrie, can you go out and get us some ice, we've run out," or ask me to help her in the kitchen or something. She was caring, in a low-key way.'

'And did she have a young man, or a young lady?' Gretchen enquired.

'Yeah.' Carrie made a face and looked away. 'I don't want to talk about him.'

'Why not, dear?'

'I just don't. We... didn't really get on.'

'But she was happy with this person?' Gretchen persisted. 'Or not?'

'They were happy,' Carrie conceded. 'I didn't think he was good enough for her. It... came between us.'

'I'm sorry to hear that. So, when she died...?' There was a question in Gretchen's voice that Carrie didn't want to answer. *When she died, had it come between you? Were you angry with Claire for being with him? Did she die without you telling her you were sorry?*

'None of that matters now.' Carrie gave Gretchen a bright smile, the tone in her voice indicating that she didn't want to talk about it anymore. She didn't. It was too raw. 'She's gone, and I miss her every day.'

'I know, dear. Loss takes a long time to ease,' Gretchen sighed. 'I lost my daughter Stella not so long ago. It's been a difficult adjustment. You don't expect your child to go before you.'

'Oh, no. I'm so sorry, Gretchen.' Carrie, shocked, took Gretchen's hand. 'How old was she?'

'She was fifty. It was also a car accident.' Gretchen clicked her tongue. 'She had an extreme nut allergy, and the doctors said that she must have accidentally eaten something containing nuts when she was driving. I mean, she would never have eaten anything with nuts in, if she'd known. She went into sudden anaphylactic shock, and there was an impact with another car. They were fine. She died almost immediately, they told me.' Gretchen sounded as though she had recounted this story many times now, but Carrie could tell that the pain of telling it hadn't receded.

'I'm so, so sorry, Gretchen,' Carrie said, quietly. 'When it happens so out of the blue like that... it's just so hard to take in. One minute they're there; the next, they're gone. You don't get to say goodbye. It's kind of... surreal.'

'Yes, I know. It's an unusual and terrible thing, like a tsunami that rips your life apart, just like that.' Gretchen snapped her fingers. 'Life is never the same after, but I can tell you, it does get better with time.'

'I hope so. What was she like? Stella?' Carrie asked.

'Beautiful. She was always beautiful. I adopted her when she was two. Never any trouble. She went to full-time day-care when she was little, because I was working. We lived in Edinburgh then, and then we moved back to the cottage when she started school. I had a nanny come and pick her up from school, make her dinner and all that, and I'd always be back by six-thirty. I made sure I put her to bed every night.' Gretchen smiled at the memory. 'We read so many books. I was definite that I was going to instil a love of books in her, and I did. She grew up to be a librarian.'

'She sounds great.' Carrie held Gretchen's hand tightly. 'I'm so sorry you lost her.'

'I had her for forty-eight years.' Gretchen let out a long sigh. 'Longer than you had your sister. I was lucky.'

'I suppose so, when you look at it like that. I guess I was lucky to have Claire for thirty-five years.'

'Exactly. That's how you've got to think about it.' Gretchen gave her a brave smile. 'You'll be all right, my dear. You've survived the tsunami. Now, she'd want you to live.'

'But what if I don't want to live without her?' Carrie said, in a low voice. 'What if... I don't know how?'

'You have to live, Carrie. Your sister didn't get to do all the things that she wanted to, probably. So, you have to. For her. All right?' Gretchen reached over, put her fingers under Carrie's chin and tilted it a little. 'Chin up, okay? You'll get there. I promise. One day, you'll wake up and it won't feel like all you want to do is hide under the covers.'

'I can't imagine that day coming,' Carrie confessed.

'It'll come, dear. I promise.' Gretchen smiled.

And, for a moment, Carrie thought, *Maybe it will.*

ELEVEN

'That was the last cover. Well done.' Rory popped his head around the kitchen door.

Carrie was stacking plates in the dishwasher and running some more hot water into the stainless-steel sink, ready to wash a pile of wine glasses. 'Thanks.' She looked up and pushed her fringe out of her eyes.

Rory disappeared for a minute and Carrie could hear the sound of him saying goodnight to the final customers, and then the restaurant door closing. She started the dishwasher, then started washing the glasses.

It had been a busy night, and keeping up with Rory and Kathy, the waitress, was a challenge. Kathy was a PhD student who waitressed at the restaurant for extra money. When they'd met, Carrie had liked her immediately: her hair was dyed black on one side of her head and shocking pink on the other, separated by a poker-straight parting down the middle. Her fringe was black, and though she wore a smart white shirt and black skirt to work in the restaurant, her various ear piercings were still visible, as was a tattoo of a tiger on her wrist. It wasn't

Carrie's style, but she liked it, and she liked Kathy, who was smart and funny and easy to get along with.

Kathy took the orders and looked after the customers, Rory was the chef and did a little front-of-house too, and Carrie was strictly in the kitchen. At just before six in the evening, she arrived at the restaurant and Rory talked her and Kathy through the menu, explaining the provenance of all the ingredients, how each dish was made and any other details he thought they should know. Then, they all had dinner   tonight it had been an aromatic duck curry and jasmine rice that was so delicious Carrie had had seconds and still wanted to lick the plate clean. She had restrained herself, however.

'Wow, I'm hungry again.' Rory pushed through the kitchen door and grinned at Carrie.

She had to admit that he looked very handsome in his chef's whites. He had undone some of the poppers of the top portion and she could see just a little dark chest hair peeking out. She looked away, feeling a little warm.

It's a kitchen. It's going to be hot, she rationalised to herself, tying her hair up in a little bunch at the back. *No other reason apart from ovens being on all the damn time.*

'You are?' Carrie realised she hadn't replied. 'Huh. I guess I am too, actually.'

Her stomach rumbled, as if to agree, and they both laughed.

'Hmm. What do we have left?' Rory looked into the fridge. 'Ah. Mac and cheese. That just needs warming through and a blast under a hot grill. Up for it?'

'Sure. I love mac and cheese.' Carrie couldn't believe she was hungry again, but clearly being on her feet for four hours without stopping meant she'd burned through her two portions of curry from earlier.

Kathy came into the kitchen and gave Rory a high five, then did the same to Carrie, whose hands were wet and soapy. 'Good job, you guys,' she grinned. 'That was a busy one, aye. Made a big difference havin' ye here, Carrie. Last week I was doin' your job as well, an' it wasnae pretty.'

'Well. I hope I did okay,' Carrie said, shyly. She had enjoyed the fast pace of the evening; it had been a nice change to feel useful. Her collarbone had ached a bit, but it wasn't as bad as she'd expected.

'You did great.' Rory pulled out a container of the cheesy carbohydrate goodness from the fridge and took some bowls from the cupboard, spooning some mixture into each.

'Kathy, Rory's making us mac and cheese. Do you want some?' Carrie asked.

'Ach, no. Goin' tae head off, an' I can't stomach carbs this time of night,' Kathy laughed. 'See you guys tomorrow.'

'Right you are. Thanks for tonight.' Rory gave her a little wave as he put both bowls into the microwave.

After Kathy left, Carrie felt a slight awkwardness at being left alone with Rory. There wasn't any reason for it, of course, but somehow Kathy had been a safe buffer. Now there was no distraction from the unsettled way he sometimes made her feel.

College talk for horny. Claire's voice popped into her mind, unbidden.

No! Definitely not, Carrie thought, as if Claire really was in her head. *I'm so far from horny that is just a ridiculous notion.*

Are you? Death makes people do it like rabbits, Claire's voice replied. *You wouldn't be the first recently bereaved person to want to climb someone like him like a tree. I definitely would.*

Shut up! Carrie thought, trying to regain control of her thoughts. *That is incredibly inappropriate.*

The microwave dinged and Rory took out both dishes to put them under the grill.

'Just to crisp the tops,' he said, breaking the silence.

'Great.' Carrie nodded, and busied herself with finishing

drying the wine glasses. She didn't want to let Claire go. She understood that was why she had her sister's voice in her head. In real life, Claire would have said all those things and more; she was never backwards at coming forwards. So, Carrie didn't hate thinking about what Claire would say because it made her feel a connection to her sister at a time when she really didn't want to believe that Claire was gone forever. Still, even though all that was true, she could have done without Claire's smutty quips in her head right now.

'Here we are.' Rory set two steaming bowls of the macaroni – complete with bubbling, dark brown tops of melted cheese mixed with crunchy breadcrumbs – on the main kitchen work-top, which, like everything in the kitchen, was stainless steel. It was efficient and easy to clean, but it lacked warmth.

Carrie took two spoons from a drawer and handed one to Rory. 'Oh. Thanks so much,' she said.

'Thank you.' He took the spoon and plunged it into the hot, gloopy mix of cheese, sauce and pasta. 'I'm going to let it cool down a bit. Might have heated it an extra wee while too long.'

'Hmm. Good point.' Carrie stuck her spoon into the bowl Rory had given her and watched as a billow of steam escaped. She blew on it a few times for good measure. As she looked up, she caught Rory watching her with a smile. 'What?' she asked.

'Nothing.' He continued smiling.

'Come on. Did I do something?' She ran her fingers through her hair self-consciously. 'Do I have something on my face? In my teeth?'

'No, you're fine.' He picked up his spoon again and poked at the molten cheese in his bowl. 'You know what we need? Garlic bread. There's some left over from the last orders, I think.' He got up and went to an oven tin that Carrie hadn't cleaned yet. 'Ha! Here we are.'

He returned with two pieces of buttery, crispy ciabatta that had been rubbed thoroughly with garlic and then buttered with garlic butter before being toasted under the grill. Carrie knew, because she'd prepped them earlier.

'There you go. Perfect accompaniment.' He sat down again, broke off a piece of garlic bread and dipped it in his mac and cheese.

Carrie did the same, spooning some of the cheesy mixture into her mouth afterwards. It was still very hot, but she huffed a few times to cool it down. 'Mmm. That's incredible,' she said, her mouth full. It really was: Rory had used three different cheeses to make the sauce, and the pasta was at the perfect consistency. The garlic bread was so tangy and mouth-watering that she wanted to cram it all into her mouth at once, but she made herself eat it like a normal person.

'So. What did you do for work before you came to Loch Cameron?' Rory asked as he ate. 'I know you showed me your resumé, but I can't remember anything about it now.'

Carrie chuckled. 'Didn't you read it?'

'I skimmed it. Honestly, as I told you, you were the only reasonable candidate I had, so it was a bit of a no-brainer. Plus, you were definitely the prettiest.' Rory continued eating, but maintained eye contact, as if waiting to see how she would take his comment.

'Oh!' Carrie looked down at her food, blushing suddenly and then mortified that she was blushing.

Oh, my! Claire's voice in her head chuckled. *Looks like you're not the only horny one around.*

Shut. Up. Carrie willed the voice to stop.

'Sorry. I didn't mean to embarrass you. You just are very pretty. Objectively speaking,' Rory said, his expression unreadable.

Was he flirting with her, or just making conversation?

'Thanks, I guess,' she responded. 'It was just a bit—'

'Inappropriate? Yes, sorry. It's been a while,' he said, and then looked uncomfortable. 'And that piece of information was also inappropriate. You're not here to talk about my love life. Or a lack of it.'

'Not really, no,' she replied.

'Sorry,' he sighed. 'You probably get this all the time. Men falling over their words around you. Not knowing where to put themselves.'

'Actually, no. I don't think that's ever happened.' Carrie laughed, despite the fact that she was still blushing and it *was* an inappropriate workplace conversation. Still, somehow, she didn't really mind.

'Really?' He gazed at her, looking genuinely astonished. 'You just can't have noticed. It probably happens all the time.'

'No, it doesn't.' Carrie frowned.

'Huh. What's wrong with men?' He shook his head.

'I don't know,' Carrie replied, truthfully.

Their eyes met, and they both started laughing at the same time. It was a reflex on her part, born of the awkwardness that stretched between them, but it also felt good to laugh.

'I'm sorry. Shall we start again?' Rory spluttered, wiping a tear from his eye. 'How's the mac and cheese? A reasonable and entirely appropriate question for a chef to ask his assistant.'

'It's really lovely. Thank you,' Carrie replied, deadpan.

'Delighted you're enjoying it,' he said, equally as formally.

'I am.'

'Good.'

There was another silence, but it was comfortable this time.

'So. Why has it been a long time?' she asked, already halfway through the bowl.

He laughed and looked up at her. 'What? I thought we agreed. No inappropriateness in the workplace.'

'I didn't agree. You apologised and I said it was okay.'

'Oh.' He raised an eyebrow. 'I see. Well, in that case... ah, it's complicated. I was away a lot for many years. Hard to have a relationship. And then I got to Loch Cameron and... I dunno. Never really met anyone here I liked.'

'Oh.' She nodded. 'But there are always people coming to the restaurant. Isn't that a good way to meet people?'

'Not really. I can't very well write my phone number on a bay leaf and hope they'll find it in their food. Or ask them out after they pay the bill. It'd be weird.'

'I hadn't thought about it that way, but I can see that.' Carrie smiled.

'You've still not told me what you did for a job before.' He pointed at her with his spoon.

'I was a temp. Just office work. Remember, you asked me at the interview and you said this job wouldn't have many opportunities to do mail merges.'

'Oh, yeah. I do remember, now.' He frowned for a moment. 'I imagined you'd have been something else. I dunno. Like a caring role or something.'

'Why?' Carrie looked up.

'Dunno. You have that vibe about you. Or it's wishful thinking. I always liked nurses.' He gave her a sudden, wicked grin.

'Hmm. No, not a nurse. Though it's strange you should say that,' she said, licking her spoon. 'That's what I always wanted to be when I was a kid.'

'Was it? See. I could tell.' He smiled. 'I've met a lot of nurses over the years. You've got that same thing about you. Kind and unflappable.'

Carrie snorted. 'Of all the words I could choose to describe myself, I think "unflappable" is the last one I'd think of.' She thought of the weeks gone by when she'd all but hidden in the cottage. Unflappable in the face of Claire's death was something she definitely wasn't.

'Nah. You took to this job like a duck to water. Didn't mind me coming in and out, disturbing you. Just got on with everything. And, I can tell that you're kind,' he observed. 'But you're sad about something.' He gave her a keen look, and then stood up and took his bowl to the sink and washed it up.

'How come you've met so many nurses over the years?' She ignored his remark and took her bowl to the sink to wash too. Wordlessly, rather than step aside and let her do her own, he held out a hand for the bowl instead and washed it for her.

'I was in the navy, remember. I saw active service,' he said, shortly. 'I was injured a few times. And there are always nurses around, anyway. Nurses and military sort of go together.'

'Oh, I see.' She stepped back and watched him as he dried the bowls with the tea cloth and put them back in the cupboard. His chef's whites were still pristine, and even though they were reasonably loose-fitting, she could see the movement of his muscular back and shoulders as he moved around. She imagined Rory in a sailor's uniform for a moment, and a sudden heat lit up her belly. 'That was why you moved around a lot.'

'Yeah. Cyprus, Iraq, Germany for a while. I trained commandos in Belize and Brunei too. Jungle training,' he added.

'Do you miss it?' she asked.

He turned around, meeting her eyes. 'Sometimes. I miss some of the people. But, generally, no.' He looked away. 'I'm done with that. I retrained as a chef. This is my life now.'

'A very different kind of life, though,' she observed. 'Loch Cameron's a tiny place to call home after you've seen so much of the world.'

'I know. But that's why I like it.' He shrugged. 'It's a good place to get away from everything. Nothing ever happens here, and I'm fine with that. I saw enough action to last me several lifetimes when I was in the navy.'

'It must be boring, though. Sometimes?' Carrie didn't understand how anyone could go from one extreme to the other. 'I mean... I like the quiet, just now. But—' She broke off, not wanting to explain why. 'Well, it suits me, at the moment, anyway,' she finished.

He gave her a curious look, but nodded. 'Yeah. It's boring, in a way. But it's also calm and beautiful and I've got a job I love. I've just had enough drama, that's all. If nothing dramatic ever happened to me again I'd be delighted. Just get up, work, go to bed. That'll do me.'

'It sounds lonely,' Carrie said, before she could stop and think.

Oh, it does, Claire's voice said sarcastically in her head. *Don't you want someone to warm your bed at night, Mr Handsome Navy Man?*

She cleared her throat. 'I mean... just working... Look, it's none of my business. Sorry.'

'It is lonely. It can be, anyway,' Rory replied, carefully. 'But that's what I want.'

'Can I ask why?' Carrie crossed her arms over her chest. She wasn't sure why she was being so inquisitive, especially given the fact that she wasn't keen to talk about her life in any way.

'I'd rather not talk about it, if that's okay with you.' Rory leaned against the worktop, facing her. 'I think you've got some stuff going on you probably don't want to talk about, and so do I. Fair?'

'That's fair.' Carrie nodded. 'Okay. Well, thanks for second dinner. I should be heading home.'

'All right. You'll be okay getting back to the cottage?' Whatever more intimate energy had been between them, Rory was back to business now. 'I'll lock up.'

'I'll be fine. It's a lovely walk, and it's quiet as anything up there.' Carrie nodded.

'All right, then. I'll see you tomorrow, Carrie.' Rory stepped forward and, unexpectedly, planted a kiss on her cheek. 'Sleep well,' he murmured in her ear, before turning away.

Instinctively, she put a hand to her cheek where he'd kissed it. 'See you tomorrow,' she replied, but his back stayed turned to her.

What? she thought, and this time it was her voice, and not Claire's. *What the hell was that?*

TWELVE

Carrie was reading a book at a table at the Loch Cameron Inn while she ate her dinner.

She liked to walk down to the inn at around five on a Sunday and Monday evening, when the street lights were just starting to come on. At this time of year, there was a cosy feel to the end of the day, before it got dark in Loch Cameron. Leaves drifted down from the trees alongside the loch and were blown into high banks at the edge of the pathway, making red-and-orange piles that children jumped into with glee.

Tonight, Eric had recommended the local sausages, and served three glistening, brown links of pork with fried potatoes and spicy beans, which he proudly told Carrie were his own recipe. She'd taken to coming for dinner at the inn on the nights she wasn't working. She wasn't a fan of cooking for one, and since she got a free dinner at the restaurant Tuesday to Saturday now, before her shift started, she was saving so much money on food that she enjoyed allowing herself at least one dinner a week at the inn too. Plus, Dotty and Eric were good company.

'Ah, I was hopin' ye'd come in, dear. I've got somethin' fer ye.' Dotty waved at Carrie across the bar and went back out to the reception desk. 'Wait a mo. They're here somewhere.'

She reappeared and approached the table, handing Carrie three faded leather notebooks.

Carrie turned them over in her hands, noting that the covers were still a dark blue, but the spines were faded to grey. They looked like they had spent a lot of time on a bookshelf: Carrie wondered where exactly they had lived for so long.

'What are these?' She looked up at Dotty.

'They were your Great-Aunt Maud's, it looks like,' Dotty answered, adjusting the waistband of her lilac tweed skirt.

'Great-Aunt Maud?' Carrie frowned. 'Why do you have them, Dotty?'

Dotty sighed. 'Well, I dinnae if ye heard, but ma very great friend Myrtle passed away. She ran the little café on the high street.'

'Oh. I'm sorry to hear that.' Carrie frowned. 'I didn't know.'

'Aye, well, no reason for ye to,' Dotty said quietly and wiped a tear from her eye. 'She wasnae very auld, just unlucky with her health. Anyway, I was up at her cottage, clearin' it oot with her family, and we found those. I was goin' tae toss them oot, but then I realised they were Maud's. And so they belong tae ye.'

'Goodness. Thanks, Dotty. That's so kind of you. I'm glad you checked.' Carrie opened one of the notebooks and surveyed the neat copperplate handwriting that filled every page. 'Oh! It's a diary! Look. There are dates all the way through it.'

'I didnae look much, but aye. That's a nice thing tae have.' Dotty smiled. 'Why don't ye read them over dinner? If ye can make oot the handwritin'.'

'I will, Dotty.' Carrie opened the first book and squinted at the page. After a moment or two she got used to the antique handwriting and settled in to read.

12th January 1958

Mother gave me this diary for Christmas, no doubt thinking I would use it to record the mundane life of a postmistress. Perhaps she thinks that the new first-class stamp or the number of passport applications I approved last week deserve recording. Or, more likely, like everyone else, she assumes I am a lifeless old maid at twenty-eight, my clothes stitched to me like a doll, never torn off in passion. And so I will be amused by something else to fill my day, seeing as a man never will.

But Mother and everyone else are wrong. I have a secret life, and I will use this book to write about it.

Wow, Carrie thought. This was already far more interesting than she had thought it would be.

William and I have been seeing each other for a year. Of course, I've known him for longer than that. Loch Cameron is a small village. William was three years ahead of me at school, but all boys were just spotty ne'er-do-wells as far as I was concerned, then.

Of course, the war came when I was nine, and William joined up like a lot of the boys when he was fourteen and I was eleven. He went off with the whole group of them and I forgot about him soon after, because why would I think of a boy I hardly knew who had gone away to war? It wasn't like we were his family. You were supposed to be sixteen to join up, but all the boys lied and the navy officers turned a blind eye, that's what everyone said.

I was too young to join anything, and by the time I was old enough, the war had ended and the boys that were left came home. William was one of them. He wasn't the boy he'd been, though.

I remember one day, seeing him standing by the loch. He

was alone, staring into the water as I passed by. I was carrying
books from the library for Mother, and I dropped them onto the
cobbles. William jumped about a mile into the air at the
clatter as they hit the ground. I laughed and said something
stupid like "Whoops a daisy," but when I looked up from
where I'd crouched down to get the books, William was white
as a sheet. I reached out and took his hand and said, "William,
are you all right?" He snatched his hand away and muttered
something. I don't know what it was, and I left him staring
into the loch.

Then he married Clara, about a year after that meeting at
the loch, in 1946. He would have been nineteen or twenty
then, and I was seventeen. Clara was just a few months older
than me; they waited until her eighteenth birthday to marry
but as soon as she walked down the aisle in the chapel, I could
see she was pregnant already. I think everyone knew, but
nobody said anything. Things were different, after the war.
William had fought unimaginable terrors already and he was
still so young. No one wanted to wait until they were married
to have sex anymore. Death had been around us for too long.
We needed to live.

After the chapel wedding, they did the deadly predictable
'passing through the stones' up at the castle. At the time, I
thought little of William, or of any man. I wanted only to get
away from the village; to see the world. But I do remember
watching him dancing solemnly around those big boulders,
and thinking of that day at the loch where I dropped the books
behind him. And the look he gave me: so scared, so lost. That
moment bonded us somehow, though I didn't know it at the
time. I didn't know that I'd seen into his soul for the first time.

Oh my goodness, thought Carrie. Great-Aunt Maud had had
a secret lover? And a married one at that! Carrie couldn't
remember a William ever being mentioned when she was a

child. What had happened to their relationship? How long had it gone on for?

Carrie put the book down and ate the rest of her dinner thoughtfully. She had no idea that her great-aunt had been this good a writer, or as perceptive a chronicler of Loch Cameron. Or such a romantic! She was intrigued to know more about who William was and the secret life he'd had with Maud. It was tragic, but also daring, which surprised her less. Even when she was a child, she'd known her great-aunt was feisty. Maybe, during and after the war years, you just took what you could get. There was so much loss. Maybe Maud had felt as though some of William was better than none at all.

THIRTEEN

'So, when we reach the chorus, we need a powerful higher voice to come in,' June called as she sat at the piano, explaining a new song to the choir. 'Now. I've noticed that Carrie has a lovely soprano, and I thought she could take the lead on this song, where the second verse comes in. As a solo.'

'Oh, no. I couldn't.' Carrie held her hands up as if to fend off June's suggestion. 'I'm happy just being in the regular chorus.'

'Tut, tut. Modesty will get you nowhere in this life, madam.' June shook her head imperiously. 'Turn to page two of the sheet music. Can you sight-read?'

'No. I used to, but I've forgotten it all now,' Carrie confessed, her heartbeat getting faster. She was the centre of attention, and it felt weird. 'Really, I'm fine. I don't really want to do a solo.'

'Well, I'd like you to give it a try,' June insisted, in her no-nonsense voice.

'Go on, lassie.' Angus patted her arm encouragingly. 'No judgement here. An' ye've got a fine voice, I've heard ye.'

'Oh, fine, okay.' Carrie cleared her throat and looked at

the music where June had told her. She didn't remember what all the musical notes meant, now. Fortunately, she knew the song – a big power ballad hit from the early 1990s. She'd always loved it, and would always sing along if it came on the radio.

For a brief moment, she thought back to that day in the car with Claire. *And when you need me in the dead of night, I'm just a minute away... ooh, ooh.*

She shook her head imperceptibly. She never wanted to hear *that* song again.

The choir began the first verse, and Carrie steeled herself to come in on her part. It was an emotive lead in to a chorus and she knew, from having listened to it for so many years, that she had to attack those first words with everything she had.

The moment in the song came, and Carrie belted out the chorus as hard as she could. Its original singer had a terrific, strong voice with an amazing range, who could really warble those high notes in something that needed a lot of drama. Carrie tried to concentrate on the song and how she'd always heard it, hearing the original singer in her head as she sang.

As she shaped the words, giving them life and power, she couldn't help thinking about Claire. The song was a romantic one, but there was a feeling in it about loss. Carrie felt the loneliness of the song resonate deep in her body. When she reached the emotional climax of the chorus, she felt something loosen in her chest. She poured everything she had into those words: *Alone, alone.*

'Well. That was stupendous.' June clapped, and Carrie opened her eyes to see everyone in the choir grinning at her. 'I thought you'd do a good job, but I wasn't quite prepared for that.'

'Oh... thanks. I like that song.' Carrie felt herself blushing. She'd really let herself go, and it had felt good. It had been... *freeing.*

'Nice job,' Angus, next to her, murmured and gave her a wink. 'I love that song, too.'

'Power ballads are my favourite.' Dotty turned around from where she was standing in front of Carrie. 'Though I have to say I dinnae think ye can beat a bit o' Bonnie Tyler.' Dotty gave them a couple of lines from the chorus of 'Total Eclipse of the Heart' in a wavery yet tuneful voice that sounded like it was more used to singing hymns.

'Ah, I met Bonnie a couple o' times.' Angus smiled under his capacious beard. 'Right stunner, she was, aye. Fair pair o' lungs on her too.'

'You met Bonnie Tyler?' Carrie was doubly distracted by feeling self-conscious about her moment in the limelight by Angus's revelation, and by Dotty's unexpected love of power ballads.

'Aye. Remind me tae tell ye aboot my colourful life before Loch Cameron, sometime.' Angus winked at her.

'I will,' Carrie murmured back.

* * *

After rehearsal, Carrie helped tidy away the chairs and the tea and coffee cups from choir practice, and walked out with June, who locked up behind them.

'Lovely day,' June breathed, smiling up at the wide blue sky above them that was, for once, cloudless. 'Just look at that sky, and the way it reflects in the loch. In October, too! You just can't find that anywhere, you know. That's what people call picture-postcard beauty. Or, they did, in my day, anyway.'

'It *is* stunning here,' Carrie agreed, as they walked along the high street; she admired the baskets of riotously colourful flowers that hung outside many of the shops. Even the railings along the walkway that protected walkers from the drop down to the loch-side shingle beach were bedecked with baskets of trailing pink roses, bright orange geraniums and purple petunias. 'The air is so clean, too. I feel like it's clearing out my lungs every time I take a breath.' She took in a deep lungful of air and let it out slowly, feeling a twinge in her collarbone. It was still sore, some days.

'It probably is,' June chuckled. 'I'd prescribe Loch Cameron for anyone with asthma. Or any breathing issues. You don't appreciate how much of an impact city pollution can have on those things. That's the ex-nurse in me talking, of course.'

'You're right. When I was in London, my snot used to go grey from the soot in the underground,' Carrie remembered. 'Can't be good for you, can it?'

'Absolutely not.' June shook her head. 'Ugh. Really?'

Carrie took in June's lined, brown skin and her bright eyes: she was living proof of the benefit of living somewhere like Loch Cameron. You heard about those Greek islands – was it Greece? Somewhere like that, anyway – where everyone lived well past 100 because of their diet and the cleanliness of the air and the water. Maybe Loch Cameron was the Scottish version of that. Although, Carrie reasoned, the diet probably wasn't as good, what with the whisky and all the hearty pies and puddings she'd been putting away since she got here.

'Really,' Carrie laughed. 'You know, it's the air, but it's more than that too, isn't it? Loch Cameron? It has these strange healing powers, somehow.'

'I've always thought so.' June nodded as they walked along. She linked her arm in Carrie's, and Carrie felt a rush of gratitude for the gesture. 'You're finding it's helping you, I can tell. You really opened up today, in rehearsal. You know, you have a lovely voice.'

'Thanks. That's kind. I just enjoy singing. Always have.'

'I'm not known for my kindness,' June sniffed. 'Just say it how I see it. You could front a band or something. Or at the very least, be a soloist somewhere more impressive than the Loch Cameron community choir.'

'Hm. Thank you, but the community choir is enough for me for now,' Carrie demurred. They walked past a group of school children at the edge of the loch who looked like they were doing some kind of nature study, holding little fishing nets and listening to their teacher who was explaining something to them. Carrie thought how nice that was; she felt a pang of regret that she and Claire hadn't gone to school in Loch Cameron. Maybe their lives would have been different. Maybe everything would have been different.

'Penny for them.' June looked at her inquisitively as they walked along. There was a cold autumnal breeze blowing in across the loch, despite it being so sunny and clear, and Carrie was grateful for June's arm in hers. They passed a tree with bright yellow leaves that drifted down on Carrie, landing on her hair as if they were confetti.

'Oh. Nothing. Just thinking it must be nice, at that little primary school. Must be small? I can't imagine there are many children in the village, compared to a good-sized town, or a city school.' Carrie brushed the leaves from her hair.

'Ah, yes. It's very small. Different type of experience, but a nice one.' June smiled at the children, and waved. 'My grandchildren go there. In a place like Loch Cameron, everyone tends to know everyone.'

'I get that, yes.' Carrie smiled, shading her eyes from the glare of the sun off the loch.

Ahead of them, a food market had set up on the high street, and Carrie's spirit was lifted by the market's colourful awnings. 'Oh, look! I didn't know Loch Cameron had a street market!'

'Oh, yes. Once or twice a month at the moment, more in the summer. Mostly food: bakery, fruit and veg, jams and chutneys, that kind of thing. Sometimes other things. Crafts, candles, you know. We even had a man selling New Age crystals a while back.'

'Wow. What does an ex-nurse think about that?' Carrie asked playfully, as they walked past a delicious-smelling bakery stall. Fat loaves lined the back of a wide table, and baskets of large Belgian buns with thick icing and luscious cherries vied for attention with a stack of gooey brownies and a huge, white coconut cake. Individually wrapped fruit loaves were stacked to one side, next to a sign that said PLEASE ASK, WE HAVE BUTTER TO GO WITH THESE.

'Oh, I don't mind a crystal. Very pretty. Can't do any harm unless you insert it into an orifice.' June rolled her eyes. 'I saw my fair share of things that shouldn't be inserted into the body when I was nursing. Let's just say that crystal eggs weren't the most inappropriate.'

'Oh, my!' Carrie stopped in front of the bakery stall and asked for a fruit loaf, some delicious-looking crusty white rolls and a block of butter, which the friendly, middle-aged woman running the stall handed to her from a small fridge.

'That's local butter, from a dairy not far from here.' June nodded approvingly. 'It's very good. Be lovely on the fruit loaf.'

'Looks delicious.' Carrie took a paper bag filled with goodies from the woman gratefully. 'Thanks so much.'

'Come again! We're here every time,' the woman replied, cheerily.

She walked on with June, who gave her an unreadable look.

'What?' Carrie asked.

'No, it's just that you look happy,' June said, stopping in front of a fruit and vegetable stall. 'Your cup is filling up. It's not full yet. But it's getting there.'

'What do you mean?'

'It's a phrase, isn't it? Your cup is full if you're happy and fulfilled.' June shrugged. 'I say it how I see it,' she repeated.

'Do you think so?' It felt like so long since Carrie had been happy that she barely recognised the emotion anymore. But, today, putting her all into that song had been really cathartic. And, in the simple pleasure of browsing the food market with June, she realised she hadn't thought about anything in particular other than how much she was looking forward to devouring that fruit loaf. She hadn't thought about Claire, or the accident. And that was a relief.

'Yes,' June answered, simply. 'Carry on filling your cup, Carrie Anderson. Life can be awful, but it's also full of gifts, if you're brave enough to grab them.'

FOURTEEN

'I'm looking for a new rain mac,' Carrie told the young woman in Fiona's Fashions, the only clothes shop in the village. 'Preferably something that doesn't make me look like a pensioner. And a few other things.'

Though Carrie wasn't exactly paying attention to her looks during her stay in Loch Cameron, she had caught her reflection in the long mirror that hung in the hallway of Gretchen Ross's cottage that morning and had been appalled at her scraggly hair and pale pallor. Usually, she liked to keep her hair in a sleek bob, and tried to wear makeup most days – if she was going to work, anyway.

She had resolved, looking at herself that morning, to try and pull herself out of the slump she'd been in since Claire had died and do something about the way she looked. *Fake it until you make it.* Wasn't that what people said?

She was faking not being a mess, in that case.

'Aye, of course. Plenty o' macs.' Fiona walked over to a rack of garments and started pulling out various sleeves. 'No' just all black or khaki, either. Pink, red, turquoise too – I've got this one in fuchsia, an' I've had compliments on it.' She pulled out a hooded mac in a blue and green star pattern and held it out to Carrie to see. 'An' what else were you wantin'? I'm Fiona, by the way. This is ma shop.'

'Oh, hi! I'm Carrie. Just staying for a little while. Gretchen Ross's cottage.' Carrie waited for the familiar *Ohh, aye* that usually followed this disclosure.

'Ah.' Fiona nodded agreeably. 'Nice wee place, isn't it? Especially since Zelda did it up.' She clicked her tongue. 'Here I am assuming ye know who I'm talkin' aboot! Zelda's an American girl who stayed there a while back. She was quite into interior décor and the Laird let her do it up when Gretchen moved into the nursing home.'

'Ah. I met her, actually. At choir rehearsal in the village hall.' It was an unusual name, and meeting an American wasn't an everyday occurrence in Loch Cameron.

'Ah, okay. She must be visitin' the Laird. Lovely couple, they are.' Fiona looked mistily out of the window.

'She seemed really nice,' Carrie agreed.

'And how is Gretchen? Have ye met her yet?'

'Yeah. She's great.' Carrie nodded. 'And that makes sense, about the cottage, because I was thinking it was quite modern, décor-wise, for Gretchen. Not that she isn't modern in her way. But you know what I mean.'

'I know what you mean. All Zelda's work. She's actually gone on to work at one of those glossy interiors magazines. I think she does interiors fer people too, sometimes. Livin' the dream.'

'Sounds amazing.' Carrie looked around her. 'But this is your little empire. That's amazing, too, having your own business.'

'Aye, I'm proud of it.' Fiona nodded. 'The Laird helps small businesses in the village. It's only because he's givin' me such a good deal on the rent, as well as a grant, that I can operate. Still, business has been good. I cannae complain.'

'That's really nice of him. The Laird. When I used to come here as a kid, my great-aunt took us up to the castle one day and I remember an old man with a white beard. He sort of appeared at one point when we were having a tour around the castle, like he didn't want to talk to us but knew he had to. I always remember that.'

'Ach, that wouldae been the current laird's faither. He passed some time back, an' the estate went tae Hal Cameron. Cameron land, this is.'

'Oh, I see. That would make sense.' Carrie nodded. 'So the Laird owns... the whole village? And the castle?'

'Aye. He's the landowner. Been that way for hundreds o' years,' Fiona sighed. 'When ye look back at Scottish history, it isnae maybe the best way to have organised things. But, it is what it is. Lots o' families sold off their land, so some of Scotland's now owned by people from other countries. At least the Laird kept it in the family. It's hard work fer him, aye. He does a lot o' the work himself.'

'Hmm. I guess so. And at least he helps the villagers out, like you said, with the grant and the low rent.'

'Aye. He does a lot fer us.' Fiona ran her hand along the top of one of the rails of skirts that hung to her left. 'So, what else d'ye need?'

'I could do with a couple of nice dresses. Practical for work, but pretty,' Carrie mused. 'I'm working at The Fat Hen, in the kitchen. I just feel like I always turn up for work looking like I got pulled through a hedge backwards. But nothing too warm, as it gets hot in there, with the ovens.'

'Hmm. Rory McCrae's place?' Fiona started flipping through a rail of brightly coloured tea dresses, buttoned down the middle. She pulled out a couple and showed them to Carrie: one green, with a small white flower design, and one red, with polka dots. 'These would look nice on you. Green's always nice on a redhead. And red on red's also fun.'

'I like both of them. Can I try them on?' Carrie asked, reaching out to touch the fabric.

'Sure thing. Dressing room just here.' Fiona hung both dresses on a hook in the cosy little room at the back of the shop and gestured to Carrie. 'Come in. I'll get you a few more. You're a size fourteen?'

'Yes. Good skills,' Carrie laughed.

'All part o' the service.' Fiona smiled.

Carrie closed the door to the dressing room and started to change.

'What d'ye think o' Rory, then?' Fiona called through the door. 'Good-lookin' fella.'

'I suppose. I don't think of him in that way,' Carrie lied, shrugging off her jumper and jeans.

'Then you'd be the only one in the village,' Fiona laughed. 'Even the auld ones talk aboot Rory an' his looks. He's easy on the eye, I cannae deny it.'

'Do they?' Carrie unbuttoned the red polka dot dress and eased it up over her thighs. She'd been trying not to think about Rory McCrae. He'd been super professional at work every night since they'd had mac and cheese after hours; there hadn't been a repeat of his oddly mixed signals.

'Aye. He seems nice enough, but he keeps himself to himself,' Fiona continued. 'No' one for bein' overly friendly. I've barely said more than a few sentences tae the man since he arrived here a few years back. Get the impression he doesnae like people that much,' she sniffed. 'He's been known tae be rude. No amount of attractiveness makes me forgive that, I'm afraid.'

'Rude? In what way?' Carrie buttoned up the dress and twirled a few times in front of the mirror so that the knee-length skirt spun around her. She remembered her first meeting with Rory in the village shop, where he had practically barged her out of the way for some fresh parsley. She'd thought he was rude, then.

'Ah, just here an' there. Demandin' things in shops, bein' rude tae people on the high street when they ask how he is. I heard him makin' fun o' the May Day party the Laird holds every year. He seems tae think he's above all of us, ye know? With his posh restaurant. No one from the village goes there. All tourists.'

'That seems a shame.' Carrie admired the dress: it fit around her waist very well and flared out over her hips nicely. She took it off and tried the green one. 'He seems fine to me, but I guess I don't know him that well.'

'Ah, well, maybe he's a nice guy. I just heard he had a bit o' a shady past in the military, an' what with him keepin' himself to himself, I guess people dinnae think anythin' else.'

'What shady past?' Carrie frowned, buttoning up the green dress. It was just as nice as the red one: she wasn't frowning at it, rather the idea that Rory had done something awful in the past.

'Dunno.' Fiona lowered her voice. 'But I heard it was somethin' tae do with a woman.'

'Oh.' Carrie looked at herself in the mirror. Rory did seem reluctant to talk about his time in the navy, and she wondered if that was why. Maybe he'd had his heart broken. Or broken someone else's heart. Or, maybe there had been something worse. You heard stories about bullying in the military. It could have been anything, or nothing.

'Well, I guess that's his business,' she said, feeling a little sorry for anyone in Loch Cameron who tried to keep a secret. She was well aware that her business had already most likely been splashed around the village. If Rory had a past, then that was up to him, wasn't it?

I don't care what Rory might or might not have done in the past, she thought. *It's of no importance to me.*

But was that entirely true? Carrie didn't like to admit it, but she was attracted to Rory. Nothing was going to happen between them, but she had found herself thinking about him more than she probably should have done. He had kissed her on the cheek, when she'd left work that time, and she kept thinking about it. What did it mean? What did she want it to mean? She didn't know. But there was a primal physical attraction there, and she was surprised by it.

She changed back into her clothes and walked back into the shop. 'I'll take both dresses, and the mac in black, I think,' she said. 'Thanks, Fiona.'

'Nae bother.' Fiona nodded and took the dresses from her. 'Let me put this all in a bag for ye.' She took the garments to the counter and started putting them through the till. 'Ten per cent discount fer new customers.' She twinkled at Carrie, as she gave her the total.

'That's very kind of you. Thanks.' Carrie paid and took her bag.

'Hope tae see you again soon,' Fiona said. 'And I hope the dresses have the desired effect,' she said, with a wink.

'But that's not why...' Carrie trailed off. 'They're for work,' she added.

'Aye. Work with Rory McCrae.' Fiona winked again. 'No judgement. He's a good-lookin' fella, like I said.'

'That's not what I was thinking,' Carrie insisted.

'Ah, dinnae worry, hen, I'm just teasin' ye,' Fiona chuckled. 'Ye enjoy yerself, that's what I say. Life's too short.'

FIFTEEN

'So, you take the bread dough and knead it like this.' Rory picked up a ball of soft dough from a stainless-steel tray of perhaps twenty identical balls. His strong hands kneaded the bread dough, stretching and pulling, in and out. Carrie found herself a little hypnotised by the motion, and Rory's hands themselves, which were large and square and somehow so muscular. She'd never particularly noticed anyone's hands as being muscular before.

Don't stare, she told herself. But, of course, she had to pay attention to Rory's instructions. And that involved watching him.

Nice work if you can get it, Claire's voice said in her ear. She ignored it.

'Now you try.' Rory handed her a lightly floured ball of bread dough.

Their fingers brushed each other's; Carrie fought the impulse to touch his hand.

'Okay. Like this?' Carrie began copying Rory.

He watched her for a moment and nodded, but reached for her hands and held them in his. 'You've almost got it. More like this.' He gently guided her hands against the dough, pushing and opening her fingers with his.

Carrie tried to concentrate, but the motion of his hands on hers was...

Intensely erotic? Claire's voice suggested.

It's something, all right, Carrie thought, hoping she wasn't blushing.

'That's it.' He caught her eye. 'Bit like that scene in *Ghost*, isn't it?' he chuckled. 'You know, with the pottery wheel.'

'Oh. Haha. Maybe.' Carrie laughed, surprised at Rory's abrupt change of mood. 'I hadn't thought about it. I haven't seen that film for years.'

'One of my favourites.' He took his hands off hers. 'So, when we've kneaded the dough, you put it into the greased, floured tin – see, you'll need to prep all these,' he pointed to a pile of small rectangular bread tins stacked neatly by the sink, 'and let it prove. Then we knead them again and bake them. All right?'

'Sure.' Carrie picked up the stack of tins from next to the sink and brought them to her workspace. 'I'll get going on these and then finish the kneading.'

'Great. Thanks. I can give you a hand for ten minutes or so, but then I've got to prep the salmon for the gravlax.'

'So. *Ghost*.' Carrie caught Rory's eye this time. 'All-time favourite, or you're just really into Whoopi Goldberg?'

'Top five. But yeah, I did also love *Sister Act*,' he confessed.

'I'm almost frightened to ask what else made it into the top five.' Carrie raised her eyebrows as she started to brush oil around the bread tins. '*Crocodile Dundee*?'

'*Crocodile Dundee* is a perfect eighties movie. Don't try to suggest it isn't.' Rory continued kneading the bread dough, a smile lifting the corner of his lip.

'I wouldn't dream of it. They fell in love and got married in real life, didn't they? The two stars,' Carrie asked, oiling the next tin. 'Maybe it was something about the scene where he saves her from the crocodile.'

'Maybe. I always liked the "That's not a knife. *That*'s a knife," scene,' Rory chuckled, picking up a bread knife from the block they used in the kitchen and doing a quick impression.

'Heroic,' Carrie giggled. 'What girl could resist?'

'Exactly. A time when men were men.' Rory shot her a little smile.

'I think men have always been men, haven't they? Unless I missed a memo somewhere,' Carrie replied, archly. 'We have moved on from the "my knife's bigger than yours" model of masculinity nowadays though, haven't we?'

'I suppose we have. Bear in mind I spent a large part of my life doing boy's own adventure stuff for a living. I lived in a very macho environment in the navy. Sometimes I forget the rest of the world's not like that.'

'Hmm. But you also like *Ghost*.' Carrie picked up a new tin. 'Not very macho.'

'You can be a man's man and a romantic as well, you know. Their love defies death!' he protested.

'Oh, I know.' Carrie thought briefly about how Patrick Swayze's character in the movie spoke to Whoopi Goldberg from beyond the grave.

Not unlike me, Claire quipped. *Maybe I have unfinished business with you.*

Carrie ignored her.

'It's nice to be a romantic,' she added. 'I never really found it worked out, though. All that... stuff...' She trailed off.

'What stuff?'

'Love, I guess.' She shrugged.

'Hm. It's a tricky beast,' he said, dropping one kneaded ball of dough into a tin and picking up another.

Carrie liked the way that they seemed to be working in synergy with each other.

'I never had much luck either,' Rory continued. 'Here and there, but...' He trailed off. 'You like to think it's out there, don't you? Like the movies kind of love? I do, anyway. Some days I believe it, some days, not so much.'

'Hmm. Mostly I don't,' Carrie admitted. 'I never found it.' She sighed. 'But, when I look back, I can see that I didn't really allow myself to find it, either. My sister and I were always really close. We were kind of like a couple, in a way. She was my go-to. Probably I just never needed anyone else.'

'You're referring to her in the past tense.' Rory frowned. 'Did you... lose her? I remember you said you'd lost someone.'

'I still don't want to talk about it, if that's okay.' She looked away to collect herself, not wanting to get upset in front of Rory. 'Can we go back to bread? Or eighties movies?'

'Of course. I'm here if you need someone to talk to, though. I mean, I am a tough guy, obviously.' He rolled his eyes, as if to indicate how ridiculous he knew it sounded to say such a thing about yourself. 'But I think I've learnt how to listen, too, over the years.'

'Thanks. That's really kind.' Carrie shot him a shy smile. 'Tell me the rest of your top five movies. That'll cheer me up. Presumably they're all awful.'

'They are absolutely NOT awful,' he argued back, grinning. 'Classics of cinema, more like.'

'Including *Crocodile Dundee*?' She shook her head.

'Most definitely *Crocodile Dundee*,' he insisted, kneading the bread. 'And in the kitchen, at least, I'm the boss. So, what I say, goes.'

'Yes, Chef,' Carrie replied, smartly, feeling a frisson of plea-sure at Rory's words: *I'm the boss*. She definitely wasn't averse to the pleasant aura of alpha male that he gave off in the kitchen, giving orders and making sure every plate went out looking and tasting perfect. It wasn't an unpleasant, shouty vibe at all – yes, Chef Rory gave orders, but only because that was his job. And he never raised his voice, just delivered everything in a calm, steady tone of voice. Carrie found that she liked knowing exactly what he wanted from her, and his praise when she did a good job. In fact, she found that there was a kind of erotic undertone to it all.

They both started laughing.

'That's more like it,' he chuckled, raising an eyebrow playfully.

* * *

That night, when Carrie got home after work, she climbed tiredly into bed and opened Maud's diary again. Rory was playing on her mind, and she needed not to think about him for a while. They'd had such a nice time together at work that evening. When the restaurant opened, Rory was all business, just like always, and she and Kathy made a good team, making sure everything happened when it needed to. But in those hours before opening, when they'd been making the bread together... that had felt both comfortable and exciting at the same time. And Carrie had never felt that way before.

This isn't why you're here, she told herself. *You came to Loch Cameron to hide. To heal. To get over losing Claire.*

Don't mind me, Claire's voice piped up. *I wouldn't want to get in the way of you getting some action at long last, Carrie.*

That's the last thing on my mind, Carrie argued.

Is it, though? Claire asked.

Carrie picked up Maud's diary as a distraction. She was enjoying reading her great-aunt's thoughts. It made her feel close to Maud, even though she had written them down so many years ago.

Why not think about him? Claire asked, butting in. *I would. If I wasn't madly in love with Graham, of course.*

'Because he's my boss,' Carrie said out loud. Now that she

was at the cottage alone, she could do weird things like talk to her dead sister's voice in her head, without anyone knowing. 'It's inappropriate. And I'm trying to read, here.'

People meet at work all the time. Where else is there, apart from the internet? Claire asked. *I met Graham at work. When are you two going to make friends, by the way? I don't like the fact you're still ignoring each other. I did die, you know. The least you could do is keep my memory alive, together.*

'I'm not likely to forget you, am I?' Carrie tutted. 'Graham and I never got on.'

You mean, you never gave him a chance. I don't think you've ever even had a proper conversation.

'Whatever. Claire, I don't want to talk to him about you,' Carrie protested. 'I can't. Not yet.'

Claire's voice went silent, and Carrie picked up Maud's diary again. If it was teaching her anything, it was that love hurt. Maud and William's affair was doomed – anyone could see that. Carrie read on, hoping she was wrong, but knowing that she likely was not.

20th January 1958

I feel like I'm writing a novel about me and William, but it is a strange story, how it all came to be. I was going to write how it worked out there for a moment, but of course it hasn't worked out at all. Clara is still alive. William and Clara are still married.

Now, of course, I don't want Clara to die. That would be appalling. But she has been ill for a long time now, and it has taken a toll on William.

I see everyone, as postmistress. When I took over the job from Mother in 1952, I was just twenty-two but somehow, that uniform gave me a kind of power over Loch Cameron. People didn't see bookish, odd Maud Rose McKinley anymore:

they saw the postmistress, someone who they thought they could entrust all their secrets to – and all those belonging to other people, in particular.

Now, I'm not one for gossip. I listen, because I have to. But I don't pass it on. Yet, when I started to hear the rumours about Clara's mystery illness, like everyone else, I wondered what it could be.

I did sometimes see them around the village. Of course, I did. Loch Cameron isn't that big. And my mother was friends with William's mother, so we even ended up at the same parties sometimes. I'd been to William and Clara's wedding, but I also ended up at the christening party for their first child, Alice. And the second, Luke.

However, William, Clara and I weren't friends, particularly. It was just that Loch Cameron was – and is – a small place, and there would be crowds of people who gathered at these kind of events all the time. I was just one of the crowd.

They seemed happy, but on the other hand, I wasn't really paying attention. Running the post office was busy, not least because it wasn't just the post office; there was the adjoining shop to take care of, and all the other things: tobacco, the newspaper orders, groceries.

And then I started to hear that Clara couldn't get out of bed. That she'd been very sick after Luke was born, and that she'd almost bled to death during the birth. My mother went round to see if she could help, and I remember she came back with terrible tales about Clara. That she just stared at the wall and refused to move. That she was neglecting her baby, and neglecting Alice. That she was as thin as a rake and hardly ate.

Still, it wasn't until William came into the post office almost two years later with both children that we had a conversation. Both children were crying, that I recall. William looked exhausted; I don't doubt that he was, considering that he was caring for the children and Clara at that time. His family did help, though.

He wanted two stamps. I tore them off the strip for him. Little Alice was running around the shop causing havoc, and Luke was still crying. I came out from behind the desk, caught Alice up in my arms and took the envelopes from William and stuck the stamps on for him. I gave both little ones some sweets, free of charge. It was something I did sometimes if I needed to quiet rowdy children. Luke was probably too young, but he seemed to take to it very happily and William didn't seem to mind.

He thanked me, and while Alice and Luke enjoyed their sweets, I asked if he wanted a cup of tea. There wasn't anyone else in the post office, and I thought he looked like he needed it. And he said yes. So we all went into the back room and I made us a cup of tea and put some biscuits out for the children too.

And William talked. For the first time he really talked to me, despite us knowing each other so long, but also never really knowing each other at all. He told me everything that had happened with Clara. That she still refused to get out of bed, and that she was so weak that she had to be spoon-fed. The doctor couldn't see anything medically wrong with her, although she had had a very traumatic birth with Luke. He stumbled over his words as he told me how Clara bled heavily all the time, so much that he'd had to buy new sheets on many occasions, and how his mother was always having to bleach Clara's blood out of them. Still, the doctor just said that it was women's problems, and that the bleeding would probably go away on its own.

I didn't know what to say to him, so I listened. It seemed like that was something he needed. He told me about how happy he and Clara had been, but that he still always had nightmares about the war. He wouldn't talk about what those nightmares were, though I found out later.

He told me he didn't know what to do. Clara didn't seem to be getting any better, and he was struggling to cope on his own, even though his mother looked after the children when he went to work. He was a boat builder. Still is. When he came back from the war, his uncle took him in and apprenticed him.

I didn't have any wisdom to offer him. I just listened, and I thought about how handsome he was, and how sad. Then he finished his tea and went home.

After that, he started staying for tea at the post office fairly frequently. He always brought the children with him, as if they were some kind of barrier between us, providing safety. Making our conversations above board.

And they were above board. Until they weren't.

SIXTEEN

1st February 1958

Saw William today at the post office. When he comes in, you'd never know we were sleeping together. I don't know if this is all part of being British and the stiff upper lip the English have, though I always wondered whether it really applied to Scots. He always greets me as "Miss McKinley" and I always say, "Hello, William," because it's all right for me to do that. Everyone knows we have known each other since we were bairns, more or less.

Sometimes he asks for some tobacco, sometimes the newspaper or he sends a letter and asks for a first-class stamp. I always give him what he wants with a smile, just like I do with everyone else. I always ask after the children, but I don't mention Clara. The casual observer might think that I'm being kind by not mentioning her. That's what people do, here – not mention difficult situations so they can pretend they're not happening. But I'm not being kind. Even though I feel sorry for her, I try not to think about the fact that William is still married, and that what we're doing is wrong in the eyes of God. Because I love him, and I don't want to stop.

Bloody hell, Carrie thought, as she hulled strawberries in the restaurant kitchen. It was the day after the bread-making with Rory and she had Maud's diary open next to her. She just couldn't stop reading it. As a precaution, not wanting to make a mess of it with strawberry juice, she'd put the book inside a transparent zip-lock food bag. It was a pain having to reach inside the bag to turn the page every time, but she was wary of keeping Great-Aunt Maud's diary in good condition. Especially because the entries were so fascinating.

'Referring to your notes?' Kathy came in and washed her hands in the sink. Today her hair was a striking yellow on one side and a vivid green on the other. Even her fringe had a poker-straight division in the middle now, where it had been all black before. 'Do you need to, to prepare strawberries? Or has he given you such strict instructions you're paranoid about getting them the wrong width?'

'Ha. No, nothing like that. It's an old diary belonging to my great-aunt,' Carrie explained. 'I didn't want to get it dirty while I was working.'

'How cool! Oh, by the way, Rory'll be here shortly. He said he wants to brief us on the specials.'

'Okay.' Carrie put the diary to one side on the counter. As she did so, Rory strode into the kitchen, rolling up his chef's white sleeves. Carrie found herself staring at his muscular forearms again, at his tanned skin and his dark hair. She blinked and looked away.

'So, the specials,' he said, placing a scrawled list of dishes on the counter in front of Carrie. 'As usual, all fresh, local and seasonal. Roast Loch Cameron salmon with sautéed potatoes and fresh greens. I'm also doing a mussel in white wine linguine, if you can prep the mussels for me, Carrie—? I'll show you how.'

Carrie nodded. 'That's fine.'

'Okay, great. And then we've got organic chicken done as a casserole, local sheep's cheese and beetroot salad with walnuts, and fresh bread. Like we did yesterday.' Rory raised his eyebrows at Carrie. 'Reckon you can manage that with me? I see you've started on the strawberries for the cranachan. I thought I'd mix it up and not use raspberries for a change.'

'I love cranachan,' Kathy sighed. 'Hope there's at least one left over at the end of service.'

'Me, too.' Carrie grinned. The traditional Scottish dessert made of cream, whisky, oats and raspberries was a delicious treat. Maud had often made it for her and Claire when they were children, without the whisky. Though, sometimes, Carrie and Claire would ask for a little bit of whisky to go into the cream, so that they didn't feel like babies. Maud would give them a long look, smile, and then tip a few drops into the cream with a smile.

'Well, it's always popular, but I do have a tarte tatin on the menu too. So, you might be lucky.' Rory looked up at Carrie, a twinkle in his eyes. 'I have to say, I love a woman who loves food.'

'Rory, don't embarrass the girl. We all love food. That's why we're here. Let's face it, it's not for the wages.' Kathy rolled her eyes.

'Whaaaat? Are you saying I don't pay you enough? I'll have you know this is the best restaurant in Loch Cameron,' he exclaimed.

'The pay's fine, and I appreciate the free food, for sure.' Carrie laughed at his mock-outraged expression. 'I'm not criticising.'

'Neither am I, Rory. Keep your hair on.' Kathy raised a

comedic eyebrow. 'Chefs, eh, Carrie? Dramatic types. Just like those cooking programmes you see on TV.'

'Hardly. I don't think I've ever raised my voice in the restaurant or the kitchen, what are you on about?' Rory protested, grinning. 'Also, I wasn't always a chef, remember? I was trained to keep calm in high-pressure situations. Timing a perfect steak isn't quite as stressful as defusing a bomb.'

'Depends who you're cooking it for. My grannie's very particular about her steak,' Kathy chuckled. 'Real tough old bird, she is.'

'Must be where you get your *joie de vivre*.' Rory gave Kathy a beatific smile.

'That feels like a veiled insult, hun,' Kathy shot back.

'Children, children!' Carrie interjected, laughing at Kathy and Rory's sibling-like banter. 'Come on. Let's concentrate on the menus.'

'See, this is why Carrie's my favourite. Focused on the food.' Rory nodded.

You're his favourite, Claire's voice piped up in her head. *That's nice, isn't it?*

He didn't mean anything by that, Carrie thought back. *Stop being so sarcastic.*

I'm not being sarcastic, Claire said. *I was merely observing that Hot Chef Rory described you as his favourite employee. Can't be bad.*

There are only two of us, to be fair, Carrie replied.

Whatever. I'm a romantic, Claire replied. *I believe in love, unlike some people.*

That's not fair.

You didn't believe I loved Graham. But I did. I do.

I don't want to talk about that now, Carrie thought, wanting to shake her head to get her sister's voice out of it all of a sudden.

'Carrie? Are you all right?' Rory was looking at her curiously.

'Yeah. I'm fine.' Carrie chewed the inside of her cheek, hoping she hadn't looked like a crazy person just then. 'What were we saying?'

'I need to run you through some of the provenance for these things.' Rory fanned out some other pieces of paper he was holding on the counter containing more of his scrawled notes. 'What's this?' He picked up Maud's diary, still in its zip-lock bag. 'Did I leave this here?' He pulled the diary out of the bag before Carrie had a chance to say anything. 'Oh. Wait. Sorry, I thought this was one of my notebooks, but—'

'It's mine.' Carrie held out her hand for the diary and Rory handed it to her. 'Well, I should say, it belonged to my great-aunt. Dotty found it in Myrtle's things after she passed away, and she gave it to me when she realised I was Maud's great-niece.'

'Oh. Sorry, I just assumed, because I leave notebooks everywhere...' Rory trailed off. 'Though I don't usually put them in zip-lock bags. That's actually a great idea.'

'You're welcome to use the patented Book in Bag formula.' Carrie gave him a shy smile.

'So, anything good in there? Maybe some old recipes?'

'No recipes yet. I'll let you know if there are. Some fairly scandalous detail about my great-aunt's sex life, though.' Carrie pulled an awkward face. 'Fascinating but also slightly uncomfortable.'

'I can imagine. How interesting, though!' Rory looked thoughtfully at the diary in Carrie's hands. 'I'd love to have a look sometime.'

'Well, I'll show you later, if you like.' Carrie shrugged. 'I wouldn't have thought anyone would be that interested.'

'Well, it's a story, isn't it? Bit of local history.' Rory grinned.

'He just wants to hear about the sex part, I bet,' Kathy chuckled.

'Not true. I'm into local history,' Rory protested.

'Smutty history,' Kathy corrected him.

'I think you're talking about yourself there.' Rory one-upped her again.

Carrie wondered if there was anything going on between them; she'd assumed that their vibe was like brother and sister, but maybe she was wrong. Kathy was good-looking and obviously very intelligent and funny.

'As if. Come on, let's do the provenance.' Kathy winked at Carrie. 'Leave Carrie's auntie's innermost thoughts alone for now.'

SEVENTEEN

'So, go on, then. Tell me about this diary.' Rory hoisted himself up onto the edge of the stainless-steel worktop and handed Carrie a spoon for her strawberry cranachan: luckily, there had been a few left that evening, after a quieter than usual service.

Kathy had already had hers and hurried home: she had a chapter to finish for her PhD supervisor. She had confided in Carrie that she was way behind on her deadline.

'Oh. You don't have to be polite, really.' Carrie laughed a little nervously. 'It's just some family stuff.'

'You said it was saucy.' Rory pointed his spoon at her. 'Don't hold out on me. I'm invested.'

'Okay. Well, to give you some background, Maud was my great-aunt. Me and my sister and our parents used to come up and visit when Claire and I were kids. She was great.' Carrie smiled for a moment, remembering. 'I always thought she was single. But it would seem that she had an affair with a married man in the village.'

'Wow. Secret lives. I love it.' Rory spooned more dessert into his mouth.

'Yeah. Though I kind of feel a little as though I'm spying on

Maud's most intimate thoughts – well, I am, really. But I'm kind of obsessed with Maud and William and their secret relationship.'

'That's the guy? William?'

'Yeah. They were at school together and she didn't think anything of him, then he married this local girl, Clara, but then she got ill and basically he and Maud got together. That's where I am.'

'Sounds like a bit of a player.' Rory frowned. 'Cheating on your sick wife? Got to be a no-no.'

'I don't know if he was a player, really. Not yet, anyway. I think they – William and Maud – were both really lonely. But I don't know. We weren't there so we can't judge.'

'Fair enough.'

'I wish...' Carrie trailed off. She'd wanted to say that she wished Claire could have read the diaries, but she didn't want that to lead in to having to explain what had happened.

'What?'

'Oh, nothing. I was just going to say I wish I'd known more about my great-aunt when she was alive. She was a warm, homely presence in my childhood. But when my mum died, our dad refused to take us to Scotland anymore. Then Maud died, and we never even knew.'

'We?'

'Me and my sister,' Carrie answered, shortly.

'Oh, that's rough. I'm so sorry.' Rory reached out and touched her arm.

'It's okay. It is what it is. But thanks,' Carrie said. 'Do you want to hear the next entry?'

'Sure. If you don't mind reading it.'

'I don't mind.' Carrie finished the last spoon of her delicious dessert and put her spoon down, wiping her fingers on a napkin. She picked up the diary and started to read the next entry aloud.

10th February 1958

Yesterday was our one-year anniversary.

Unlike other couples who can celebrate their special days openly, we can't have house parties or dance around the stone circle up at Loch Cameron Castle. So, we had a secret evening away from Loch Cameron altogether.

William picked me up in his car and drove us to a little bed and breakfast in Loch Awe. On the way, he wordlessly handed me a wedding ring. I put it on my finger just as silently. I knew that it must be Clara's, but I didn't ask. I also knew that if I wasn't wearing it when we got to the bed and breakfast, no doubt eyebrows would have been raised at the notion that we really were Mr and Mrs William Graves.

When we got there, we went straight up to our room and lay on the double bed. William took me in his arms but I was mindful of the silence in the building: married couples don't roll around in the throes of passion as soon as entering a bed and breakfast. I knew that. It would be unseemly. So, I made us lie there, fully clothed, and talk and sound normal until it was a decent time to go to the local pub for dinner.

I don't think William liked that too much, but he indulged me. He has a sweet nature.

Still, when we got home after a very nice dinner and some wine, William made it clear that he had waited long enough and he took me upstairs to our room and fulfilled his 'husbandly' duty very well indeed.

It wasn't the first time, of course. The first time we made love was a couple of months after that first conversation in the post office. I still live with Mother and Father at the cottage, and one night when I was reading in my room, I heard the sound of something hitting my windowpane. I looked out, and there was William, standing to the side of the cottage, half-

hidden in the hedge. He had thrown pebbles at my window to attract my attention.

I snuck out, of course. By this time, I was fully aware that he was a handsome man whose wife was not able to fulfil her marital duties. Combined with the fact that William was paying me a great deal of attention, and that we had talked a lot and got to know each other quite well, I had almost been expecting something like this to happen.

When I got outside, he pulled me into the hedge with him and kissed me. It was immediate; I don't think he even said anything, and neither did I. Years of frustration had driven him to it, and I responded with the pent-up passion of a woman who had never so much as been kissed before.

After that, William came for me every week on the same night. After that first time, when we made love half bent over in the bushes, we found better places: in the forest on a blanket during the summer, and when it got colder William would pick me up at the end of the lane in his car and drive us somewhere remote. It wasn't ideal, but it was all we had. His children were always at home, and Clara lying ever-present in her bed, slowly wasting away.

6th March 1958

I felt sick all day today. I wasn't sick, though, and by the end of the day I felt a little better.

18th March 1958

I have not had my monthly visitor, and it was due two weeks ago. I still feel nauseous every day. I dread what this might mean.

23rd March 1958

I have booked an appointment with the doctor. William says it is probably nothing, but I know. I know I am pregnant with his child. And if I am, I don't know what this will mean for me or for us. I am trying to stay calm, especially at work, but the knowledge weighs heavily on me. William says there is no point in worrying until we know for sure, but I can't not think about it.

Carrie turned the page, but the diary had finished – there were only empty pages that followed.

'What happened next?' Rory was literally at the edge of his seat, perched on the stainless-steel counter.

'That's all there is.' Carrie showed Rory the empty pages that followed the last entry. 'There were two other books, but I looked at those already and one just contained Maud's post office records. The other one was from when she was much younger. There were some sweet notes in it about her friends at school, but nothing about William and the baby.'

'So, Great-Aunt Maud got pregnant from her affair with William?' Rory steepled his fingers together. 'Did you know that? Did she have the baby?'

'Maud never had children. Not that I was aware of, anyway.'

'So, what? She miscarried, maybe. Or even had an abortion? Was that a thing then?'

'Not really. I think you could go to an illegal abortionist, but that would have been fraught with danger. Maybe she had the baby in secret somehow. That seems more likely,' Carrie mused.

Rory looked as though he was going to say something more when Carrie's phone buzzed. She looked at the screen.

Hi, Carrie. Wondered if you wanted to talk. I know you hate me, but Claire would have wanted us to be friends. I miss her like hell and I know it must be even worse for you. Give me a call if you want. Graham.

Carrie stared at the message for a while, and then deleted it without answering. 'Nope,' she muttered under her breath. She wasn't ready to be friends with Graham yet. She still didn't have the bandwidth to empathise with someone else; she was still finding her way through her grief. Graham would have to wait.

'Anything important?' Rory nodded at her phone.

'What? Oh, no. Just family stuff,' Carrie said, vaguely. She didn't want to talk about it because thinking about Graham unlocked other things in her mind that she didn't want to think about at all. As long as she could keep that particular cupboard locked, then all was well.

It won't stay locked forever, Claire's voice said, suddenly, in a warning tone. *You need to deal with what's in there. Don't kid yourself.*

Carrie ignored her sister's warning. She couldn't think about that now.

'So, this is quite the mystery, huh? You must be so intrigued. A whole story about your family I'm guessing you never knew.' Rory jumped off the counter and took both of their bowls and spoons to the sink.

'Hmm. I know. I could have a relative somewhere in Loch Cameron still.' The thought dawned on Carrie, and she felt somehow vulnerable at its arrival.

'You could ask Dotty. She got you the diaries in the first place, right? She knows everyone and everything.'

'Right...' Carrie was thoughtful. 'I mean, it's weird that if Maud had a child, she never mentioned it to us.' She held the book in her hand, as if weighing its importance.

'But you were kids. Your mum and dad might have known.' Rory returned from the sink, wiping his hands on a cloth. 'Didn't you say that your aunt passed when you were still quite young? Adults don't talk about this kind of stuff with children.'

'That's true. I wonder if Mum knew,' Carrie mused. 'She might have.'

'And your mum also... passed?'

Rory came to stand next to her; she was suddenly and almost painfully aware of his physical presence. It was as if he exuded some kind of manly sexual aura that made her body react to him: all she wanted to do, in that moment, was melt into his body.

Instead, she cleared her throat and sat up straighter, as if signalling how clearly she *wasn't* affected by Rory's presence. 'Yes. I was quite young.'

'Sorry. That's awful.' His hand grazed hers.

She looked up into his deep brown eyes. 'Thanks,' she breathed.

There was a moment of pause between them, where their eyes seemed to say everything they weren't saying with words. Rory's gaze on hers was intense, and Carrie felt as though she was dissolving.

Without saying anything, he reached up to her mouth and stroked the edge of her lip. 'You had some cream there,' he explained, his fingertip resting for a moment just above her chin, before he took it away.

'Oh.' Carrie was unable to think of any other reply. Rory's touch was electric and unexpected: it resonated deliciously on her skin.

'Taken care of,' he added, his arm returning to his side.

He retained eye contact with her, and they stood there, staring at each other. Carrie felt slightly breathless. When she tried to think of anything to say, she drew a blank.

Great.

Something fell from the book onto the floor. It had hardly made a sound, but Carrie was still holding the book and she felt something dislodge from the pages. Frowning, she bent to pick up the paper that had fallen out. She fanned the pages of the book open again and looked between them carefully, but there was nothing else loose inside it. Just this one thing.

A photo.

She turned it over and looked at it carefully. 'Huh?' Her eyes widened and she showed it to Rory. 'This might answer some of our questions, maybe.'

It was a sepia-toned picture of the kind from a long time ago: a posed image, featuring a little boy in a sailor suit sitting on a chair. His decidedly sulky expression reflected the likelihood that he was probably being told to sit still, or else.

Carrie turned the photo over. On the back, someone had written *L, 1960* but nothing more.

'Look! 1960. That's a couple of years after these entries.' She passed the photo to Rory.

'It must be the kid. Her child.' Rory studied the picture. 'Has to be.'

'It would have to be more than a coincidence – that she's writing about being pregnant, and there's a picture of a baby,' Carrie admitted. 'So, she had the baby. It looks that way, anyway.'

'Yeah. But you didn't know him when you used to visit; he wasn't here. So, what happened to him?'

'I don't know,' Carrie mused. 'I never knew Maud had a child. She never said anything to us, and there was no one else living with her.'

'Bit of a mystery, then.' Rory handed back the photo.

'I mean, I suppose, given the circumstances, there would have been a local scandal if people knew Maud and William had had a baby together, given that he was already married, with kids. And that his wife was sick. People would gossip now, never mind in the sixties.'

'Yeah. So maybe she gave him away to be adopted or something.' Rory shrugged. 'I mean, I'm not an expert in this kind of stuff. But that seems like something that could have happened, right?'

'Yes. It definitely could have.' Carrie stared at the picture again. 'If he was born in 1959 – she got pregnant in 1958 – he'd only be, what? In his sixties, still?' She looked up, hopefully, at Rory. 'He'd be my... what would he be?'

'Your first cousin, once removed? He would have been your mum's cousin. I think that's right.' Rory closed his eyes for a minute, working it out. 'Yeah. I'm pretty sure that's it.'

'Well, he would be... family, anyway...' Carrie trailed off. 'And he might be alive, still.'

'But if he was adopted, he probably isn't in Loch Cameron anymore,' Rory said. 'I mean, it stands to reason.'

The realisation that she might have a family member she never knew she'd had, alive, somewhere, was like a hammer blow to Carrie's heart. She didn't know what to make of the idea. When she'd lost Claire, she'd lost everything. Her mum was already gone, her dad might as well have been for all the contact he had with either of the girls, Maud had gone, and there was no one else. Carrie had been mourning Claire, but she'd also been mourning the loss of all her family.

With Claire gone, she felt as though her tether to the real world had finally broken. There was nothing and no one keeping her attached to reality. That was partly why she'd come to Loch Cameron: it was a place that held memories, and she could attempt to tether herself to those. And, at the same time, it was a place where she could lose herself, a place where she could hide from reality.

She had been slowly recovering, day by day, with the choir and the fresh air and long walks that made her feel more centred and whole. But now, she felt completely adrift again. Maud had had this whole life Carrie had never known about, and now it looked like Carrie might still have some living family somewhere.

But instead of feeling excited, it made her feel unsettled. *They lied to us. To me*, she thought. *Maud lied about her baby. We never knew.*

Dad had prevented her and Claire from visiting Maud once their mother had died. *We could have had family. We could have not felt so damn alone,* she thought, ashamed of the tears that sprang to her throat.

'Carrie? You okay?' Rory laid his hand on her arm.

'I'm all right.' She cleared her throat and took a deep breath, steadying her emotions. 'It's just... a lot. I thought about my family in a certain way, and now... I don't know. I feel like I don't know anything anymore. Everything's moving, shifting under me.'

'I'm sorry. I can see that would be upsetting,' Rory said, carefully.

Carrie was aware that she hadn't told Rory about Claire, and the knowledge hung uncomfortably in her mind. Part of her wanted to unburden herself to him, but she couldn't quite bring herself to do it. 'I'd better go home,' she said instead, and picked up the diary. 'See you tomorrow, then.'

'Oh... sure.' Rory looked surprised.

Carrie knew it was sudden, that she was leaving a little dramatically, but she couldn't stay. If she stayed, she would have to talk about Claire, and she didn't want to. Couldn't.

She bundled on her new black mac and picked up her bag. 'Okay. Night, then,' she said, awkwardly. 'Thanks for the dessert.'

'Anytime.' Rory's voice was low; was there an urgency there, or was she imagining it? 'See you tomorrow, Carrie.'

EIGHTEEN

In her dream, Carrie found herself in Maud's cottage. She looked down at herself: she was wearing her favourite dress from when she was nine – a red and white polka-dot smock with a lace collar – and her frayed red slippers.

She stood in the kitchen, watching Maud, who was stirring a hot chocolate.

Of course, this Graham is very like William, Maud said, continuing to stir. *Don't you think so, dear?*

Carrie looked down at her dress, wondering how it still fit her, because she was grown up now – wasn't she? *Why am I here?* she wondered.

Graham, Claire's boyfriend? Carrie asked her aunt. Part of her brain knew that Maud was dead; part of her wanted to hug her and bury her head in Maud's shoulder and take in her familiar smell. But another part of her was in that present-dreamer state, where she followed along with wherever the dream took her.

Just like William, Maud said, smiling over at Carrie. *You changed your hair.*

Why is Graham like William? Carrie asked.

He lost Claire just like William lost Clara, Maud said, mistily. *Such sadness. I could never fully heal William's heart, though I tried.*

But you loved each other, Carrie said, immersed in her memory of Maud's kitchen: the mismatched plates, the row of colourful ceramic teapots on a shelf. *Whatever happened between you, you loved William and he loved you.*

Yes, dearest. But we were both heartbroken by forces outside our control, Maud said, evenly. Carrie looked at Maud's hands: now, she was hulling strawberries, just like Carrie had done in the kitchen for Rory. *You should be kinder to him.*

I don't want to, Carrie replied, knowing she was a little girl in the dream. She knew she sounded petulant.

You know how he feels. And you have to open your little locked door, Maud said, pointing to a door that had mysteriously appeared in the wall on the other side of the kitchen. *There it is now.*

Carrie *could* empathise with Graham. That was the truth of it. She knew exactly what Graham was feeling, but she didn't want to face someone else's grief alongside her own.

However, in an odd way, reading Maud's diary had made her feel more receptive to him. Perhaps it was because she knew, deep down, that Maud would have welcomed him into her home and treated him like one of the family if she'd still been alive. Or the fact that Carrie now understood better, from reading Maud's diary, how transitory love could be and how heartbreaking it was to lose the person you thought you were destined for. She knew that was how Graham and Claire had felt about each other: she'd seen it in their eyes every time they were together. That was the reason she had felt so threatened.

What's behind the door? she asked Maud, in the dream. It was a fairy tale door, small, with an odd handle made of a bread roll.

Maud shrugged, and continued making jam. *Only you know*, she replied. *Only you can open it.*

Carrie felt a wave of unease flood her as she stared at the door. *But I don't want to*, she told Maud. *I don't want to.*

That's up to you, Maud said.

* * *

Carrie woke up, staring at the ceiling as the dream faded. The feeling of unease stayed with her. What was behind the door? It didn't matter, she supposed. It was just a dream. Dreams didn't mean anything.

Only, this one had. She felt as though Maud had given her a clear message about Graham, and she could guess at what was behind the strange little fairy tale door.

It was guilt, rattling the strange handle made of bread, trying to take her over.

You know, she thought. *You know it's your fault your sister died. You made her crash and then you couldn't save her. You failed her.*

Carrie picked up her phone and stared at it. What would she even say to Graham? She had no idea; she hadn't a clue how to cope with losing Claire. To talk about it with someone who had known her as well as Graham had was terrifying. But the guilt was part of it, too. She didn't want to talk to Graham, because then she'd have to acknowledge her role in Claire's death. Because Graham knew Claire as well as she did, there would be no hiding with him.

She found Graham's number in her contacts and pressed the icon for a new message. Her fingers hovered over the screen.

Hi, Graham she tapped out. *I don't know what to say to you right now. I miss Claire. And I know you miss her too. But I'm not ready to talk about it yet.*

She looked at the message for a moment, feeling conflicted.

Part of her wanted to reach out to Graham, but she was scared to. That was the truth of it. She was scared that Graham would know it was her fault that Claire died.

She deleted the message, and stared at the blank screen for a long time, until she felt the grief in her heart almost overwhelm her.

NINETEEN

It was the end of a busy Thursday night's service, and Carrie had stepped into the lovely kitchen garden behind the restaurant for a breath of fresh air before she finished clearing up. The night was unseasonably warm and it had got very hot in the kitchen, mostly because Rory had added lobster to the menu and all night she'd had to keep a huge silver pan of water at a roiling boil, ready for him to drop in the lobster to order.

Carrie had to admit that she wasn't overly fond of the fact that the lobsters were alive when they went in the pot, or the way they still moved when Rory got them out of the freezer, but he was the boss. If Rory said lobsters were on the menu, then they were on the menu.

She fanned herself with a linen napkin, untying her apron and pulling her pink gingham cotton dress up at the front to get some air underneath it. She'd got so sweaty in the kitchen that she could feel her hair sticking to her neck. She pulled it into a messy short ponytail and secured it with the hairband she had around her wrist, thinking that she really had to find a hairdresser's soon so she could get her colour redone. The deep red she usually preferred had washed out a lot and was currently looking more auburn than anything.

Loch Cameron seemed to be having one of those autumns that stayed warm long past where it should have. *Climate change, most likely*, Carrie thought, but it was difficult not to enjoy the warm sun and the dry evenings like this one. Leaves drifted down from an oak tree at the end of Rory's kitchen garden, covering the herbs. She watched them, enjoying the beauty of the moment and feeling the cool evening air on her stomach and thighs.

'Not interrupting, I hope?' Rory stood in the doorway behind her, a slow smile on his face.

Mortified, Carrie dropped the hem of her dress. 'Oh! No. I was just cooling off. Since we've ended service.' She cleared her throat, hoping he hadn't seen anything he shouldn't.

I bet he'd like to, Claire's voice suggested slyly. *Naughty boy. He would like nothing of the sort,* Carrie thought, crossly.

'It's okay. You're allowed to take a break whenever you want.' Rory folded his muscular arms over his chest and leaned on the doorframe. 'Busy again tonight.'

'Yeah. The lobster was popular.' Carrie took up the thread of the offered conversation, grateful for the distraction away from her exposing herself in the garden.

'You didn't like it, did you? Me boiling them?'

Carrie didn't want to be rude, but she also disliked not being honest. 'No. But it's not my decision.'

'I got a great deal on them and it's always popular on the menu,' he explained. 'But I understand watching them be cooked isn't for everyone. I appreciate your professionalism, anyway. Just getting on with it.'

'Well, that's what I'm here for.' She shrugged. 'You're the boss, I'm just the minion.'

'I don't see it like that. We're all part of the same team.'

'Listen, I don't mind taking orders. It's easier if you can just tell me what you want me to do,' Carrie said. 'I like not having to think too much about anything right now. It's good to lose myself in something boring and repetitive.'

Rory looked her up and down. 'You would have done well in the navy,' he said.

Carrie felt herself blushing under his stare. 'What are you looking at me like that for?' she asked.

'I'm imagining you in the uniform. Not that it would do much for a pretty girl like you.'

'Oh, please.' She rolled her eyes. 'If you like the uniform so much, why did you leave?'

'It's not just wearing a uniform. You do actually have to do some difficult things,' he countered, the smile disappearing from his face.

'Like what?'

'Nothing I want to talk about.' He looked away.

'You can talk to me. I've... I know what it's like to experience difficult things,' Carrie said, watching his expression. He was guarded, closed off suddenly. She knew what it was to feel that way. That was exactly what she'd been doing in Loch Cameron: hiding. Not wanting to talk or share her feelings about Claire. She still hadn't replied to Graham's text. She had gone to do it a couple of times, but had stopped at the last minute on both attempts and deleted her message.

'I don't want to talk to you. Not about that.' He met her eyes, and she saw something dark in his expression. A shadow of pain.

'Why not? I'm a human. So are you.' She folded her arms across her chest, realising that she was mimicking his protective body language.

'I hardly know you, I'm your boss, and I don't want to talk about the navy,' Rory said, an edge in his voice. 'So, no.'

'There's no need to be rude,' Carrie said, feeling slightly annoyed. 'I was just trying to be nice.'

'Well, don't,' he growled. 'I don't need your sympathy. Or anyone else's.'

'I wasn't—' Carrie began, but he cut her off.

'These dishes need sorting, when you're ready.' He turned and went back into the kitchen.

Carrie felt wrong-footed and annoyed. *What just happened?* she asked herself. She had just been trying to be nice; to pass on some of the kindness she herself had received from Dotty and Gretchen and the other villagers since she'd arrived. But Rory had thrown her kindness back in her face. Now she saw what Fiona had meant about Rory being standoffish. Not even that: he'd been downright rude. She had seen it, herself, that first time in the shop. Maybe her first impression of him had been right, after all.

She returned inside. Rory was in the large larder, his back to the kitchen, so she returned to the sink and finished loading up the dishwasher and put it on. He re-emerged, nodded to her and walked into the restaurant without a word.

Oh. That's not going to be awkward at all, Carrie thought, taking off her apron and tossing it into the basket for used aprons, napkins and tablecloths. At the end of every week, they got taken off by a laundry service and replaced with a stack of clean, starched white garments and cloths. She took a deep breath, took her jacket and bag from the little cupboard where they kept their belongings during service, and went out into the main restaurant.

Rory was standing by the door, obviously waiting for her to leave so he could lock up. Kathy, as usual, had left first. Carrie had never seen Rory quite like this before, and she didn't know how to be with him.

'Right, then. See you tomorrow,' she said, abruptly.

'Carrie. I'm sorry. About that, just now,' Rory took her arm as she reached for the door handle. A frisson of something – electricity? – shot through her.

Not actual electricity. That would be dumb, Claire's voice said in her mind. *But what the hell was THAT?*

I don't know, Carrie thought, looking up into Rory's eyes.

'It's okay. I shouldn't have been so personal,' she said, quietly. His hand stayed on her arm, and she could feel an immense warmth from his touch. She was reminded, close up, how soft his deep brown eyes were with their long lashes.

There was a definite chemistry between them; it was as though the air around them was thick with anticipation. Carrie's lips tingled, and she licked them with her tongue to wet them. She noticed that Rory watched her as she did it, and his eyes widened just a little.

Nice, Claire's voice said.

I didn't do it to be sexy. It was just a reflex.

Yeah, right.

Rory cleared his throat and released her arm. 'No. You were just being a friend, and I was being rude. Please, forgive me,' he murmured.

'There's nothing to forgive,' she said, quietly.

'Well, I'm still sorry.'

'Okay.'

'All right. See you tomorrow, then.' Rory cleared his throat again and opened the door for her.

'See you tomorrow,' she said, looking behind her as she stepped out into the street, and meeting his gaze.

There was another moment of something that passed between them.

'Until then,' he replied.

Carrie walked away, along the street and turned at the bottom of the road. When she looked back, Rory was still standing in the restaurant door, watching her walk away. She felt a tug at her heart. She didn't quite know why, but in that moment, she had to fight the impulse to run back up the street, grab Rory and kiss him.

Instead, she followed the way home to the cottage.

Well, that was interesting, Claire said. *I'd follow that up if I were you. No sense in being miserable and alone when you could be satisfying yourself with THAT.*

Shut up, Claire, Carrie thought.

You agree with me. I know you do, her sister's voice insisted.

It doesn't matter if I do or not, Carrie thought. *I'm not going to do anything about it. Rory's my boss.*

Chicken, Claire responded.

Are we ever going to talk about what happened? Carrie asked her sister's voice, knowing that it was stupid to be talking to her dead sister in her head but needing to do it anyway.

What do you mean?

You know what I mean. You're in my head. You know everything, apparently. The crash.

There was no answer.

Claire?

I don't want to talk about it, Claire's voice replied. *It's in the past. Let's just leave it.*

But Carrie couldn't just leave it. She'd failed Claire, and then Claire had died and she'd never had a chance to say she was sorry.

'And that's part of what's eating me alive,' Carrie said, out loud. 'I failed you, Claire. And I'm sorry.'

There was no answer.

'I'm sorry. I'm so sorry, Claire.' Carrie's voice broke, and she started to sob. 'Please forgive me.'

But, for once, her sister's voice was silent.

TWENTY

I need a hand at the vegetable supplier today – don't suppose you're free? Can pay you extra of course.

Carrie looked at her phone, reading the text from Rory. She'd just got out of the shower and was towelling her hair dry when she saw the phone light up.

She was surprised to hear from him, given that they'd left things in a slightly uncomfortable place the night before.

Nothing happened, really, Carrie thought. *Except for the fact that we had a little argument.*

Lovers' tiff, Claire's voice interrupted her.

Oh, shut up, Carrie thought. She looked at the text message again. This would be a trip in a car, most likely, and Carrie still wasn't that great in cars. It wasn't so bad if she drove, but she wasn't sure how she'd be with someone else at the wheel. The idea of it brought her out in a cold sweat. She wouldn't be in control. And that terrified her.

You have to be able to get in a car with someone else, Claire's voice told her sternly. *What happened with me was a freak accident.*

I know, but I can't help the way I feel, Carrie responded.

You have to try, Claire's voice told her. *Be brave.*

Carrie didn't want to be brave. She wanted to hide away in Gretchen's cottage forever and pretend the past months hadn't happened. But she knew she couldn't do that.

She tapped out a reply before she could think too much about it.

Happy to. What time?

She pressed send. *There.* That was her, being fearless. Her stomach twisted with tension, but there was a kind of wild freedom there too. *I did it.*

In an hour? I'll pick you up in the car, he replied, immediately.

Okay, she replied, her heart thrumming in her chest.

Brave girl, Claire said.

* * *

'Morning. Thanks for this.' Rory leaned over and opened the passenger door to his black jeep, pushing a pile of papers off the seat and onto the floor.

'No problem,' Carrie lied, her heart beating so hard that she thought Rory might hear it. 'I could do with the extra money, and I had the time free.' She stepped into the jeep gingerly and sat down. 'Don't you want all these?' She leaned forward and gathered some of the papers in her hand, offering them to him.

He made a face. 'Mostly bills. Chuck them on the back seat.'

'Right you are.' She threw them behind her. 'You know, you should probably open them,' she added, noticing that many of the envelopes were still sealed. She swallowed hard, as if she could subdue the anxiety in her stomach that way.

'Hmm. When I'm really bored, I will.' He started the engine and they followed the narrow track road along Queen's Point, moving away from the loch and the village.

'I've never been far down this road,' Carrie said, putting on her seatbelt and pulling it tight to test it. She fought to keep her voice steady.

'Yeah. It's a lovely drive, actually,' he said, not seeming to notice her tension.

Carrie nodded, looking out at the trees at the side of the road and focusing on them, rather than thinking about the road and all the dangers that might be lurking on it. The road was overshadowed by trees in a leafy tunnel for a while, like something from a fairy tale. Then, suddenly, the trees – mostly evergreens – thinned, and she could see across the fields to a range of soft, purple hills in the far distance. More importantly, Carrie could see the road reaching out in front of them, with no cars on it at all. Being able to see the road ahead calmed her, as did the fact that Rory seemed to be a careful driver.

'What a beautiful day,' he said, sighing. 'Music?' He leaned over and turned on the radio, brushing her arm accidentally as he did so.

Carrie felt a shiver of something resonate through her as he did so; he looked over, very briefly, and caught her eye.

'You all right?' He frowned, catching something in her expression. 'You look... worried about something.'

'Oh. No, I'm okay,' she lied. 'Just a bit warm.'

'Oh. Well, open the window, if you want.' He nodded towards a button on her armrest. 'You've got the controls there.'

'Thanks.' Carrie pressed the button and a blast of sharp, autumnal highland air blew her hair in her face a little. She took a deep breath and felt its calming effect; she took several more, and felt better again.

'No lobsters, you'll be relieved to hear.' Rory watched her for a moment and then turned his attention back to the road, a smile playing on his lips.

'What?' Carrie asked, temporarily distracted. She was feeling far less anxious, and that was leaving space for the other energy between her and Rory. Why was it that every time Rory was near, there was this electricity in the air? She'd never experienced it before. It was unsettling.

Lust, Claire's voice said, in her mind.

It's not lust, Carrie argued with her sister, half-heartedly.

Well, what is it, then?

Carrie didn't have an answer for that.

'Lobsters. We aren't picking any more up,' Rory repeated, putting the jeep into low gear to go around the corner. 'Just vegetables today. And some fruit.'

Carrie glanced at his arm; his tanned, muscular forearm tensed and released. Today, as usual when he wasn't wearing his chef's whites, he wore a black T-shirt under a red tartan shirt which he had left unbuttoned, and black jeans. The T-shirt wasn't fitted or obviously trying to be sexy in any way, but she could still see the outline of his muscular chest underneath it.

She cleared her throat. 'Oh. Right. Vegetables. I can cope with that. Aubergines don't try and crawl out of the pot when you're cooking them.'

'Not usually, no,' he laughed. 'I think you'll like the farm we're going to today. I get all the veg from there, and a lot of the fruit. It's all grown without chemicals. They've got goats for milk, eggs, that kind of thing. There's even a little petting zoo for kids. It's cute.'

'Is that why you brought me? Because you thought I'd like playing with some fluffy bunnies?' She smiled, relieved to be having a conversation and keeping her mind off the road. *Look at me, I'm in a car and not freaking out!* she thought. *Progress.* Still, she'd be glad when they got to the farm and she could get out of Rory's jeep.

'The very fact you called them bunnies leads me to believe it was a good choice, yeah,' he chuckled.

'Shut up. I meant rabbits.'

'Well, as glad as I am that you love little fluffy animals,' he chuckled again, looking at her out of the corner of his eye, 'I mostly need a hand carrying crates today. If that's all right.'

'I should be okay, but I would warn you that I broke my collarbone recently,' Carrie said, shortly. 'Don't give me the heaviest crates, I guess.'

'Oh! I didn't know. You should have said. I would have asked someone else.' Rory shot her a concerned glance. 'Are you okay?'

'I'm fine, really.' Carrie glanced at him and then stared back at the road.

'If you're sure.'

There was a slightly uncomfortable silence as Rory drove on.

After a few moments, he put on his indicator and pulled into a dirt track with a sign that said APPLEGATES FARM – ORGANIC FRUIT AND VEGETABLES.

'Here we are,' he murmured, and drove up the track, parking at the end in front of a series of long white polytunnels.

Carrie closed her window and let out a long sigh of relief. She'd made it, and she hadn't had a meltdown. Maybe there was hope for her still. 'Thank goodness,' she said.

'Was my driving that bad?' Rory looked concerned. 'Are you all right? Really?'

'I'm okay.' Carrie smiled, and opened the passenger door. 'Let's go get some vegetables.'

TWENTY-ONE

'Oh, Rory, look!' Carrie knelt down next to a wooden and wire mesh enclosure where three long-haired, lop-eared rabbits were industriously chewing lettuce leaves. 'They're adorable! Look at their widdle ears!' Without meaning to, Carrie had lapsed into a baby-talk voice as she spoke to the rabbits. 'You're just too cute, awwen't you? Yes, you are! Yes, you are!'

Rory watched her, a grin spreading over his face. He waved to a friendly looking man with a beard and wearing a knitted hat and a sweatshirt.

'Hey, Jon. Can we pick the rabbits up?' he called. 'My friend's not too old, right?'

'Hey, Rory.' Jon jogged over. 'Sure thing. Floof is for everyone.' He reached into the enclosure and picked up the fluffiest rabbit – a sandy coloured thing with white feet and very long ears – and handed it to Carrie, who squealed a little as she took it.

'I'm Carrie, by the way,' she said, trying to act like an adult for a minute at least.

'Jon. Great to meet you. This is Benjamin. That's Jemima

and Ducky.' Jon pointed out the other two rabbits. 'They're super friendly. Won't bite.'

'Awwww, Benjamin!' Carrie crooned at the rabbit, all of her tension in the car forgotten. 'He's so soft! Look at his ears!' she exclaimed to both men, who grinned.

Rory stroked the rabbit's ears. 'Super soft,' he agreed.

'If you want to pet some of the other animals, we also have a goat, some hamsters and there are a couple of farm cats roaming around,' Jon said. 'We also have chinchillas, if you like soft things. Mind you, they're nocturnal, so they're usually asleep around now.'

'The bunny is fine, thanks. I am actually here to work,' Carrie laughed, nuzzling Benjamin. 'I just want to take him home, though! It's been years since I picked up a rabbit. Or any animal, I think.'

'Take your time. It tends to be quiet here when the kids are in school,' Jon said. 'Here for the usual, Rory? Thomas was saying we've got some great purple sprouting if you're interested.'

'That'd be great, yeah. We'll go up in a minute and see what there is.' Rory watched Carrie with amusement. 'When I can separate this one from the new love of her life.'

'Aww. But Benjamin's so cuuute,' Carrie crooned, stroking the rabbit's ears. 'I really want to take him home with me.'

'Carrie. Think of the children,' Rory said, faux-sternly.

'Oh, I know, I know,' she sighed. 'I suppose we'd better get on with what we came here for.'

'You can come back and see Benjamin whenever you want.' Jon took the rabbit from Carrie gently.

'It's fine,' Carrie laughed. 'Though I do think it's sweet you guys have this for the kids.'

'Ah, well. It's not much, but it's something to do for the little ones. And sometimes the school brings a little group up here and we do projects with them about planting, sustainable farming, that kind of thing.'

'That's so nice.'

Carrie and Rory watched as Jon returned Benjamin to his rabbit friends, and they all walked past the rest of the animal enclosures and along a dirt pathway towards the polytunnels.

'Yeah, it's a good place to work. The air's so clean up here, and we all get a free organic lunch every day. Can't complain.' Jon adjusted his knitted hat. 'Anyway. Duty calls! I'll see you guys later. Good to meet you, Carrie.'

'And you,' Carrie called after him. 'Seems a nice guy,' she added, to Rory.

'Yeah. Salt of the earth. They all are, up here.' They walked along companionably. 'Here. You've got rabbit fluff on you.' Rory reached across and brushed her sweatshirt gently, and she recoiled slightly at his sudden intimacy.

'Sorry, I just...' She blushed. 'I wasn't expecting you to...' She trailed off.

'Yeah. Sorry, I don't know why I did that.' Rory looked awkward. 'It was just an instinct. I didn't mean anything by it.'

'I know,' she said. There was a brief silence, in which Carrie thought, *Is he embarrassed because he sort of did mean something by it, or am I overthinking that?*

Definitely not overthinking it, Claire's voice said. *Mr Hot Chef over here clearly has the hots for you.*

He does not, Carrie argued, weakly.

It was the rabbit that did it, Claire added. *Men love a woman who goes gooey over small, furry things.*

Shut up, idiot, Carrie willed the voice.

'Come on. Veggies await,' she said, instead, walking on and admiring the farm.

The three white polytunnels sat at the centre of fields, and to the right, far back, there was a large red brick farmhouse where

Carrie guessed that the owners lived. Crops grew in the fields, stretching into the distance: on one stretch, Carrie could see the orange humps of pumpkins like night lights under their wide leaves.

As they walked into the polytunnel, Carrie took in a breath of surprise.

'Impressive, huh?' Rory nodded. 'I was the same when I first came here.'

Carrie nodded, gazing at the rows of perfectly ordered vegetables that seemed to explode in a riot of colour before her eyes. Yellow and orange peppers hung from firm green stalks on one side of where they stood, while a profusion of deep purple and green sprouting broccoli stood tall, further along in the orderly beds. To Carrie's left, large-leafed plants displayed huge, long, deep and light green courgettes under them, and a raised bed with a canopy displayed green and purple lettuces. A further bed was filled with orange, green and purple leaves, which Rory pointed to.

'Chard. Look at how rainbow-coloured it is.' He grinned. 'Almost a shame to cook it.'

'This is amazing,' Carrie marvelled. 'I can see why you like to come here.'

'Yeah. There's a whole other tunnel just dedicated to herbs, too, and another one for fruit. Everything they can grow in season, and some out of season too,' he said, as they walked along. Rory was making some notes in pencil on a small notepad he'd pulled out of his pocket. 'Shopping list,' he explained. 'They also have potatoes, onions, carrots – all the usual things. I buy those ready bagged.'

'What do we do with this stuff?' Carrie gestured to the vegetables around her.

'We can choose what we want, and they'll put it all into some crates for us.' Rory scribbled something down on the paper. 'I like to look at the produce and think about what I can make with it. That's how I do the menu, most of the time. So, today I'm thinking, stuffed peppers, maybe. And something with the chard. It's good with anchovies and chilli, maybe with spaghetti or tagliatelle.' He chewed the end of his pencil.

'That sounds delicious.' Carrie's stomach rumbled. 'I could eat that now.'

'Me, too, actually,' Rory agreed. 'Okay. Let's get the order sorted, and then I'll make you lunch when we get back. How's that for a deal?'

'It's good.' Carrie nodded. 'Let's do it.'

* * *

'Look, I'm sorry I was a bit of an idiot to you last night at work.' Rory edged in the last crate and closed up the back of the jeep. He hadn't let her carry any of them to the back of the jeep, doing all the heavy lifting himself.

'You weren't.' Carrie dusted off her hands and got back in the jeep. She'd been so relaxed at the farm, but now she was facing another drive, she could feel the tension returning.

'I guess I wanted to explain, a little.' Rory got in to the driver's seat and turned to her. 'When I was in the navy... I was kind of a different person. I loved it, loved the adventure, but...' He trailed off. 'I look back and I don't like who I was then.' He looked like he wanted to say something more, but he shook his head and started the engine. 'Anyway. I can be a bit touchy talking about it, I guess.'

'We've all got difficult things in our past,' Carrie said, trying to keep her voice even. 'And we've all changed from when we were younger. Don't they say that your body essentially replaces itself every seven years, or something? Regrows, renews itself? Or, parts of the body, anyway? So, in many ways, you're not the person you were seven years ago. Mentally and emotionally too, probably.'

'I didn't know that. That's quite a thought.' Rory raised an eyebrow in consideration as he reversed slowly onto the dirt track that led in and out of the farm.

'I hope it's true, anyway,' Carrie sighed. 'I could do with not being the same person I was six months ago.'

Rory pulled onto the quiet country road at the bottom of the dirt track and shot her a concerned look. 'What does that mean?'

'Nothing.' She opened the window again and let the cool air wash over her, taking in a few deep breaths.

'You sure?' He glanced at her as he changed gear. 'Sounds kind of a dark thing to say.'

'Yeah, well. I've been in a dark place, I suppose.'

'But you still don't want to talk about it?'

'Not really.' She sighed. 'Though, to be honest, I guess everyone else in the village knows already. I told Dotty, and I suspect she'd told everyone else.'

'Oh, for sure. Dotty's the nexus of all gossip in the village,' Rory chuckled wryly.

'Hm. Well, maybe she'll tell you, then. I'm not really up for talking about it right now. You know that I lost someone very close to me and... it's not been easy.'

'I know, and I'm sorry.' Rory looked over at her for a long moment. 'I mean, I don't know the details. But it's rough.'

Ahead of them, a farm truck was approaching. It was the first large vehicle they'd seen on their journey, and though it was on its own side of the road, it was wide, and Carrie could see that Rory would have to pull over a little to the verge to make way for it.

Yet, he was still looking at her.

'Keep your eyes on the road, for goodness' sake!' Carrie raised her voice in panic.

'Okay, okay.' He gave her an odd look and slowed down, seeing the truck and pulling aside just as Carrie had imagined he should.

It wasn't a big deal. It was just a normal moment, on a road, in a car. Yet Carrie's heart was banging wildly in her chest.

'Are you okay?' he asked, looking alarmed. 'Because you don't seem okay. Do you want me to stop the car?'

'No. Sorry. I'm kind of anxious in cars,' she said, not wanting to explain. 'Just carry on. I want to get back.'

'Okay. I can see that.'

They drove on in silence; Carrie concentrated on the road ahead and on breathing plenty of lungsful of the cool, calming highland air. Neither of them said anything else until they pulled up outside the restaurant.

'Well, here we are,' he said.

Carrie opened the car door gratefully and jumped out. 'Thanks,' she blurted, then stood there awkwardly, realising that he'd promised to make her lunch and that she'd agreed. And that they still had to get the crates of fruit, veg and herbs out of the car.

She took a few deep breaths as Rory straightened up the jeep. He probably thought she was a complete headcase, but there wasn't much she could do about that now.

'You all right?' he repeated, as he got out of the jeep. 'What just happened?'

'Nothing. I told you, I'm anxious in cars, that's all,' she said.

Oh, babes, Claire's voice sighed. *What are we going to do with you?*

Carrie ignored her sister's voice.

'Bring those bags in, if you don't mind, and I'll do the crates. They're a bit heavy.' Rory picked up one crate, his biceps bulging, and carried it into the restaurant.

Carrie looked away so that she didn't end up staring at them inappropriately. She followed with a couple of bags of potatoes and dumped them on the worktop. Rory had taken the crates of vegetables he'd brought into the large, cold larder. He went back out to the car and brought in another; Carrie followed and brought back a hessian sack of carrots.

'That's a nice top, by the way. Suits you,' he observed.

Carrie had put on jeans with a white top she'd got from Fiona's Fashions today; she'd worn walking boots with it, though, so it didn't exactly feel dressy. The top had a scoop neck and long sleeves, but fitted nicely.

Tight, you mean, Claire's voice interrupted.

'Oh. Thanks.' She dumped the sack on the counter.

'Now. Are you going to tell me why you're as skittish as a horse, or will it remain a mystery?' Rory folded his considerable arms over his chest and gave her a patient frown. 'You said you'd lost someone close to you. Is that why you're here? What you're so upset about?'

'Yes,' she whispered.

'What happened, Carrie?' he asked, quietly. 'Tell me, for goodness' sake.'

Carrie tasted the tears in her throat. *I guess this is happening*, she thought. 'If you were more of a gossip you'd know by now. I expect Dotty's told everyone within a five-mile radius.'

'Well, I'm not. I like to keep to myself as much as possible.' He gave her an odd look. 'Quite frankly, it's not like me to ask you about your past. I don't usually like to get too close to people, but you...' He trailed off. 'You seem to have a strange effect on me. I... I like being around you.'

'I like being around you too,' Carrie replied, quietly.

'You can trust me with whatever you want to tell me,' he said.

'I know,' she sighed. And she did know, somehow, that she could trust Rory. She felt it, instinctively. 'Claire... I had a sister. A year older than me. We were involved in a c-car crash. And Claire...'

'She didn't make it?' Rory asked, his voice low.

'No.' Carrie looked at her hands. It didn't get any easier, talking about what had happened.

'I'm so sorry.' He took her hands in his. 'Carrie, that's terrible. Now I understand why you were so tense in the car earlier. Why didn't you say anything?'

'I didn't want to. I have to be able to be in cars again. I can't develop a phobia. It's impractical.' She shook her head, impatient with herself.

'It's not impractical. It's human,' Rory said, softly.

'Yeah, well. I didn't want to talk about it. I still don't, really. But I have to. So, I'll tell you. It was my fault she died. I was playing the stereo really loud and being an arse, and she was trying to concentrate on the road. It was terrible weather. She could hardly see. It was my fault,' Carrie repeated the mantra, a sliver of steel piercing her heart every time she did so. 'And then...' A sob escaped her. 'And then, when it had happened, I could have donated a kidney she needed, but they didn't take it and I was unconscious and she... she died before I woke up.'

Carrie started to cry, desperately trying to stop herself and failing. The emotion felt like a black balloon of bitterness that filled her chest. She imagined a pit, and throwing herself in it. That was all she was good for. To drown in her own sorrow.

'Oh, Carrie. Come here.' He held her tight against him, and she didn't resist.

The wave of sorrow engulfed her, and she sobbed loudly against his chest.

He stroked her hair gently and continued to hold her tight. 'I've got you. I'm not going anywhere,' he breathed.

And she clung to him gratefully, like a buoy in a storm-ridden sea.

TWENTY-TWO

'I'm glad ye popped by. I was thinkin' I should come over and see ye, check in, like.' Angus ushered her into the hallway of his cottage.

Not for the first time, Carrie thought about how unsuited this huge Viking was for the tiny whitewashed house. He towered above her, having to stoop in the hallway where the ceiling was low.

She had woken up that morning with Maud on her mind. Perhaps it was all a distraction from having to think about Claire, but after she had opened up to Rory the night before, Carrie felt like she needed some answers about her great-aunt. Anything not to think about that day in the car.

And when you need me in the dead of night, I'm just a minute away... ooh, ooh.

Carrie shook her head imperceptibly to get the song out of her head. She'd be grateful if she never heard it again.

'Come in, come in. Time for a cuppa?'

'I'd love one, thanks.' Carrie followed him, noting that the layout of Angus's cottage was the same as Gretchen's. 'So, these cottages were all built at the same time, I'm guessing?'

'Aye, I think so. These were end o' the nineteenth century, but there's been dwellins up on Queens Point for hundreds o' years.' Angus led her into the small sitting room and gestured to an aged, wine-coloured corduroy sofa. 'Take a seat, dear. I'll make the tea. Or d'ye prefer coffee? I have the good stuff. None o' ye instant.'

'A coffee would be great, then, thank you.' Carrie settled herself gratefully into the sofa and looked around her. She needed a distraction. She needed *company*, and Angus had offered, after all.

Angus's cottage was decorated in what she privately recognised as Single Man Style, which meant that there were several expensive-looking electric guitars hanging from wooden holders on one wall, an untidy pile of paperwork on the coffee table, along with several dirty cups, but a pristine shelving unit containing what looked like hundreds of CDs. On a wooden shelf to her right, a number of small metal sculptures were arranged neatly. She remembered Angus saying something about his workshop at the back of the house: they could be ornaments he'd made. His furniture was dated but clean and comfortable, and though the cottage didn't have the cosy, girly feel of Gretchen's, she decided she still liked it.

Angus returned with a tray, holding two steaming mugs of coffee and a plate of chocolate biscuits.

'Ooh, biscuits!' Carrie smiled, taking a mug.

'Och, aye. I wouldnae hold back wi' the chocolate when a young lady visits,' he chuckled. 'I didnae know if ye wanted sugar, so I brought the bowl.'

'Thanks.' Carrie helped herself to a spoonful of brown sugar and stirred it into her coffee.

'So what prompted the visit?' Angus asked.

'Well, I guess I was wondering if you could tell me anything more about my great-aunt,' Carrie confessed. Since reading Maud's diary, she had so many unanswered questions. What had happened to Maud's baby? And to William and Clara? What had Maud done about being pregnant and single at the end of the 1950s? How had she coped? And had she and William carried on seeing each other – or had he gone back to Clara and never gone into the post office ever again?

'Oh. I expect so. I hope you're enjoyin' the choir, by the way. I find it fun.'

'Yeah. It's really good, I love it.' Carrie sipped her drink. 'It's cathartic. Like you said.'

'Aye. Glad ye think so.' Angus nodded at the guitars. 'I was always into music. When I was younger, I was in a band. Still got the long hair,' he chuckled. 'Used to plait it, have it shaved up the sides like a Viking. The ladies liked that.'

'I bet they did,' Carrie laughed. 'When was that?'

'Oh, the seventies. It was a wild time.' He took a biscuit and crunched it. 'Toured most of Europe. Not that I remember half o' it.'

'Wow. So were you famous?' Carrie asked, looking at the rows of CDs.

'For a while, aye. No one remembers us much now.' He named a band that Carrie had vaguely heard of. 'We supported some big bands. It was my life for a long time.'

'Bonnie Tyler. That's how you met her.' Carrie remembered that day at choir, after she'd belted out the chorus to 'Alone' by Heart.

'Aye, that's right. Nice woman.'

'Any stories about her?' Carrie raised an eyebrow. 'Come on, Angus. You must have a lot.'

'A gentleman never tells.' He gave Carrie a smile that suggested there were definitely stories he could tell about his former life.

'You played the guitar?' Carrie pointed to them hanging on the wall.

'Aye. Axe man. But the choir's about as much music as I do nowadays. I keep ma hand in, but nothin' much.'

'Do you know if Maud was musical? Did you know her well?' Carrie asked, keen to bring the conversation back around to her great-aunt. 'I've been given some of her old diaries and it's made me want to know as much as I can about her.'

'Oh, we were good friends.' Angus nodded. 'In fact, when I moved here, we were a bit more than that, for a while.'

Carrie looked up, surprised. 'What do you mean?'

'We were a bit of an item, on and off. She was a bit older than me, but when I moved here in the eighties she was about fifty or so and I was – what – early thirties. She was a fine-lookin' woman. We got on well.' He shrugged, smiling. 'Boy meets girl. You can imagine the rest.'

'Maud and you...?' Carrie was flabbergasted.

'Aye. Dinnae look so surprised. Middle-aged people have sex, ye know,' he chided her.

'No, it's just more that...' Carrie trailed off. 'I didn't know Maud had any boyfriends. I found out some stuff from her diary, but later in life, I just assumed...'

'You assumed she just waited for death, like a nun or something? No. Maud was a sexual woman. I wasnae exactly her boyfriend, but we had an arrangement. Nowadays you might call it "friends with benefits". She used tae make me dinner once or twice a week, which I appreciated, because I'm not a cook. An' usually we'd end up in bed. We were never in love, but it was nice, ye know. Company.'

'Wow!' Carrie took a biscuit. 'I had no idea.'

'No, well. You wouldnae,' he laughed. 'She wouldn't exactly tell her young great-nieces what she was up to. That would have been inappropriate.'

'Oh, of course,' Carrie agreed. 'No, it's just more that... I feel like I didn't know very much about her at all, and I wish I did.'

'Ach, well, that's how she was. We had that arrangement

goin' fer years, but she never really told me much about herself. She'd had a child, that I know. She told me one night when we had a couple o' glasses of wine wi' dinner. Told me putting the bairn up for adoption was the hardest thing she'd ever done.' He gave a sad smile.

'Do you know anything else about the baby? Did she ever have a relationship with the baby's father?' Carrie was desperate to know more about what had happened to Maud.

'Dunno. In the time we were seein' each other, she never saw anyone else as far as I know. An' she never talked about the baby. I did have girlfriends later, after we stopped. No one special, mind ye.' He shrugged. 'But Maud an' I just always kept what we had quiet. It gets lonely, bein' on yer own. We kept each other company.'

'You were probably right to keep it quiet in a place like Loch Cameron.' Carrie raised an eyebrow. 'I can imagine the gossip.' She felt disappointed that Angus didn't have anything much to say on the subject of Maud's baby. Maybe he knew things he wasn't saying, but Carrie thought he seemed like a pretty open person.

'Aye. That was the main thing. Gretchen knew, I think, because she'd see me goin' over there sometimes. But she was never a one tae say anythin'.'

'No. I can only imagine how many secrets Gretchen knows.' Carrie sipped her coffee.

'Exactly. She wasnae left out of the rumour mill, anyway, bein' a single mother by choice an' adoptin' a baby.' Angus nodded. 'Loch Cameron's got a lot more diverse nowadays but, back then, there was a lot o' disapprovin' goin on. She rose above it, o' course.'

'Seems like you ended up living next door to some pretty brilliant, independent women,' Carrie observed. 'But I never would have imagined someone with a crazy sex, drugs and rock 'n' roll lifestyle choosing to live here, Angus!'

'Haha. I know. But that's exactly why Loch Cameron appealed, an' why I stayed. The landscape's stunnin', for one thing. An' I was burnt out from years on the road. I *did* do all the sex, drugs and rock 'n' roll, that was the problem. I needed somewhere quiet, to heal. The air an' the loch did that. I'm sure o' it.' He smiled fondly at the view from the cottage window.

'I can relate to that.' Carrie nodded. 'I always notice the air. June said it should be available on prescription.'

'Ha. June would say that, but she's no' wrong,' Angus chuckled.

'What did you do for work, after you got here?'

'I didnae,' he laughed, self-consciously. 'I had money from the music days tae live off. Did some odd jobs fer people, but nothin' much. Mostly I just work in ma workshop, go to the choir, potter about here. That's enough fer me, aye.'

'And you had Maud,' Carrie added.

'Aye. I was sad when she passed. She missed you and your sister, and your mum,' he said. 'I remember ye, actually, visitin'. No' least because I was told in no uncertain terms that dinner wasnae on for however long ye were there.' He laughed, good-naturedly. 'She looked forward tae seein' ye so much. She really didnae like yer faither, though. Forgive me for sayin'.'

'Oh, no. I already know that.' Carrie rolled her eyes. 'He was – is – a difficult man.'

'Hmm. Liked the drink, as I recall.'

'Yeah. Still does, I suppose. I hardly see him.'

'That's a shame.'

There was a moment of silence, as Carrie thought about her dad for a moment. He'd hardly been in touch after Claire's death. She wondered whether she should check in with him, but instinctively, she didn't want to.

Let him check up on me if he's bothered, she thought. *He's the grown-up here.*

'You never had kids?' she asked Angus instead.

'Me? Naw. Never met the right girl. Also, I guess I never felt like I was that much of a responsible guy. Or, by the time I felt like I was, it was too late.' He shrugged. 'That's okay. I've got a nice little life.'

'Seems a shame that you can't be my dad,' Carrie laughed wryly. 'I feel like you'd make a better job of it than my actual father.'

'Haha. Ach, well, lassie. Ye always know where I am, if ye want an aged Viking's worldly wisdom. Or a coffee an' some biscuits. Or both.' Angus put his huge arm around her shoulder and gave her an affectionate hug. 'Ye cannae say anythin' that'll shock me, that's fer sure. An' I'd never judge ye for anythin'. I'm more than happy tae be yer good neighbour an' friend, if that helps.'

'It does help. A lot, actually.' Carrie put her head on Angus's shoulder. 'Thanks.'

And when you need me in the dead of night, I'm just a minute away... ooh, ooh.

The song played again in her mind. The vision of Claire jerking violently forward in her seat, her neck as soft and pliant as a rag doll. Carrie's final vision of the car that had hit them, through the windscreen, so much closer than it should have been. Before she blacked out, she had heard screaming. Only later had she realised it was her own voice.

'Aye, yer welcome anytime, lassie,' Angus rumbled. 'Very welcome indeed.'

TWENTY-THREE

'Oh, good. You're here.' Rory stepped back into his hallway and ushered her in. 'Sorry for the mess. Everything's a bit all over the place,' he said, frowning. He was holding a pile of clean laundry and absent-mindedly stacked it on a chair by the door.

'I was free, though I have to say that you cut into my very important sitting around time,' Carrie joked. 'What's up?' She was keen to project an air of cheery indifference after the events of two nights ago. The night before, Rory had said nothing about the fact that after their trip to the farm she had clung to him like a limpet and cried her heart out – he was all business – and she'd scurried off after service the night before rather than hang around and for things to be uncomfortable.

'Come in. I called Kathy but she didn't answer, so I'm going to have to catch up with her on the phone later.' Rory led her down a hallway with a black and white tiled floor which Carrie barely had the opportunity to admire, and walls that were painted a dark blue, with the woodwork finished in the same colour. 'Are you feeling all right?' he asked. 'I was worried about you the other night. We haven't had a chance to talk, since.'

They came into a wide, cosy lounge with two plain white

sofas which shone out against the same blue walls as in the hallway.

'I'm fine, thanks.' Carrie put her hands in the back pockets of her jeans, feeling slightly awkward. 'Sorry for crying all over you.'

'Don't apologise. I didn't mind at all.'

The lounge's floorboards had been varnished and a mustard rug stretched between the two sofas. A wall of bookshelves stood opposite. Carrie resisted the urge to look surprised that Rory was such a reader, and also to go over and look at the books he'd read.

'Take a seat.' He offered her one of the sofas. 'Coffee? Tea? Glass of wine?'

Carrie looked at her watch. 'It's two forty p.m. Maybe a little early for wine.'

'Oh, right. Sorry. I've been up all night, sorting things out. Sort of lost track of time.' Rory ran a hand through his black hair and exhaled. 'Coffee, then? I could do with one.'

'Sounds like you could. I'll help.' She followed him into an adjoining kitchen, which contained a dining table and chairs that were piled up with more laundry, and a large rucksack. 'Going somewhere?'

'Yeah. That's what I wanted to talk to you about, actually.' He flicked on the kettle and got a silver canister of filter coffee out of the fridge, spooning a generous amount into a cafetiere, then took two blue mugs from a shelf and poured milk into one. 'Do you take it black, or white?'

'White, one sugar.' Carrie watched him, admiring the way that he moved with almost balletic grace around the kitchen.

'No problemo.'

They made small talk while they waited a few minutes for the coffee to brew. Carrie was grateful for the fact he wasn't making her talk about Claire. When Rory deemed the coffee ready, he pushed down the plunger, humming under his breath while he did so.

'Here.' He handed her a mug. 'Do you want to sit down in the lounge? These stools aren't as comfortable as the sofa.'

'I know, but I'm not as worried about spilling coffee on them,' Carrie said, taking the mug and lowering herself onto the tall metal stool. 'Those are two blinding white sofas in there. Only a childless man would choose such an impractical colour.'

Rory frowned for a brief second. Carrie suddenly wondered if she'd made some kind of terrible *faux pas* mentioning the fact that he didn't have children, but then he smiled, and, just like every time Rory smiled, it was as though rainy clouds had been blown away and the sun had come out.

'You're right. They looked great in the showroom. That's all I really thought about.' He stood on the other side of the white marble kitchen island and took a long slug of his coffee. 'Plus, it's just me here.'

'It's really nice, though,' Carrie said, and meant it. The kitchen had wide bifold doors that opened onto a long garden, which started with a patio area. 'Is that a kitchen garden out there, too? Like outside the restaurant?'

'Yeah. I try to keep it up when I have time. Just some standard herbs, potatoes, broccoli, chard, onions. Nothing much.'

'That sounds like a lot.' Carrie glanced back at the dining table piled up with clothes. 'So. You're going away?'

'Yeah,' Rory sighed. 'Look. You know I was in the navy, right?'

'I remember.'

'Yeah. Well, I left, but I stayed in the Reserves. That means I can theoretically get called up if needed, until I get too old to be useful.'

'Right. And?'

'I got called back, would you believe.' He raised an eyebrow. 'Haven't seen active service for years. But I've been asked to provide some specialist training for the thing I used to do. I'm going early tomorrow.'

Carrie's eyes widened. 'Oh, goodness. Where?'

'I can't say, I'm afraid. It's unusual to be asked to come out of retirement, but not unheard of when your skills are quite niche.'

'What are your skills?' Carrie sipped her coffee. 'Or is that on a strictly need-to-know basis as well?'

'Ha. I was a navy diver. I specialised in neutralising bombs underwater.'

'Oh. Wow.'

'It's not as impressive as it sounds.' He shrugged.

'I think it probably is.' Carrie briefly imagined Rory in a wet suit and noticed her pulse quicken. 'When you say neutralising, you mean...'

'Defusing them, yes. I mean, that's not all I did. Intelligence-gathering was a large part of the job, too.'

'How do you do that from underwater?' Carrie leaned forward on her elbows, genuinely fascinated.

'You do it in pairs, usually. There's specialist equipment. Swim underwater into a particular area and then pop above the water, take a reading, go back under again. I'm simplifying the process, of course.'

'Wow. That really is Boy's Own Adventure stuff.'

He gave a small smile. 'Anyway, I'm going to be away, maybe for a few weeks, maybe longer. So, I have to close the restaurant. I'm so sorry. You've only just started.'

'Oh. I see.' Carrie nodded. Of course, the restaurant couldn't run without the head chef.

'I can pay you a bit while we're closed. Not full wages, but maybe half? I'm sorry. I just can't afford more than that.' He wrung his hands, looking anxious. 'I don't want to go, but I have to.'

'I understand. It's okay. And you don't have to pay me anything while you're gone,' Carrie offered.

He shook his head vehemently. 'No, I want to give you something. It's not fair, just having to close this suddenly.'

'But I understand,' Carrie said, taking another sip of her coffee. 'It sounds like it's just the way things are in your profession – well, reserve-profession. So, you don't know how long you'll be away?'

'No. As I say, definitely weeks. Maybe longer.' He sighed. 'Honestly, it's bringing up a lot of stuff for me, but I'm trying not to think about it.'

'What stuff?' she asked, before realising it was too personal a question. 'Sorry. Ignore that.'

'No, it's okay.' Rory sighed again. 'I never talk about it, but I've started seeing a therapist, and she says I should.'

'A therapist?' Carrie shook her head. 'Sorry. I didn't mean to sound surprised. That's good. More people should see therapists. I should, probably,' she added. 'Anyway, I'm happy to listen if you do want to tell me.'

'Okay, well...' He trailed off. 'I was away a lot with work. You get posted abroad, as you can imagine.'

'Sure.'

'I worked in some very far-flung places. I saw active duty in the Gulf, in the Indian Ocean, in the Mediterranean. I can't tell you what I did specifically.'

'Okay.' Carrie finished her coffee. The stool was pretty uncomfortable, but she didn't want to move. 'Traumatic things? I know it's not uncommon for people in the military to have PTSD.'

'No, it's not uncommon. A few of my old mates got that, but for me, it was never the job. I loved the job. Made me feel alive.' He blinked. 'No. I was in a relationship when I joined up, and we stayed together for the first few years. It was hard, keeping the long-distance thing going, but we tried – I'd get leave, and sometimes I'd be working somewhere like the Caribbean, and she could come out and join me. Those times were pretty nice. But then we broke up.' His face darkened at those words.

'What happened?' Carrie asked, gently.

'Hmm. It was... a bad break-up, I guess you'd say.' He looked uncomfortable. 'So, I don't mind being asked to go back and deliver this specialist training, but it's just making me think about all this stuff again. Like, I always do anyway, because of the therapy, but this is bringing other things back.' He drummed his fingertips on the counter top. 'Stuff I used to do when I was in service. Not, like, terrible things in terms of killing people or anything. But the ways I used to cope, I suppose.'

'We've all done things we're not proud of.' Carrie's expression darkened as she thought of the moments in the car before the accident: of her turning up the music, knowing that Claire was having trouble concentrating.

And when you need me in the dead of night, I'm just a minute away... ooh, ooh.

She had been trying to irritate her sister. And that distraction had meant that Claire had died. Carrie's gorge rose: for a moment she thought she was going to be sick at the sudden memory of the accident. She must have made a strange noise, because Rory shot her an odd look.

'Are you okay?' he asked. 'You look terrible, suddenly.'

'I'm okay.' Carrie cleared her throat. 'I just... it doesn't matter.'

'Are you sure?' Rory looked concerned. 'Do you feel ill?'

'No, it's not that. I just...' She trailed off. 'I just know what you mean. About... what you do to cope with difficult feelings. I try not to think about Claire, but pretty regularly it kind of overwhelms me, you know?'

'I do.' Rory frowned. 'Are you sure you're all right? Would you like a glass of water? I'm sorry if what I said was triggering for you in some way... I can be thoughtless.' He went to the cupboard next to the sink and took out a glass, filling it under the cold tap and bringing it back to the kitchen island. 'Here. Drink this.' He watched her take a sip.

'I'm all right, Rory. Really,' Carrie protested. 'It's just...' She paused for a moment. 'I just have a lot I'm dealing with at the moment,' she finished, lamely.

'Do you want to talk about Claire?' He reached out and put his hand on hers. 'I'm a good listener too. It's a sign of someone who's been therapised to death, but I've learnt how to listen and ask the right questions. I think, anyway.' He gave her a gentle smile.

Carrie looked up at him, desperately trying to blink back the tears that filled her eyes. 'I can't right now. I know I just asked you to explain yourself, but for me it's too soon. I'm sorry.'

'Never be sorry for your feelings, Carrie,' Rory murmured, and he squeezed her hand.

Despite the fact that she felt awful, Carrie felt a warmth in Rory's presence, and his hand on hers felt... right. She really did feel better for that one small touch.

Rory moved to sit down on the stool next to hers. 'By the way, could I ask you not to tell anyone I go to a therapist? It's not something I broadcast,' he said.

'Of course, I won't,' Carrie replied, seriously. 'The important thing is that you're working through whatever it is. I'm hardly a good example of how to do that. I moved up here to run away from it all. So, I'd never judge someone else.'

She thought briefly about her conversation with June, about becoming a nurse. Rory had said to her, before, that he could imagine her being one. She wondered whether she'd be any good at listening to people's problems; the bedside manner, as it was called. It was true that she didn't believe in judging anyone else, now, not after what she'd been through. Was that enough to make her good at a job like that? She'd have to have the training, of course. But she thought, maybe, that she *could* do it. And the thought filled her with a thread of hope.

'That's a very kind point of view.' Rory picked up her coffee mug. 'Refill? I've got some biscuits too, if you want. You look a bit peaky.'

'Thanks. I'd love a refill.' Carrie nodded. 'What did you mean, ways you used to cope?'

'Agh, Carrie.' Rory shook his head as he turned away to go through the same procedure of coffee-making as before. 'I just meant the ways I used to manage my emotions, back then. I used to do things to hurt myself on purpose if I was depressed or felt low. Act recklessly on manoeuvres and missions. I wanted to get hurt. Like it would be a distraction, or something.' He took in a deep breath and let it go slowly.

'It was a dark time for me. Not edifying. I've left that guy in the past. Still, I'm worried when I go back, that I might feel like that again. I don't think I will, but I haven't been put in an extreme situation for a long time. I've been playing it safe, here in Loch Cameron.'

'Believe me, I've done some unedifying things in my life,' Carrie said, grimly.

And when you need me in the dead of night, I'm just a minute away... ooh, ooh

Carrie. Turn it off. I need to concentrate.

The air con isn't working. The screen's fogging up.

She closed her eyes, as if she could stop the scene repeating before them.

'I guess you won't know until you go,' she offered, after a moment. 'What does your therapist think?'

'She says she thinks I'll be okay as long as I stay present and focused. I've been meditating a lot, and I can also have remote sessions with her, which I'm going to do weekly, if I can.'

'Will you be able to get WiFi underwater, or wherever you're going to be?'

'Haha. I will be spending some time on dry land. I'm not a fish.' He handed her a new cup of coffee, opened a drawer and took out a packet of plain digestives.

'Not the chocolate ones?' she asked, attempting to lighten the mood.

'No. Plain only. The manly choice.' He cracked a smile. 'Sorry. I feel like I just kind of vomited all of my trauma onto you. You thought you were here for a friendly coffee.'

'That's all right.' Carrie took a biscuit from the packet. 'Remember when I freaked out on you the other day, in the car? Plus, if anything, I suppose I feel like I know you a bit better.'

'Please don't worry about the other day. But it's a relief to know you don't think your boss is some kind of maniac.'

'I don't. Anyway, you won't be my boss for much longer, as it turns out.' She raised her eyebrows playfully.

'I know. But, to be clear, I'm not sacking you, I just have to put you on paid leave for a while. But... either way... I don't want you to think badly of me.' Rory held her gaze for a moment before looking away.

Is there something more than friendliness behind that look? she wondered. *Am I imagining it, or was there an intensity there?* Carrie again felt a connection blazing between them. It was a sensation she hadn't ever felt with anyone else: it was as though time slowed, and she and Rory were the only two people on the planet.

'I don't,' she said, shortly, looking away and breaking the moment.

Rory was just an intense kind of guy, Carrie rationalised. She had thought that about him since she'd first seen him in the village shop. On that day, she'd thought he was rude. Since working with him, she'd learnt he was passionate about the restaurant and about food, but that he was also kind and funny. The villagers thought he was standoffish, but Carrie knew better. She thought so, anyway. And the fact that he was dealing with his demons was commendable.

She decided to change the subject. 'Why don't you tell me about this house? It's really beautiful, you know. This kitchen alone must have cost you an arm and a leg.' She looked around again at the modern space with its marble worktops and collection of top-of-the-range food mixers, bread makers, the coffee machine and various other gadgets.

She could tell from the look in his eyes that he knew what she was trying to do, but he acquiesced gracefully.

'Thank you. It's been a labour of love. I bought it when I moved to Loch Cameron six years ago and took my time renovating it. It was a seventies nightmare when I moved in. Avocado bathroom, orange flock wallpaper, brown carpets. The lot.'

'Wow,' Carrie chuckled. 'Lucky you had these lovely natural floorboards underneath. And the fireplace in the front room is gorgeous.'

'Yeah. Come on, I'll give you the tour.' He put down his coffee mug and stood up. 'Then I should get back to sorting things out. There's not much to pack, but I have to do things like leave a spare key with a neighbour, empty the fridge, that kind of thing.'

'Well, if you've got anything I can take, let me know. I've got hardly any food in,' Carrie joked.

But he nodded seriously. 'Oh, absolutely. You'd be doing me a favour. I'll put a bag together for you.'

'I wasn't serious,' Carrie laughed. 'Give it to... I don't know. Someone who needs it.'

'You just said you don't have any food in. Ergo, you need it.' He flashed Carrie a grin which gave her a glowy feeling. 'Happy to help a damsel in distress. I'm a navy man, remember.'

'Real *Officer and a Gentleman* stuff, huh.' Carrie was trying hard not to imagine Rory in a navy dress uniform with the shiny buttons and smart epaulettes, and failing miserably.

'Sure.' He gave her an unreadable look under his long eyelashes and she felt her stomach turn to jelly again. 'Come on, then, let's go upstairs.' He walked to the hallway and bowed theatrically. 'I'd carry you up, *Officer and a Gentleman* style, but you might get the wrong idea.'

'What? Oh, right.' Carrie had temporarily forgotten that Rory had offered to give her a tour of the house. For a brief moment, she'd been distracted by his suggestion they go upstairs. She blushed, and was instantly mortified for doing so.

Dear lord, Claire's voice surfaced in her mind. *Stop blushing all the time and kiss the guy. He obviously wants you to.*

No, he doesn't, Carrie argued with Claire. *Stop making comments about my love life – or, my lack of one. If you're going to be here, then let's have a proper conversation. About what happened. Do you want that?*

Claire's voice went silent. Carrie sighed to herself. Was she going mad? She hoped she wasn't, but it was entirely possible.

TWENTY-FOUR

Carrie followed Rory into the hall and up the wide wooden staircase, which featured a carved wooden banister varnished in a dark nut brown. The woodwork gleamed against the dark blue walls. At the top of the stairs, a long, wide hallway reached out in front of Carrie. Along the walls, there were a number of framed prints of landscapes: a desert, a beach, some jungle. When Carrie looked closer, she realised that they were in fact photographs, and each one had Rory in them, grinning into the camera. In some, he wore his navy uniform. In others, he wore shorts or casual clothes.

'These are you!' Carrie exclaimed, looking more closely at the photo of Rory in the jungle. In that one he was wearing some khaki shorts with pockets and no shirt; Carrie tried not to stare at the image of his toned, muscular chest.

'Yeah. My adventures.' He grinned, standing behind her and looking at the photo.

'While you were in the navy?' She was very aware of him standing so close to her; she could sense his body's heat.

'Yeah. That's Brazil, the Gulf, Jamaica.' He pointed them

out one by one. 'The job took me to some amazing places, all right.'

'Are they sending you back somewhere like that?' Carrie half turned to him and looked up into his dark eyes. The urge to lean into him overtook her, and she fought against it. There was just something so warm and familiar about him, even though he wasn't familiar at all. Not in that way. *Maybe I just need the touch of a man after all this time,* she thought. *A non-specific man. And Rory is the closest one right now.*

She was aware that it wasn't exactly a *nice* thought, or at least, not a usual one for her. She'd always supposed women weren't meant to *need* a man in that kind of way. But she realised she needed something right now. Comfort, perhaps. Or simply basic human touch. Being held. Being *alive*. She had come so close to death herself, after all. It could have been her who had died in the crash.

'No. Sadly not.' Rory's voice broke over her thoughts. 'It'll be a lot colder where I'm going.' He folded his arms over his chest. 'But I can assure you it's nowhere that exciting.' He blew out his cheeks.

Carrie's eyes caressed the bulge of his biceps. She looked back at the photos to avoid them. She was surprised her sister's voice didn't have something to say about this.

'So, as far as the tour goes: bathroom, office, guest room, another guest room, master bedroom.' Rory pointed to the different doorways leading off the hall.

'Can I see?' she asked.

He nodded, leading her to the first room, which was one of the guest bedrooms. Inside, it was very neat, and the blue paint Rory seemed to favour on the walls had been substituted for clean white. The bed in this room had an expensive-looking upholstered baby-pink velvet bedstead, and it was made up with a crisp white cotton pintucked bed set. In the corner of the room there was an antique white chair with a painted spindle back and a rattan seat.

'I wouldn't have put you down as a pink bed guy,' Carrie chuckled. 'It's pretty, though.'

'My sister chose it. It's where she sleeps when she comes to stay. I don't mind,' he said, with a shrug. 'I'm secure enough in my masculinity to have a pink bed in the house and not lose any sleep over it.'

'Fair enough.'

They walked on to the next door, which was a neat bathroom, tiled in white, then on down the hall.

'And this is the master bedroom.' Rory indicated the next room offhandedly. 'I put in an ensuite as well.'

'Wow, Rory. This is beautiful.' Carrie walked in to get a really good look: she had to admit, she was curious about what Rory's bedroom would look like. *Not for any particular reason,* she thought, feeling she had to make a pre-emptive comment before Claire's voice piped up, but her sister was mercifully silent.

The room's focal point was a huge bed: Carrie guessed that it was probably at least a super king size, like the ones you saw in posh hotels. Unlike the pretty pink bed in the guest room, this one had a tall black headboard, and the sheets were a dark copper. However, it was still neatly made, and the room itself showed Rory's military training: there were no clothes strewn on the floor; no untidiness anywhere. The floor was the same type of stained floorboards as the lounge, and the only real decorative piece in the room was a large, elaborate copper-coloured lampshade which hung from a beautiful central rose on the ceiling.

She turned to look out of one of the windows and made a small gasp.

'Yeah. It's some view, huh? That's most of the reason I bought it in the first place.' Rory stood beside her, looking down at the village spread below, and the loch, glinting in the after-noon sun. The late autumn sun was low already, but there was a goldenness to it still that made the loch look like the picture postcard Carrie remembered June describing it as. A couple of sailing boats tacked at a distance, out beyond the village and the castle, their white sails taking up the always-available wind. Carrie imagined how free she would feel, out on the water of the loch with the wind in her hair.

The house was on the hill behind the village, where a lot of the newer homes had been built in more recent years. Gretchen's cottage had a more immediate view of the loch, being right on Queen's Point, but even though Rory's house sat further back, the view from the two wide bay windows in the bedroom was stunning.

'It really is,' Carrie breathed. 'This is a beautiful room, too. The cornicing is lovely.' She looked up to the high ceiling, where the edges of the walls met the ceiling in a white curve of plaster.

'Thank you,' Rory said, his voice low.

Carrie shivered with pleasure just hearing it. Instinctively, she turned to him, just at the moment he also turned to her.

There was something in the air between them, sudden and electric. It was as if a switch had been flipped. Carrie felt as if there was a hiatus in ordinary life; a moment of stillness, where, somehow, she and Rory were totally alone, together, in a brief time of possibility.

He stepped towards her and looked down, intensely, into her eyes. 'Carrie?' His voice was gravelly with desire. 'I...'

Before he could finish, she went to him, reaching for him in an instinctive way, knowing that was what he wanted. And that it was what she wanted, too.

As soon as their hands touched, he drew her to him in a firm embrace. She let out an involuntary sigh, partly in surprise, but partly from desire too. The urge to be held, as purely and as simply as Rory was holding her, was powerful. It made her feel alive, and she realised suddenly and all at once how much she had missed simply being touched by another person.

He met her eyes with a furious passion blazing in his. Without saying anything more, he kissed her, gently, and as soon as his lips met hers, Carrie felt as though she might melt completely into the floor. The sensation of his arms firmly around her was intoxicating. She had never felt this degree of heat or passion from the presence or touch of a man.

Even though Rory's kiss was soft, there was an intensity to it and she felt herself responding; kissing him back, communicating with her lips and hands, in the unspoken way of lovers.

His breath grew more ragged, and his kiss deeper. 'Carrie.' He whispered her name as he kissed her. 'I want... I want you. Now. I've wanted you so long,' he breathed, one hand leaving her waist and caressing her cheek.

'I want you too.' Carrie wrapped her arms around his neck, pressing her body against his. She wanted Rory, too, in that moment, and gave herself up to it. If she allowed herself to rationalise what she was doing, then the moment would be lost, and she didn't want that, because the moment was beautiful. Carrie needed Rory, right now, right here, and for once she was going to allow herself to have what she needed.

He led her to the bed, and they fell onto it, wrapped in each other. Rory kissed her neck, his hands finding her breasts; he groaned as he touched them.

'Carrie... oh...' He unbuttoned the top of her dress, reaching his hand inside. She gasped, not from shock, but from the raw pleasure of Rory's touch on her skin.

'Oh, Rory...' she murmured, her whole body full of the warmth of his touch. She kissed him, again, more deeply, and felt his smile under her lips.

TWENTY-FIVE

The choir was rehearsing in the community centre and June had told them all to take a ten-minute break. It was just as well, because Carrie couldn't concentrate at all, after the night before with Rory.

She'd woken up in his bed in the very early hours of the morning, with him stroking her cheek gently.

Hey, beautiful. I've got to go.

She hadn't known where she was at first, and then she'd remembered. She and Rory had made love in the afternoon, up in his room, and then lay in each other's arms and talked until it got dark. Rory had been going to get up and make them something to eat, but they must have fallen asleep instead.

Waking up, she had been disoriented, and then... then, it was all just a little... awkward.

It was four in the morning when Carrie had got back to Gretchen's cottage and slid into her own bed. Rory was still rushing around at his house when she'd left him, trying to get all his jobs done before he left. He'd been sweet to her, but it was impossible to hide the fact that he was leaving and he needed her to go pretty fast too.

Had he taken advantage of her? No, that wasn't what had happened. It had been a genuinely spontaneous moment between them, and they had both wanted it. There had been an attraction between them and it had been building over the weeks they'd been working together. Carrie had wanted... *needed* Rory yesterday, and it had been... so blessed. It was a kind of cliché, but that really was how it had felt.

And now, he was gone, and though he was coming back at some point, she had no idea when. She had to admit she felt abandoned. Even though she knew, rationally, that wasn't what had happened, her heart wasn't rational. She had shared herself with Rory and they'd connected in a way she had never felt with anyone else before.

And then he'd left.

Carrie got a cup of tea and a biscuit and sat down next to Dotty, who offered her a throat lozenge.

'Helps ma vocal cords stay limber,' she advised. 'Little secret o' mine.'

'I think the tea will do it, but thanks.' Carrie tried not to let her glumness show; the last thing she wanted was for all the gossips of Loch Cameron to know that she and Rory had slept together last night. 'How are you, Dotty? I haven't seen you for a while.'

'Ah, mustn't grumble.' Dotty nodded. 'And ye? How've ye been gettin' on? I've been thinking o' ye.'

'I'm okay, thanks. Taking things slowly. The choir helps.'

'Aye. I like coming. Good fer the soul tae blast out a tune.' Dotty chuckled.

'Hm. I'll have a lot more time to practise, now that I don't have a job anymore. You're not hiring at the inn, are you?' Carrie bit the edge off a custard cream biscuit, thinking about Rory. The way he had held her. The way he'd looked into her eyes.

'No, dear. Why don't ye have a job? Were ye not workin' at The Fat Hen?' Dotty crinkled her eyes in concern.

'I was, but Rory has to close up temporarily. The navy called him back to do some kind of special project. He was vague on the details.'

'Oh, my!' Dotty's eyes lit up, probably at the gossip potential, Carrie thought. 'How excitin'.'

'Hm. I guess so.' Carrie nodded. It was sort of heroic, when she stopped to think about it. But mostly, she just felt abandoned.

Seeing June at the piano, Carrie remembered the conversation they'd had before, about nursing. Perhaps this gap in her time was there for a reason; her old flatmates, Patty and Marcus, were all about there always being a reason why rubbish things happened. Frankly, Carrie had always thought it was an attitude that refused to accept that sometimes life was just crappy, but maybe she would benefit from being a bit more positive in her outlook. Being free from the restaurant could mean that she was freer to think about taking up a caring profession. She'd thought about it a little, here and there, since her and June's conversation, but she'd been so busy with the restaurant and thinking about Claire that she hadn't really concentrated her thoughts enough.

'I'm just going to say a quick hello to June. Back in a minute,' she excused herself and went over.

'Hi, June,' she greeted the older woman, who was today dressed in a long grey knitted dress and a black pashmina. She wore gold-rimmed glasses which were pushed halfway down her nose for reading the sheet music for the choir. Today, they'd been running through 'Alone' once more, and Carrie had sung the chorus as a solo again. She'd done it several times now and everyone seemed to love it. She had been listening to other power ballads at home on a playlist on her phone, and belting them out around the cottage. There was something life-affirming about it.

'Ah, hello. Carrie. How's things? Enjoying the song today?'

'Yes, thanks.' In fact, Carrie hadn't been at all in the mood to come to choir practice today – she hadn't really gone back to sleep after getting in so early from Rory's, so she was tired and grumpy – but she knew she should come, and it had in fact been a little cathartic to *blast out some tunes*, as Dotty put it. And at least if she was at choir, she could try not to think about Rory.

'Actually, I was wanting to ask you about nursing, June. Were you serious about taking me to the hospital you used to work at? I'd really like that, if you thought it would be okay. It would be really good to get a sense of what it's really like, from the people who do it.'

'Oh, of course, dear. In fact, I'm going next week, because it's one of the girls' birthdays. I still keep in touch with them all, even though I've been retired a good while. I did a lot of teaching, you see, well into my seventies. I only stopped that fairly recently because my hip couldn't stand being on my feet that long, and, you know, the mental strain. Not that I'm not still as sharp as a tack.' She raised an imperious eyebrow.

'Oh, I have no doubt of that at all,' Carrie laughed. 'Well, that would be great, as long as you don't mind. I'd love to come along.'

'You'd be more than welcome, dear. Wednesday morning next week all right for you?'

'That's fine. I haven't got anything else on. Not even work, now that Rory's had to close the restaurant while he's away.'

'Ah. I heard about that. Very sudden.' June turned over a couple of pages of her sheet music and replaced it on the holder with a frown. 'What happened?'

'He got asked to go back to do some navy training,' Carrie explained. 'It was very sudden. Apparently, he has skills that are in high demand.' She wondered exactly how June had heard about it – he'd only just left. The rumour mill turned fast in Loch Cameron, she supposed.

'Hmm.' June narrowed her eyes, regarding Carrie's face for a moment. 'Must be annoying that you just started that job and now he's gone.'

'Yeah. Well, he's paying me half pay while he's away, so it could be worse.'

'Hmm,' June repeated, her eyes like gimlets. 'Missing him, are you? Good-looking boy.'

'He's hardly a boy,' Carrie argued, self-consciously. Could June tell she'd slept with Rory?

Don't be ridiculous, she told herself. Still, she felt as though she might blush, and that would be a sure sign. *Don't blush*, she told herself sternly. *For goodness' sake.*

'Man, then,' June continued. 'Fair few eyes on him in the village, I'd say. Course, I'm too old for that kind of thing. But it doesn't mean I don't notice an attractive young man.'

'Well, I wouldn't know about that,' Carrie said, shortly. She was only half lying; she hadn't noticed women falling all over Rory, though he was always polite and charming to the customers in the restaurant. That was his job. But she also knew that the main thrust of June's comment was that Rory was attractive, and that it would be understandable if Carrie had been taken in by his considerable charms. Which, of course, she had. But she didn't want to tell June that. It would have been all round the village by dinner time. That was just the way Loch Cameron was.

Carrie wasn't ashamed that she and Rory had slept together. It had been amazing. But, now that he'd disappeared, Carrie wasn't particularly up for playing the role of the jilted lover or for having the whole village gossip about her, either. They were probably already doing that, just because she was the new stranger in town. Dotty had likely filled everyone in with Carrie's story: how she'd lost her mum and now Claire, and come back to Loch Cameron, the place where she'd spent the best parts of her childhood. That story was probably irresistible.

Carrie noticed her phone light up in the bag at her feet, and she excused herself for a moment, lifting it out to check who was calling or texting her. It was another message from Graham.

I know it's hard to talk. But I think we should. Call me when you're ready.

She looked at the message for a minute, then put the phone back in the pocket of her bag. She still wasn't ready to deal with Graham. Not yet.

'Ah, well, then,' June said. 'Wednesday it is, hen. I'll see you outside the main entrance. Let's say... ten thirty? I've got some errands to do that day, so that suits me if it's okay with you.'

'That sounds fine. Thanks, June.'

'No bother, lassie.' June winked at her. 'We'll make you a nurse yet.'

TWENTY-SIX

'So. Anythin' interestin' in Maud's auld diaries?' Dotty popped another lozenge into her mouth.

'Hmm? Oh, right. There was, actually.' Carrie got another cup of tea from the table and came back to sit by Dotty. All the attendees stood while they were singing in the choir, but some of the more elderly members, like Dotty and June, also had a seat nearby in the event that they got tired. 'But what I don't know is why Myrtle had them.'

'Hmm. Well, I might know the answer to that.' Dotty lowered her voice. 'But if I tell ye, ye've got tae keep it under yer hat. Okay?'

'All right.' Carrie looked around them, but no one was nearby. 'What is it, then?'

'Well,' Dotty said, looking from side to side and leaning in towards Carrie. 'No' tha' it's ma business, but Myrtle was ma friend, an' over the years, we talked. As friends do.'

'Of course.' Carrie nodded, sipping her tea.

'Well. Ye probably dinnae know but Myrtle took over the premises of the café from auld Len, whose place it was before her. But he didnae run a café. That was Myrtle's invention.'

'Oh. What was the place before, then?' Carrie leaned in too, feeling as though they were sharing official secrets and not just gossiping about Dotty's best friend. *Talk about cloak and dagger*, she thought, amused.

'Well, Len had a barber's. He'd cut women's hair as well, mind, as long as it wasnae anythin' too fancy. But what he did the most was run a bit o' black-market tradin' on the side.' Dotty had lowered her voice even more so that Carrie had to really concentrate on what she was saying.

'Black market?'

'Aye. He'd get ye what ye needed, anythin' from an engagement ring to a sofa, cheap. No one asked questions. For a lot o' people in the village it was the only way to get a new washin' machine or a tumble dryer or whatever. Len would let ye pay monthly, over time. Lot o' poor people in Loch Cameron, especially twenty, thirty years back. It's improved a bit now, but folks still find things hard.'

'I had no idea,' Carrie confessed. 'Did the police know? What about the Laird?'

'Aye, they knew. Everyone knew. Just one o' those open secrets in the village. As far as I know, the police didnae mind as long as Len didnae bring any trouble intae the village, an' he never did.'

'But... where was he getting those things from? The engagement rings and washing machines?' Carrie asked in a low voice. 'Were they stolen?'

'Dunno. I never asked Len and neither did Myrtle. He was a gentleman. It didnae feel right tae ask.' Dotty shrugged.

Carrie frowned. 'So, why are you telling me this? Did he come by Maud's diaries somehow? Were they stolen or something? Not exactly your usual black-market goods.'

'No. He didnae get them from someone.' Dotty gave Carrie a look. 'They belonged to him.'

'What do you mean, they belonged to him?' Carrie frowned. 'They were Maud's.'

'Aye. An' that's what I'm tryin' tae tell ye,' Dotty said, patiently. 'Len was Maud's son. An' I think, if ye've read the diaries by now, that you'll know how that came aboot.'

'Len was Maud's son?' Carrie sat back in her seat. 'You mean... William's son? Maud's baby?'

'Aye. She had William's baby.' Dotty nodded sagely, keeping her voice low. 'I know all this from Myrtle. She found the diaries in Len's things when he died and she took over the café. But they'd been friends too before that and she knew. He'd told her. Course, Myrtle never knew Maud, but I did. As soon as she told me, I could see the resemblance.'

'So, Len who ran the barber's and the black market... he was related to me?' Carrie couldn't believe it. This was definitely a good distraction from the Rory situation. 'But he died.'

'Aye, sadly. He would have been, what...? Your great-aunt's son, so... your cousin, once removed.'

'Goodness. I can't believe it.'

'Aye. He wouldae been in the village when you visited, as a child.' Dotty tutted. 'Do ye remember him at all? She wouldae introduced ye, maybe?'

Carrie thought back for a moment. 'D'you know, I do remember a man. That could have been his name. Every time Maud took me and Claire into the village, she'd take us into this dingy little shop, with big chairs in it. It was strange because the window was made of these different coloured panels of stained glass. I used to like looking at those, but I wondered what the big chairs were for.'

'Uh-huh. That would've been Len.' Dotty nodded. 'Did she not explain who he was?'

'Not that I remember. We used to go in and play on the chairs and they'd have a chat. Maud always came away with something she needed, something for the house, or what have you. I remember that. Sometimes he gave us ice lollies.' Carrie tried to remember more. 'Sometimes there was a little girl there too, about our age. Wow, I haven't thought about this in years, but we used to go out and play by the loch, sometimes, if we were allowed. I don't remember her name. She had dark hair.'

'Hmm.' Dotty nodded. 'There's a lot you shouldae been told, I'd say.'

'The diary finished at the point where Maud realised she was pregnant. Perhaps she thought she should stop writing it then for some reason. Maybe she was worried it would be too incriminating if anyone found it.' Carrie put her china teacup back on its saucer and placed it carefully under her chair.

'Maybe,' Dotty sighed. 'What I know is that she didnae feel that she could bring Len up herself: the scandal wouldae been too great. So, she gave Len to William and Clara, believe it or not.'

'William and Clara? That's insane! Clara wouldn't have wanted to take in her husband's illegitimate child, surely?' Carrie gaped at Dotty.

The old woman sighed and ran her fingers through her immaculately coiffed hair. 'I dunno what happened, exactly, hen. All's I know is that Len grew up with William and Clara's kids. Clara got better, slowly, over time, but she was never strong. I suspect William gave her little choice. An' she needed him, because she couldnae cope wi' the kids on her own.'

'If that's true, that's an awful choice to have to make,' Carrie said, appalled. 'Lose your husband – if he threatened to leave her – or bring up his child from another woman?'

'Aye, well. People do things ye would never think,' Dotty admitted. 'They never told Len he was Maud's, and I guess she never told him either. But William kept those diaries. I guess Maud gave them to him at some point, aye. At some point, Len found them and he read what you've read. And he realised

Maud was his mother, not Clara. He told Myrtle one day. And she told me.'

'So, did you know William?' Carrie asked.

'I knew him, yes. Sad story. William Black, married to Clara Black. They had the two children. She was ill most of her life. Course, nowadays, the doc'd say she had post-natal depression, and no doubt some other gynaecological matters. In those days, she was just left to it. Poor thing. You can only imagine what that marriage was like, aye.'

'I know. It's terribly sad,' Carrie agreed. 'And especially more so because Maud and William seemed to have a really close connection. But he was married, and that was that. Not like now, where maybe he could have got a divorce or even have an open relationship.' Carrie frowned. 'In the diary Maud said he gave the name Graves when they stayed at a hotel together. I suppose that was a fake name. To avoid being found out.'

'I'd think so, dearie,' Dotty nodded sagely. 'Very different times. Anyway, the Black family lived in the village a long time. Len has just passed, of course. William and Clara's two other kids moved away some time back. I was friendly with the girl, Alice. We were about the same age. We did keep in touch for a while after she moved, but you know how it is. People fall away, lives are busy.' Carrie nodded.

'But, of course, Bess lives close by,' Dotty added. 'You know Bess, don't you? Maybe you haven't met each other, mind you,' she mused.

'Who's Bess?' Carrie frowned. 'I don't think I've met anyone of that name.'

'Ach, listen tae me, runnin' on at the mouth. I havenae told ye the most important thing, then. Len had a daughter. Not far off your age, aye. She lives with her partner in the next village, but she works all around. Handyman work. Handy*woman*, I should say.' Dotty laughed, correcting herself.

'Len... has a daughter?' Carrie gaped at Dotty. 'And she lives close by?'

'Aye. Bess Black. I'll introduce ye. I'm guessin' yer, what... second cousins or somethin'? Distant family, but still family.' Dotty squeezed Carrie's hand.

'The girl from the shop...' Carrie trailed off, remembering the dark-haired girl she and Claire sometimes played with when they visited Loch Cameron. 'That was her? Bess?'

'Aye, very probably.' Dotty nodded. 'I'd say that even if Maud and William never told Len she was his real mother, Maud wanted tae be around him as much as she could. So it makes sense she'd always be in there, wantin' things fer the house or what have ye. An excuse to see her son and her grand-daughter.'

'Wow. Thanks for telling me.' Carrie breathed out a long exhalation.

'Nae bother,' Dotty said. 'Thought ye should know. I'm just sorry ye never got tae know your cousin, once removed. He was a nice fella. I'll introduce ye tae Bess. Lovely girl, she is. Her partner, Sally, works at the distillery, an' Bess is our local plumber, painter, odd jobs lassie. I'd be lost without her, that's no word o' a lie.'

'I'm sorry I never had the chance to meet Len.' Carrie sighed. 'But it still makes me feel like I belong here a bit more. Knowing I have family here.'

'Of course ye do, poppet.' Dotty squeezed her hand. 'Ye should think of Loch Cameron as yer home, whether ye end up stayin' or not. Ye belong here as much as I do. An' I'm like the fixtures an' fittin's,' she said, with a laugh.

'I don't think I've ever felt like I belonged anywhere,' Carrie said, quietly.

Dotty gave her an impromptu hug. 'Well, ye belong here,' she repeated. 'Now. Come and stand next tae me an' sing "Total Eclipse of the Heart" like yer life depended on it.'

TWENTY-SEVEN

After choir, Carrie had been so inundated with thoughts about Len and Bess that she had almost forgotten she was supposed to be going to clear out Claire's flat in Edinburgh the next day.

Claire's landlord had rented the flat to a new tenant, and unless someone moved Claire's stuff out, Carrie had been informed by email that Claire's things would be *disposed of.* She had been dreading it, and had put it off for as long as she could, but it had to be done. At least Dotty's revelations at choir practice the day before had distracted Carrie in the lead-up to this daunting task.

Dotty had given her Bess's number, and before she'd got in the car that morning, Carrie had drafted a message several times, rewriting it so often it had started to sound nonsensical. In the end, she settled on:

Hi Bess. Sorry for the out-of-the-blue message, but Dotty gave me your number. My name's Carrie. Maud McKinley was my great-aunt and I think you and I knew each other as children. I know you're Len's daughter – I'm so sorry for your loss. I've recently discovered that we're related. I'd love to meet and talk, if you had some free time?

Writing and rewriting the text was a distraction from having to get in the car in the first place, and from the idea of having to sort through Claire's things. Carrie would still prefer not to be in a car, but at least if she could drive, it helped her feel she was in control. Being a passenger was worse, like when she'd freaked out in the car with Rory that time. She'd been a passenger when the crash had happened. She hadn't been able to do anything to save her sister. She hadn't been in control.

Then, just as bad as the car journey, when she got to Claire's flat she was going to have to pack up all her stuff.

She was dreading it.

Carrie looked at her phone for a minute, wondering if Bess would reply straight away, but the screen remained empty of messages. She sighed and put it in her pocket.

No more distractions, she thought. *Just go, do the thing, and then by the time you get home tonight, it'll be over.*

She really didn't want to leave the cottage: it was safe here, her little sanctuary. But she knew she had to go.

* * *

'I can do this. You don't need to be here,' Carrie snapped at Graham as he opened Claire's wardrobe.

They both stared at the racks of her clothes hung haphazardly on the rail. There was silence as they both took in the scent of Claire: the washing detergent she used, the faint trace of her perfume that was still on some of the dresses and coats and blouses that hung there.

'I want to be here,' Graham muttered, refusing to look at Carrie. 'I know you hate me, even though I still don't understand why. But I have every right to be here. As much right as you.'

'You do not have anywhere *near* as much right as me to be

here, so don't even pretend,' Carrie spat back at him. 'I was her sister. Who were you? Some guy she was sleeping with.'

'Carrie. You know we were engaged. I spent more time in this flat than you ever did,' he said, keeping his voice even. 'Let's not argue. Okay? I can't, right now. I just don't have it in me to be here, and argue with you as well.'

'Then leave.' Carrie turned to him, feeling her heart wrench and the tears spring to her eyes. Carrie had had no intention of talking to Graham at all if she could help it, but he'd been at the flat when she'd let herself in with her spare key. 'Why are you even here? It's not your flat.'

'Because I miss her. I wanted... to be around her things.' Graham sat down on the edge of the bed. 'Is that so wrong? Not everyone reacted to losing Claire like you did, just upping sticks and running away. I wanted to stay as close to her as I could.'

'So, you've been living here? In her flat? That's a little twisted, don't you think?' Carrie frowned. 'I didn't say you could be here. I don't want you here, Graham.'

'Tough. I am here.' He looked up at her. 'Why have you never liked me?'

Carrie looked away, grief blocking her throat. How could she explain? She'd found it so hard to get in the car to drive all the way to Claire's flat today, for one thing. And then the hours it took to get to Edinburgh from Loch Cameron were intensely stressful: negotiating the country roads, expecting a car to come around the corner too fast on the wrong side of the road any minute. She was in a cold sweat the whole time and shaking for most of it.

Then, when she'd finally got to Edinburgh, she'd had to stop at a storage centre and organise a place to put all of Claire's stuff until she had a home for it. She'd bought a ton of flat-pack boxes and tape and parked outside Claire's flat in the city centre, lugging it all up four flights of stairs, dreading opening the front door and seeing Claire's belongings. Never mind the fact that the physical effort made her collarbone ache terribly.

'Graham. This isn't about you. It was hard enough to come here today. I just want to get this done as best I can. I can't deal with you right now.' Carrie blinked back the tears, reaching into Claire's wardrobe and pulling out dresses, throwing them on the bed next to Graham. 'And you shouldn't be living here. It's ghoulish.' She didn't explain why she'd gone to Loch Cameron. She didn't have it in her to make Graham understand that escaping to the place she and Claire had been happiest as children had been the only thing she could think of. The only place she could be, right now.

'Carrie, one day you'll realise that I'm not the enemy here.' Graham got up, shaking his head. 'Just know that I loved your sister, okay? No matter what you think about me, you have to admit that I made her happy. She made me happy too.' His voice broke, and he started to cry. 'I loved her, Carrie, and I miss her so damn much.'

Carrie couldn't comfort him. If it had been anyone else, she would have, but with Graham, she just couldn't.

Graham got up and walked out; Carrie sat on the bed and stared at Claire's clothes and burst into silent tears. She knew why she'd always been awful to Graham. It was obvious, and she hated admitting it, but she was jealous. So very jealous of him, and the fact that Claire loved him. Because Claire had always been hers, first and foremost.

She'd hated him from the moment Claire had introduced them, in a bar in Edinburgh. Carrie had seen the look in her sister's eyes as she looked up at him, and had felt a stab of anger in her stomach. She'd known Claire was seeing someone, but, usually, it was casual and ended within a few months. But Graham was different. Carrie had seen that immediately. Claire looked at him as if he was the most remarkable person in the world, and not an accountant from Manchester. The way they'd touched each other, as if being away from the comfort of each other's presence was a kind of torture. The lingering looks Claire gave him when she thought no one was looking; Carrie had never seen her sister give anyone those before.

So, Carrie had been brittle and unfriendly to Graham that night, and ever since. That was why she and Claire had been edgy with each other the day of the crash; because Carrie had been avoiding her sister for months. Their relationship had gone from talking to each other on the phone or seeing each other every day to keeping in touch with the odd text message once or twice a month.

How are you?

Fine.

Want to come for dinner? I'd love you to get to know Graham more.

I'll let you know. Busy with work.

When the invitation to the wedding of an old family friend had arrived, Carrie had assumed Claire would want to take Graham, but she'd suggested they go together instead and have some *quality sister time*. Carrie had cautiously accepted. She knew she had pushed Claire away, but she'd felt unable to do anything else.

In the car, it had been strained. That was why Carrie had been annoying her sister with the radio, refusing to turn it down. She hadn't known how to be with Claire anymore, because she was too angry. Angry because Claire had replaced her in her heart. Or, that was how she had felt, anyway.

And that anger had made the accident happen. Carrie had caused it. Because she was jealous.

Her phone lit up, taking her attention. A message flashed on the screen.

Hi, Carrie. What a bolt from the blue! Yes, Len was my dad. You think we're related? How? Happy to chat and maybe meet for a coffee. Bess x

Carrie stared at the message for a minute, temporarily distracted. However, she didn't have the bandwidth to reply. *I'll text back later*, she thought, and started removing Claire's dresses from their hangers and folding them up, trying to stop crying. She could hear Graham in the lounge, moving things around. Why wouldn't he just go?

Carrie folded some more clothes, but the knowledge that Graham was out there, touching Claire's things, made her antsy. She couldn't cope with his presence.

She stormed into the lounge and found him kneeling next to Claire's bookshelf.

'Some of these are mine,' he said, taking a book out and adding it to a small pile by his feet. 'I'm taking them home. And I want to take some of her things. To remember her by.'

'You can take anything that was yours originally. But that's all.' Carrie crossed her arms over her chest.

'Carrie, don't be unreasonable.'

Graham looked like a ghost. There were black rings around his eyes; he didn't look like he'd slept. Carrie wondered how long he'd been in Claire's flat. Whether he'd been sleeping in her bed. The thought was awful. Not that Carrie didn't know that Graham would have spent many nights here with Claire; it was more the thought that no one should be sleeping in their dead partner's flat. It wasn't healthy. Reluctantly, Carrie allowed herself to feel a glimmer of sympathy for him. *No one should be living like this*, she thought. *Not even Graham.*

She sat down on the sofa and sighed. 'This is hard for me, too, you know,' she said. 'Please understand how hard it is for me to be here. And you can take some things. Just...' Carrie trailed off. 'I-I just don't want to let any part of her go. That's all.'

'I know.' Graham sighed. 'Look, Carrie. We don't have to be friends. We never were, even though I wanted to be, and Claire wanted us to be. But that's okay. After today we never have to see each other. But I want to be here and sort out her things. I need this closure. Agreed?'

'Agreed.' Carrie needed the help; there was so much to do. 'But I still don't like you.'

'I know.' Graham nodded, and gave her a small smile.

TWENTY-EIGHT

Carrie checked her phone for the millionth time that day: nothing. She refreshed her messages, pulling down the screen and hoping that Rory's name would pop up to the top, but there was nothing.

She sighed. She knew that Rory was away doing some kind of secret navy training mission, but was he really so busy that he couldn't manage a single, *Hi, how are you, thinking of you xx* message? Would that have been so hard?

She had replied to Bess, though, and arranged to meet for a walk along the loch in a couple of days' time. Carrie didn't know what to think about potentially having a new living relative but, overall, it felt good.

Carrie stood at the entrance to St Bernadette's Hospital, watching June approach. It was ten thirty exactly, and it was raining heavily in the way that it only could in Scotland: seeming to come in sideways, underneath Carrie's brolly. However, despite the weather – she rationalised that it was November now, and the fine October they'd been having had to run out eventually – Carrie was enjoying wearing the red polka-dot dress she'd bought at Fiona's Fashions. June wore a long rain mac and a plastic headscarf of the kind that only elderly ladies seemed to wear.

Carrie still had her eye on quite a few things in the shop, including some other lovely dresses that would be perfect for dates.

Not that you're likely to be going on any dates, she thought, a little glumly. *Not with Rory, anyway.*

'Carrie! You look lovely. Excited to see what it's all about?' June took her arm.

'Yes! Let's go,' Carrie allowed herself to be marched inside, and put Rory out of her mind.

* * *

The small hospital was busy, but Carrie's first impression was of calm and friendly efficiency. Inside the automatic double doors, there sat a small reception area with a couple of members of staff behind a large desk. June approached it, and one of the staff, a middle-aged man with a ginger beard and a name tag that said Dr Daniel Musgrove, looked up and broke into a huge smile.

'Junie! How are you?' He beamed. 'Did you bring me any brownies? I rely on you, you know.'

'Dr Dan, I'd hardly forget you,' June said, primly. She reached into her capacious brown leather handbag, produced a Tupperware container and handed it to him.

'Oh, amazing. I'm eternally in your debt,' Dr Dan cooed. 'Brought a friend today, I see. Hello, I'm Dan. Nice to meet you.' The doctor held out his hand.

Carrie shook it. She noticed that Dr Dan was very handsome: tall, and under his blue tunic, he had very muscular arms. 'Carrie Anderson. Hi.'

'Carrie's interested in nursing training,' June explained. 'So,

I said I'd show her around, if that's all right? Give her a sense of what it's really like?'

'Of course. Anything for June.' Dan gestured towards the wide corridor behind him that led off the reception area. 'The hospital is your oyster. And if you fancy giving us a hand, let me know. We're a bit understaffed.'

'Me?' Carrie placed her hand on her chest. 'Oh, I couldn't! I don't know how to do anything.'

'Well, I meant June, really. But you're welcome to help us at lunchtime, if you like. Do the rounds with the food. And there's always cleaning that needs doing. No qualifications needed for that.' Dan laughed at Carrie's expression. 'Oh, I'm teasing! I'm not going to make you clean the wards. I can't, anyway. You'd need to be a member of staff. But, look around, get a feel for the place, and if you have any questions, I'm happy to help. You can help at lunchtime, though. We'll consider you a volunteer.'

'Okay. I can probably manage that,' Carrie said, relieved.

'Great. You're in good hands, here. You know, June trained most of the nurses here. We miss her like mad.' Dan beamed at June, who looked uncomfortable at the praise, but also a little pleased.

'Get away with you. I just did my job, that's all. Come on, then, Carrie.' June led her away, down the corridor that Dan had indicated. 'We'll see what's going on, see if we can look in on some assessments in triage first. Do you know what that is?'

Memories of waking up in the hospital after the accident flashed into Carrie's mind. The stark room; not knowing where she was. The beeping of the machines, the smell of antiseptic. Was it crazy, coming into a hospital again so soon after such a traumatic experience? Where she'd had to stay for what seemed like forever with her broken collarbone, that hurt every time she breathed, that was still sore now? Where she had learned that Claire had passed away, and had stared stupidly at the nurse as she'd delivered the news.

'No. I mean, I think it's a kind of assessment, maybe in A&E? I don't really know.'

'That's right. It's just a word that means assessment. We have a couple of rooms set aside here for that; fortunately, it's not a hugely busy A&E service, but people do come in with emergencies and we can see them in here.' June led Carrie into one of two curtained-off areas on a corridor. Neither were currently being used. 'You'll probably have been in one of these yourself at some point. It's just a preliminary area where we can look you over,' June explained. 'In triage, we look at the patient first. You can see if people are pale, or they look sweaty or touch their hands to feel their body temperature. That can be an indicator of fever, of course, but also vascular disease and other things. We can touch – we call it palpate – an area if people are complaining of pain. Take your pulse, of course. We use one of these,' June reached into a drawer and produced a familiar-looking plastic monitor, 'and pop it on your finger to measure the oxygen saturation level in the blood. That's called a pulse oximeter.'

'I've had one of these before.' Perhaps coming to the hospital had been a bad idea. The smell of the place was starting to get to her.

'Yes, I expect you have,' June ran on. 'Other useful things we have in here: stethoscope, of course. For listening to the heart, lungs, other areas that might need investigation. This is a sphygmomanometer. We use it to measure blood pressure.' June picked up the familiar inflating cuff Carrie had seen before. 'Then there's other things here, like a nasal speculum, if we have to look up someone's nose. You wouldn't believe the number of kids I've seen with beads and small toys pushed up their nostrils, over the years.'

'I can imagine.' Carrie smiled, trying to focus on what June was saying.

'Are you all right, dear?' June looked at her carefully. 'You actually look a bit peaky. Here, sit on the bed.'

Carrie sat. 'I'm okay. It's just... I was in an accident recently, and... I guess being in a hospital again is bringing it all back,' she explained.

'Hmm.' June sat down on the bed next to her and took her hand. 'I know, dear. I heard. It's terrible, what happened.'

Carrie hadn't spoken to June about the accident, but she wasn't surprised that word had got around by now for the choir to know what had brought her to Loch Cameron.

'I'm sorry, I—' Carrie broke off as a nurse opened the curtain.

'Ah. Sorry, I didn't know this was being occupied,' the nurse said. 'I'll go next door.'

'No, that's all right, Bobbi.' June stood up. 'I was just showing Carrie around; she's thinking about nursing training. We'll get out of your way.'

'Oh, aye. Well, hang on. I've got Mr Jones here. He's had a fall but I dinnae think it's anythin' terrible. He might not mind if ye want to sit in. Get a feel for things, like.'

Bobbi, who was short and stocky, had short black hair and an immediately friendly, calm demeanour, brought in an elderly man in a wheelchair who was gamely holding a bag of peas on his elbow.

'Are you sure? We don't want to get in your way,' June said.

'Ach, nae bother.' Bobbi wheeled Mr Jones into the room. 'Now, Mr Jones, do ye mind if these lovely ladies sit in while I look at yer elbow?'

'That's all right with me.' Mr Jones looked positively delighted at the extra attention. 'I've never said no to a nurse and I don't intend to start now.'

'That's the spirit,' Bobbi chuckled. 'Now then, let's look at this elbow, shall we? Have ye taken anythin' for the pain?'

Gently she took away the bag of peas and put it on a nearby side table.

Mr Jones flinched. 'Naw. Never taken pills and I'm not about to start now,' he replied, bravely.

Carrie suppressed a smile. *Bless him*, she thought. He was probably eighty, but the experience of being in the presence of three women was still bringing out the alpha male in Mr Jones.

'And how did you injure the elbow?' Bobbi gently rolled Mr Jones's flannel shirt back so that the elbow was exposed. Carrie couldn't see any bone sticking out and there didn't seem to be any blood, but she did think it looked rather swollen.

'Fell in the kitchen. I need to replace the lightbulb. It was my own fault for rummaging around in the kitchen in the dark, but I woke up in the night hungry and I was looking for a biscuit. Lost my balance when I opened the high cupboard.' He sighed. 'I hate being old. I used to run marathons. Worked on an oil rig. I was as tough as they come, you know.' He raised an eyebrow at Carrie, who couldn't help but giggle. 'Now, look at me. Falling over while getting a biscuit in the night.'

'It comes to all of us, dear,' June chuckled. 'Of course, nowadays, if I fall over, it's "a fall". I'm at that stage now too.'

'Hmm. You're right.' Mr Jones winced as Bobbi gently manipulated his arm. 'Ouch.'

'It's the way of the world,' June replied, watching Bobbi.

'Aye. You're a nurse, are you? Bet you could teach these two a thing or two.' Mr Jones twinkled at June. 'Always loved a lady in uniform, me. But you're not wearing one. Supervisor, or something?' Carrie realised that Mr Jones was flirting with June.

'No, dear, I've retired,' June replied, crisply, but not without a certain warmth. 'I'm just showing my friend what it's like being a nurse. And that includes men of all ages making passes at you.' She turned to Carrie. 'Now, Mr Jones is really quite sweet. But I have to admit, I've been on the receiving end of many experiences with patients that were less than charming.'

'Oh, I didn't mean to offend.' Mr Jones looked discomfited.

'I know you didn't, dear, and I'm not offended at all.' June patted him gently on the knee, and he glowed with pleasure. 'Just explaining to my friend here what can happen. Still, Carrie, it shouldn't put you off. You've got to remember that our role is to help people at difficult times. Sometimes, that means people aren't their normal selves. We have to allow for that, and be kind.'

Carrie thought back again to the nurses that had looked after her in hospital, after Claire died. One, Pamela, had stayed with her on more than one night when she couldn't get to sleep because of the pain from her collarbone, but also from the sheer, heart-numbing exhaustion of grief that had overcome her. She had sobbed her heart out, uncontrollably, and Pamela had handed her tissues, listened, and – though she couldn't hug Carrie because of her injury – patted her knee consolingly. Pamela had been incredibly kind at a time when Carrie hadn't been her usual self, and she would always appreciate that. And, she found that when she thought about that kindness, and the kindness Bobbi was showing to Mr Jones, then she didn't feel panicky about being at the hospital anymore.

'Can you move your fingers for me?' Bobbi watched as Mr Jones wiggled his fingers. 'All right. I think ye've got away with anythin' big, but we're goin' tae have to x-ray ye and just check you havenae got a small fracture. Okay? I'll wheel you up there now.'

'Right you are, nurse,' Mr Jones sighed. 'I was going to the betting shop and then the pub later, but I suppose that's out of the question for now.'

'Probably for today, my pet,' Bobbi chuckled. 'Come on, then. We'll leave these ladies to it, aye. Nice tae meet ye, Carrie.'

'And you,' Carrie called after Bobbi, who expertly wheeled Mr Jones up the corridor.

Mr Jones's arrival had distracted her from her feelings, which she was grateful for, but it had done something more: it had given Carrie an insight into something else within her. Yes, nursing had been an ambition when she was a child, but she had lost herself along the way and ended up temping through a variety of jobs she didn't really enjoy. Nursing might be difficult, and not well paid, but it might offer her the thing that she needed in her life. She realised now she hadn't ever been looking for a set of particular skills that she could practice and enjoy in her work, but rather something more emotional. A feeling that she could inhabit. And now she realised what that feeling was: compassion. She felt a vast wellspring of compassion within her that needed an outlet.

Part of that, she realised, was a need to feel compassion for herself – to forgive herself for failing her sister. She couldn't quite do that yet, but perhaps in the meantime she could start taking steps that would allow her to offer it to others.

TWENTY-NINE

'So, because this is a small local hospital, we don't tend to have many separate wards like you would in a larger one,' June explained, as they walked up the corridor through the middle of the main ward area.

On each side of the bright white corridor, three sets of double doors led off into long rooms, each with about ten beds. There were also a couple of single occupancy rooms with large windows that looked out onto green woodland outside.

'Most of the wards are mixed in terms of what's up with people, though of course we keep men on one side and ladies on the other. The single rooms are for people that might be highly contagious, or if we're providing end-of-life care, or perhaps if we have someone like a nursing mother in. Depends on the situation.'

'Right. I see.' Carrie looked through the glass top of the door leading into one ward; she could see a few of the beds were occupied, though not all. In one, an elderly woman was asleep, and in another, a middle-aged woman was sitting up, reading a novel. 'It all seems very calm up here.'

'Well, it's up and down. It's quiet at the moment, but the

wards can get full. In the pandemic, obviously, we were at capacity. I was drafted in to help then.' June shook her head. 'Not an easy time. I was shattered, too. Too old for it really, but Dan needed all the help he could get, bless him.'

'Wow. You would have been at high risk, being around such contagious patients.' Carrie wrapped her arms around herself self-consciously.

'I know. I'm old. But I'm as strong as an ox. I wasn't going to stand by and not help,' June said with a sniff. 'I wore all the protection and doused myself in antiseptic at the end of a shift, and then again when I got home. I smelt like rubbing alcohol, but that was the least of anyone's problems, wasn't it?'

'Indeed.' Carrie followed June as they walked along.

'The thing about nursing is that it's all hands on deck when you're needed,' June explained. 'Obviously, in the pandemic, people had to make their choices. I chose to be here, and I was careful, but I was damn lucky as well. But I just thought, at the end of the day, I'm old. If it gets me, then at least I go out doing what I was supposed to do in this life. Helping others survive. Warrior spirit.' She tapped her heart.

June was just like Rory, Claire realised. They both had that in them, the special something that made them help people in need. Rory's job was different, admittedly, but it was the same ballpark: being heroic.

'Wow. June. That's amazing,' Carrie breathed. 'I don't know if I have that in me.'

'Course you do.' June fixed Carrie with a gimlet stare. 'As I said, I know about your terrible accident and loss recently. And the very fact that you're standing in a hospital now, talking to me about becoming a nurse, shows me exactly the kind of fighting spirit you've got in you. We need more like you, Carrie. And, believe me, sadness doesn't make you weak. We all experience pain at some point in our lives. What makes us warriors is carrying on anyway.'

'I... thank you. That's kind of you to say.' Carrie was slightly taken aback that June had read her mind so clearly. Was she that transparent?

'I'm kind, when it's needed,' June laughed. 'But I mostly just say it how I see it.'

Carrie had the sudden image of the little door in the wall that she'd seen in her dream. She'd forgotten all about it, but it came back to her suddenly as she stood there, talking to June.

What's behind the door?

A fairy tale door, small, with an odd handle made of a bread roll. Maud had said, *Only you know. Only you can open it.*

She hadn't wanted to open the door then, and she didn't want to now, but she realised what lay beyond it, and she knew, suddenly, that she had to ask the question that had been playing on her mind ever since Claire's death.

'June?' Carrie asked, after they'd walked on a little further.

'What is it, dear?'

'If someone... was in an accident. And they needed an urgent transplant to survive,' Carrie began. 'If a donor couldn't be found in enough time...' She trailed off.

June stopped in the hallway, looking at Carrie with an expectant expression. 'Yes?'

'If...' Carrie found the words difficult. She needed to ask the question, but she was afraid to. So afraid for her fears to be confirmed. That she could have saved Claire's life.

'Just say the words, dear. It's okay.' June reached for her hand and squeezed it. 'I'll never judge you.'

'If... my sister... Could I have saved her life if I had been conscious enough to consent to a kidney transplant?' Carrie got the words out, though it was hard.

This was the question that had been haunting her for all this time, and now that it was out there, spoken, she recoiled from the implications of June's answer. Yet, she also felt strangely at peace just for having spoken the words.

'I can't answer that question, dear,' June said, softly. 'I take it both her kidneys were damaged beyond repair?'

'Yes,' Carrie breathed, the pain she'd been holding moving from her stomach into her heart. She took some deep breaths, and imagined breathing out the pain through her nose and mouth, like a black cloud escaping her. 'Though she actually died of a heart attack. That's what the doctor said. But I can't help but wonder if I'd been an organ donor, if I'd had that card in my purse like people do, they could have taken my kidney and given it to her...' Carrie trailed off. 'I could have saved her. She might not have had the heart attack, maybe. If her body had had a kidney.'

'Oh, darling.' June took Carrie's other hand, so that she was holding both in her lined palms. 'Listen to me. Are you listening?'

Carrie nodded, crying, but letting herself cry.

'You couldn't have saved her,' June said, clearly and calmly. She squeezed Carrie's hands. 'All right? Listen to me. You need to hear what I'm saying. She had a heart attack. She was severely injured in the crash. It was an accident. It was no one's fault. Even if you'd been conscious and donated a kidney, it wouldn't have been enough. It wasn't your fault. Okay? It wasn't your fault. Sometimes, horrible accidents just happen.'

Carrie felt the floodgates open then, and a huge wave of emotion overcame her completely.

It wasn't your fault.

She had needed to hear those words for so long.

June gathered her into her arms, and they stood there, in the middle of the two sets of wards in a small hospital in rural Scotland, and Carrie sobbed her heart out. For Claire, for the loss of the most important person in her life, and for herself, and how alone she felt.

'It wasn't your fault, dear,' June repeated, rubbing circles on Carrie's back. 'You know, deep down, it wasn't.'

They stood like that for longer than Carrie knew, until her sobs tailed off into hiccups. She felt wrung out and exhausted, but also strangely free.

'I know. Well, I think I do.' Carrie wiped her eyes with the back of her hand.

June reached into her capacious brown leather handbag and handed Carrie a pack of tissues. 'You will,' she said. 'It's very common to feel the way you do after losing a loved one. Whatever the situation, when we love someone, we always feel that we could have done something to help them. We could have stopped them suffering. But the truth is that the world is full of suffering. All we can do is be there for each other and be the best sisters, friends, mothers that we can be. And offer the rest up to God.'

'Do you think it's possible for someone to recover, after that kind of loss?' Carrie asked June. 'She was my sister. We were so close. I've even been hearing her voice in my head since she died. I miss her so much.' Her voice cracked again, but she controlled it.

'Of course you do, darling. And, yes, you'll recover. You'll always miss her, of course, but there will be a time when you realise you haven't thought about the loss of her for a while. And, more and more, when you think of her, which will be often, it will only be the good things. The times she made you laugh, or the sweet times you spent together as children. Time heals all wounds.' June gave Carrie a gentle smile. 'Take it from someone old.'

'Thanks, June. You're an amazing nurse.' Carrie blew her nose. 'I wish I could be just like you.'

'Well, there's nothing stopping you,' June said, back to her normal brisk self. 'Just remember that.'

THIRTY

'So, what d'you think?' June turned around on her piano stool to Dr Dan, who was perched on one of the community centre's plastic chairs.

'Bravo!' He clapped enthusiastically. 'I had no idea you were all so good!'

Carrie had almost not recognised Dr Dan when he'd tiptoed into the hall while they were all halfway through 'Total Eclipse of the Heart', mostly because instead of the doctor's uniform of a loose, blue, short-sleeved top and trousers, he was wearing jeans and a sweatshirt with a rainbow unicorn on the front and sunglasses, which he removed when he walked in and sat down.

Carrie had been concentrating on her part in the song – June had assigned her and Angus to sing it as a duet, and the rest of the choir to support – and when they got to the end, she knew she'd done a good job. There was that same feeling of catharsis, of freedom, of the letting go of feelings.

She let out a long, satisfied sigh.

Singing just felt *good*.

'Hi, Dr Dan.' Carrie waved, going over to say hello. 'I didn't know you were visiting. Just in the neighbourhood, or you're a big Bonnie Tyler fan and couldn't resist as you walked past?'

'You were awesome, Carrie!' Dan gave her a hug. 'No, June asked me to pop in. We were thinking about doing a concert for patients at the hospital and she wanted me to see the kind of thing you were doing. I have to say, I'm impressed!'

'Oh, thanks.' Carrie felt a little self-conscious, but the praise was nice to hear. 'We've been working on our power ballad medley. It's fun. Blows out the cobwebs.'

'I can see that. You look all flushed and sparkly!' Dan laughed. 'And, Angus! Resplendent!'

'Oh, thank ye,' Angus chuckled as he walked past. 'But Carrie did all the work. I was just the pretty face, aye.'

'Ha. Indeed.' Dan grinned. 'So, Carrie. Are you going to come and train with us, at the hospital? I can probably wangle it for you to do at least some of the on-the-job stuff with us, if you wanted. We're chronically understaffed, so please know that I'm being completely selfish in offering that.'

'I don't know. I've thought about it a bit. Looked into doing a nursing degree. It's something I always wanted.' Carrie watched as the other choir members milled around the tea urn. 'It seems like it would be hard, though. I still don't know if I've got it in me. I'm not like June.'

'Who is, darling?' Dan fluttered his eyes, making Carrie smile. 'That woman is a legend. But she learnt to be a nurse. She didn't come out of the egg knowing the phrase "Just a sharp scratch".'

'That's true, I suppose.'

'Yes, it is. Listen. Yes, the training is hard. Yes, the job is horrendously long hours and even more horrifyingly low pay. There are days when I wonder why I'm doing it. But you do know, in your heart. I know. Because if I wasn't doing it, it would feel wrong. Being a doctor fulfils something in me. A need to help others. You have that in you, too. I can see it.'

'How can you see it?' Carrie asked, mystified.

'I just can.' Dr Dan made a twinkly gesture with his fingers around her head. 'It's in your aura. If I believed in such things.'

'Well, thanks. I think,' Carrie chuckled.

'Do look into the nursing degree. You're still young enough and you can get help with the money side of things these days. I can help with recommending good places to study. But if you're worried about not getting onto the course, don't be. They'd snap you up.' Dan gave her an earnest look. 'I'm serious. I think it's important to encourage people into the profession, if they think it's for them.'

'That's reassuring. Thanks, Dr Dan.'

'Dan, please. And, like I said, I'm also being selfish here.' He shrugged.

'So. Are we good enough for the patients?' June came to stand next to Carrie and flicked Dan her curious, birdlike glance. 'You two look thick as thieves.'

'You're *wonderful* for the patients, Junie,' Dan said, enveloping June in a hug. 'I was just saying to Carrie that we'd love to have you all come down to the hospital for a bit of a sing-song. And I was trying to persuade Carrie to start her nursing degree, too.'

'Yes, I think she should. But it's her decision.' June looked over the rims of her reading glasses, which were halfway down her nose, at Carrie. 'Let things happen in their own time, Dan. Don't rush the girl.'

'I'm not!' Dan protested. 'I mean, I am horribly under-staffed, but that's beside the point.'

'Yes, it is.' June gave him a firm look. 'Carrie, you make your own decision in your own time. Don't let Dan talk you into it if you're not sure or you're not ready.'

'June? Do you really think I could do it?' Carrie asked the older woman. She trusted June. Yes, she could make her own decisions, but she valued June's opinion.

'Yes, you would make a wonderful nurse, Carrie. You just need to believe in yourself a little.' June smiled at her gently. 'Just like with the solos. You didn't think you could do it, but I gave you a little push, and now look at you. Belting it out better than Bonnie herself.'

'That's hardly true,' Carrie laughed. 'But, yes, I do see what you mean. I do feel more confident, nowadays. And the singing has really helped.'

'You've really blossomed.' June nodded, briskly. 'I think Loch Cameron was just what you needed. Goodness knows you needed some peace and quiet and a place to start again, after what happened to you. You've got your whole life ahead of you now. Don't forget that.'

'I won't, June.' Carrie nodded, feeling happily tearful. June gave her a gentle pat on the shoulder.

'Now, now. You'll be all right. Dan, come and get some cake. I made your favourite.' She led Dr Dan over to the refreshments table. 'And you, miss. There's enough for everyone,' June called, in that no-nonsense way she had.

'Just coming,' Carrie replied. It didn't do to disobey June – but, of course, she always knew best. *Maybe one day I could be like her*, Carrie thought as she followed Dan. June was an inspiration. And it felt good to be inspired.

THIRTY-ONE

The bar of the Loch Cameron Inn was really the only place in the village to meet anyone for coffee, now that Myrtle's Café was closed. Carrie felt she'd missed out on not visiting Myrtle's because, from the outside, it certainly looked like an interesting place when she'd passed by on her way to the community centre for choir, or to the shops for provisions. The wooden door was painted red, but boasted a glass panel featuring a rising sun over water, and a rainbow beyond it. The café windows were a patchwork of coloured squares of glass joined by black lead piping: cornflower-blue, rose-pink and bottle-green glass reflecting the loch. Carrie had peered inside the door out of curiosity one day and seen four sets of mismatched tables and chairs, and the walls seemed to be covered in shelves full of millinery heads wearing hats, as well as postcards and books.

Carrie remembered the place when it had been Len's barber shop. She thought of her Great-Aunt Maud and how, perhaps, she'd wanted Carrie and Claire to know Len, and had taken them there. Carrie really didn't remember much about those visits, apart from the barber shop chairs and the strange glass in the windows. Again, she thought about how sad it was that she had missed out on knowing Len.

'Thanks for coming.' Carrie stood up as Graham entered. She'd considered inviting him to the cottage, but it had felt too personal. She wanted this meeting to be on neutral ground rather than anywhere that reminded her of Claire. This was going to be a difficult enough conversation.

'Hi, Carrie. Thanks for the invite.' Graham looked around him at the wooden bar and the tartan-topped stools, at the crackling fire in the fireplace, and nodded at Eric, who was wiping down the bar. Graham planted an awkward kiss on her cheek. 'This is quite a place! I've never been to the village, even though Claire and I always wanted to come. She told me all about it. She had very fond memories of the place from when you were kids.'

They went to the bar, and Eric smiled warmly at Carrie. 'Cannae keep away, Carrie. What'll it be?'

'I'll just have a lime and soda, thanks, Eric. This is Graham, he's my sister's... fiancé,' she added, to be polite.

Eric beamed at Graham. 'Ah, family, is it? Yer most welcome. What can I get ye?'

'A pint of lager. Thanks.'

Graham leaned a little on the bar; Carrie could tell he felt awkward, and so did she.

'So,' she said, trying to marshal her thoughts a little.

'So...' Graham nodded, smiling shyly. 'Thanks for replying. I didn't think you would, if I'm honest.'

'Well, I got there in the end.' Carrie thanked Eric for her drink with a smile and took a sip. 'Shall we sit at one of the tables? The chairs are comfier.'

'Sure.' Graham accepted his pint from Eric and they settled themselves at one of the low tables with aged brown leather armchairs.

'Well, first, I want to say I'm sorry.' Carrie took in a deep breath as she started the speech she'd prepared. 'I was awful to you and you didn't deserve it.'

'Well, thanks. I appreciate that.' Graham sipped his pint. 'But, if I can interrupt you for a minute, I do understand. Particularly since Claire... passed.' He took a deep breath and Carrie could see how difficult the conversation was for him. 'Nothing about that has been easy. And I should have reached out to you more. I didn't come and see you in the hospital, because I was... in shock, I guess. But you were seriously injured, and grieving just as much as I was. I should have looked after you. It was my responsibility.'

'I didn't let you, Graham. I wouldn't have let you anywhere near me if you'd have tried.' Carrie smiled, wryly. 'You know that.'

'I know, but you lost her too. And I know how close you were,' Graham sighed. 'We wanted... when Claire and I got together, she made it very clear to me that you guys were incredibly close, and that she wanted you and me to have a good relationship. When it turned out that you didn't want that, she was really broken-hearted. I'm sorry. I shouldn't have... that was too much.' He looked down at the table. 'What I'm trying to say is that I get it. I know how much you miss her.'

'I do miss Claire. There's not a day that I don't, and I don't think there ever will be. She was everything to me,' Carrie began, trying to keep her voice steady. 'But I shouldn't have been so awful to you both. I was... I was jealous. Claire had always been... well, it was just the two of us. That was how it was, always. We lost our mum, Dad was terrible and basically ignored us after that; we lost our great-aunt, and by the time we were old enough to come up here and visit her ourselves, she'd died. Neither of us ever had a serious boyfriend before Claire and you got together. I just didn't know how to deal with it. I felt like I was losing her.'

'You weren't.' Graham looked up, sadness in his eyes. 'You

never lost her. She loved you so much. It really hurt her that you pulled away like you did over the past two years.'

'I know.' Carrie swallowed the lump that thickened her throat. 'I... I was wrong. I've had to start working through a lot of stuff.' She thought of June, at the hospital, holding her in her arms and saying, *It wasn't your fault. It wasn't your fault.* Carrie wondered how long it would be until she truly believed that. 'I thought... I was blaming myself for the accident, too. And I guess I thought you blamed me. I was in the car and I survived.'

'Why on earth would I blame you? It was an accident. That boy was speeding, he went straight into you. You're lucky to be alive.' Graham looked dumbfounded. 'Is that what was worrying you, all this time?'

'Partly.' Carrie looked away, into the little room with the television that led off the bar. There was no one in it today; in fact, they were the only people in the bar. 'After the accident... I thought I could have saved her too. I thought she could have had one of my kidneys but that my being unconscious had stopped that happening,' she sighed. 'I realise now that I couldn't have saved her.'

'You couldn't have. She... the damage, it was...' He paused, his voice breaking. 'You know what I'm saying.'

'I know.' Carrie took another sip of her drink and placed it back down on the table carefully. There was a silence; she didn't know what else to say.

'What did you do with her stuff, in the end?' Graham cleared his throat. He had taken some things that were special to him, Carrie knew.

'It's mostly in storage. I don't know what to do with it, really. Some of the stuff I'll take wherever I end up moving to. Her clothes, personal stuff like jewellery... I just can't bring myself to get rid of them yet, you know?' Carrie's stomach twisted, thinking about all of Claire's things, alone and unloved, in boxes in the soulless storage facility she was hiring. 'The other part of that is, I don't know what I'm doing next. I came here to escape, but I can't stay here forever. Especially as I had a little part-time job tiding me over, but that's not happening now either. I need to... I dunno. Rejoin life.' She blew a raspberry. 'Life hasn't been so kind, though, recently.'

'I know what you mean. I could do with escaping to Loch Cameron myself.' Graham looked out of the window at the loch outside. 'It's gorgeous. Even in the rain. So, your great-aunt had a cottage here, Claire said?'

'Yeah. It was rented, like most of the places are here. The place I'm staying at is just nearby. Looks out onto the loch.'

'I'd like to see that,' he said. 'It'd be nice to see the place Claire always talked about. She had such happy memories of Loch Cameron.'

'I do, too.' Carrie waved to Dotty as she appeared at the inn's reception desk outside the main bar, carrying a handheld vacuum. 'And, since I've been here, it's really felt like home. I've made new friends. Even joined a choir.' She laughed a little self-consciously.

'That's great, Carrie. I'm really happy to hear that.' Graham tapped her hand, cautiously, as if he was petting an angry dog. 'And I'm so glad we're talking. I don't expect us to be best friends, or anything. But maybe we can be in touch, chat now and again. Support each other a bit.'

'I'd like that.' Carrie ventured a smile. 'Do you want to see Maud's old cottage? You can't go in, but you can see it from the outside, if you'd like.' She found that she didn't hate the idea of taking Graham up to Queen's Point anymore.

'I'd love that.' Graham looked surprised and pleased. 'Thanks, Carrie.'

'That's okay,' she said, and meant it.

'So, what will you do now?' Graham picked at the spare beer mat next to his pint glass. 'Like you said, you can't stay here forever, not really working. What was it you were doing, part time?'

'I was just working in a restaurant kitchen,' she said, thinking of Rory, sadly. She'd given up on any notion of hearing from him now. She knew he would have to come back at some point, but he was clearly avoiding her in terms of talking about what had happened between them. 'But that ended. I've never really known what I wanted to do. I temped for years.'

'I know. Claire told me.'

'Hmm. Well, the only thing I ever really wanted to do was be a nurse,' Carrie said, thinking about her day in the hospital with June and Dr Dan, and her conversation with Dan at rehearsal. 'And so I'm thinking of starting nursing training, actually.'

'You are? That's awesome!' Graham's face lit up. 'That sounds really positive. Good for you.'

'Yeah. It is, isn't it?' Carrie felt a small glow of pride light up in her belly. She hadn't actually made her mind up until that moment, but suddenly, she knew it felt right. And, out of the blue, there was Claire's voice in her head, echoing Graham's words: *Good for you, Carrie. All those times you bandaged me against my will, finally paying off.*

Carrie smiled. She didn't mind hearing Claire's voice in her mind; she never had. It was a way to stay connected to her sister.

Thanks, she replied. *And look at me, playing nice with Graham.*

I always knew you had it in you.

Shut up. He's all right, I suppose.

You shut up. And, I know.

Carrie smiled to herself. 'When you've finished your drink, let's walk up to the cottage,' she said to Graham. 'There's someone I want you to meet.'

THIRTY-TWO

They met Bess at the end of the loch-side path that turned up the incline to Queen's Point and toward Gretchen's and Maud's cottages. It was raining again, but there was a freshness to it as the water bounced off the loch's glassy top that felt alive and good, somehow; like rain that made everything new. A sprinkling of boats dotted the loch here and there; a couple of teens had rowed past in a dinghy as they'd walked along, and further out the coastguard patrolled.

'That must be her.' Carrie gave a shy wave from under her umbrella to the short-haired woman striding towards her and Graham. She turned away from the direction of the rain slightly, grateful that the parka she'd bought from Fiona's Fashions had a hood.

As they'd walked along the village high street, she'd explained the story of Maud's diaries and Len to her sister's boyfriend. Though Claire's voice had quieted in her head now, she still felt that her sister would be pleased that she and Graham were becoming friends, and that Carrie was sharing this new part of the family puzzle with him.

'Bess?' Carrie held out her hand. 'I'm Carrie Anderson. This is my... friend, Graham.'

How else was she supposed to describe Graham? *My dead sister's fiancé?* It was a lot for an introduction.

'Good to meet you.' Bess shook hands with both of them, politely. She had short, curly black hair and dark brown eyes and wore slouchy jeans, work boots and a buttoned-up flannel shirt under her coat. 'I have to say I was surprised to get your text.'

'I can imagine.' Carrie nodded. 'We were heading up to the cottage I'm renting – on Queen's Point? Why don't you walk up with us?'

'Oh, are you at Gretchen Ross's place?' Predictably by now, Bess, like everyone else in the village, seemed to know where Carrie was staying as soon as she mentioned she was renting a cottage. But that was likely because it was the only one that was rented to tourists, as far as Carrie knew.

'Yes. I've been there a while now. I came when my sister passed away.' Carrie took a deep breath and started to tell her story to Bess as they walked. As she did so, Graham reached for her hand and folded it in his. It was a protective gesture: nothing more, but when he took her hand, she broke off what she was saying and looked up at him gratefully. He nodded, as if to say, *I got you.*

By the time they'd got to the cottage and Carrie had let them in, stamping their wet and muddy boots on the welcome mat as they did so, she'd explained about Claire. While Graham was making them tea, finding his way around the cosy kitchen, Carrie went to her bedroom and brought back Maud's diaries.

'Your dad gave these to Myrtle for some reason, and when she passed recently, Dotty gave them to me. They belonged to my great-aunt who used to live a few cottages along. But if you read them, you'll realise that she was your grandmother. Len was her son. Illegitimate, but hers.' She handed the diary to Bess, who took it in surprise.

'So, you're saying...' she opened the book and cast her gaze over the carefully handwritten pages, '... your great-aunt was my grandmother?'

'It looks that way, yes.' Carrie sat on the sofa opposite where Bess stood, holding the diary. 'I'm sorry for this coming kind of out of the blue.'

'That's... okay, I guess.' Bess looked around her a little blearily and perched on the edge of the pink chaise longue. 'So...? What happened? Can you give me the main gist?'

'Of course.' Carrie launched into the story of Maud and William and Clara, and how Maud gave Len to William and Clara to raise.

'My grandparents, yes,' Bess said, then stopped herself. 'Well. If what you're saying is true, William was my grandfather. Clara wasn't my grandmother. Biologically.'

'Not biologically, no. But you knew her as your grandmother, and that hasn't changed.' Carrie watched Bess's face, looking for a family resemblance. 'You know, you do have the look of Maud, a little. Wait a minute, I'll show you.' She went to her room, where the pile of things she'd taken from Claire's flat lay piled in boxes, and searched through for the photo album she remembered bringing back. Claire had been better than her at finding and keeping old photos, even though there never were many. What there were, she'd preserved.

Carrie returned to the sitting room where Graham was pouring tea from the ancient ceramic teapot into mismatched mugs.

'Look.' She flicked through the album until she found one of Maud, taken in the kitchen of her cottage one jam-making day. Next to Maud, Claire stood, flour in her hair and an adult-sized apron knotted around her tiny middle, holding aloft a jam-covered silver spoon. They were both laughing. Carrie stood on the other side of Maud, solemnly looking into the camera, obviously not a part of whatever joke was being enjoyed.

She touched the picture fondly, not remembering the moment it was taken, but remembering the photo, though she hadn't seen it for a long time. She and Claire had always tried to remember who had taken it: Claire thought it must have been Mum, because Dad was never in the cottage if he could avoid it.

'You look like her. Maud.' Carrie tapped the photo and handed it to Bess, who peered at the photo curiously. 'Same curly hair. Same smile.'

'Huh.' Bess shook her head in recognition. 'Look at that. I can see it, you know. But it's more that I can see my dad in her. You know, I remember Maud, kinda. She used to come in to the barber's when I was there sometimes. Chat to Dad.' Bess looked up at Carrie. 'She used to bring in a couple of wee girls sometimes. We played out by the loch sometimes.'

'That was me and Claire.' Carrie nodded, smiling.

'Goodness, this is so weird,' Bess chuckled. 'Look at us now, all grown up! I remember you then. You and your sister.' She paused, looking over at Graham who had sat next to Carrie on the sofa, letting Carrie take the lead. 'I'm sorry. So, you guys are together, or... you said friends?'

'Oh, no. Not together.' Carrie realised that she'd sounded horrified at the thought, and tried to explain. 'Graham was Claire's fiancé,' she blundered on. 'My dad's alive, but he's hardly been a parent for years. Forever, really. Graham and I... we didn't always get on, when my sister was alive, but that was totally my fault. I guess now I've come to my senses. I want to be around the few people I have left that are family. Or, almost family.'

'For me it's a way to stay connected to Claire, being friends with Carrie. I'm just sorry we couldn't get closer before...' Graham trailed off. 'You know.'

'I see. I guess I can understand that,' Bess sighed. 'I'm an only child. My mum left us when I was five; she and Dad never really should have been together, but they had me and tried to make it work, I guess, like people do. It's been hard since Dad passed away. I did feel alone, but I have my partner, Sally. She's been a godsend. And... Loch Cameron, too, you know? The community here really rallied around when Dad died. It's what they do.'

'I've felt that too,' Carrie said, thinking about June and that day at the hospital when she had enveloped Carrie in her arms and held her as she cried. 'So... I dunno. When I realised you existed, I kind of wanted to connect. At least show you the diary.'

'I appreciate it.' Bess nodded. 'And... thanks. It's weird, and a lot to take in. But... I feel the same.'

There was an awkward moment where none of them seemed to know what to do. Carrie wondered whether she should hug Bess, or indeed Graham, but it felt a little too new.

She nodded, instead. 'Well, that's good.'

Graham was the one who solved the problem by raising his mug of tea. 'To Claire, Maud and Len,' he said, solemnly. 'Loved and missed, always.'

Carrie felt the tug in her heart as he said Claire's name; she saw the corresponding sadness in his eyes as he said it too. But she was also glad to talk about her sister.

They all stood, and did a solemn toast with their tea mugs.

'So, what do we do now?' Bess asked, catching Carrie's eye. 'Cheers to the dead. A thousand per cent. Now what?'

Something in her expression made Carrie burst out laughing, unexpectedly, and the seriousness of the moment was dispelled. Something seemed to burst, gently, in the room – a tense energy that had built up, and had now disappeared like a bubble popping.

Bess smiled. 'What are you laughing at?' she asked, chuckling.

'Cheers to the dead?' Carrie echoed Bess. 'A thousand per cent?' She started laughing harder.

'What?' Bess was still chuckling.

Graham gave Carrie a look like he thought she was vaguely unhinged. *Possibly, I am*, she thought.

'I don't know. I just thought... you reminded me of Claire just then. My sister. She would have said something like that. She was never serious.'

'Ha. Sally always accuses me of being too quippy. Too irreverent.' Bess raised an eyebrow. 'I like to keep it light. Life's too short, right?'

'It certainly is.' Graham put his mug down and strode to the kitchen. 'Wait. I'll be back,' he called over his shoulder. He returned almost immediately, holding a half-full bottle of brandy.

'Where did you get that?' Carrie asked, surprised.

'Found it at the back of one of the cupboards when I was looking for the teapot,' he explained. 'Come on. Let's toast them in style, this time.'

They drained their mugs of tea, and Graham poured a slosh of brandy into each one.

'Cheers to the dead. A thousand per cent,' he repeated, seriously, and clinked his mug against Carrie's and Bess's.

They all drank.

Making new traditions, Carrie thought. *This is what families do.* She realised she was glad, and she was grateful for the feeling. It had been a long time since she was glad of anything. 'I'm glad you're both here,' she said, out loud.

'Me, too,' Graham agreed.

Bess nodded, blinking owlishly as she downed the remaining brandy in her mug. 'Me, too,' she echoed. 'I'm gonna be pished before long, though.'

Carrie giggled and topped up all their mugs. 'Come on, then. We might as well.'

THIRTY-THREE

Carrie was cleaning the cottage bathroom when she was interrupted by a knock on the door. Swearing quietly to herself, since she was right in the middle of descaling the taps and the rather vintage shower, she stepped out of the bath in her bare feet and went to the door.

Since she was cleaning, she had on her house-cleaning attire, which consisted of a pair of pyjama shorts she didn't care about getting bleach on and a loose T-shirt she tended to sleep in. It featured a picture of two bears cuddling each other, and the phrase I LOVE BEAR HUGS at the top. Her hair was tied back with a rainbow-coloured scrunchie and she wore rubber gloves.

She opened the door, thinking it was probably the postman with a package for Gretchen; publishers still sent her books now and again for her opinion, even though she'd been retired from her high-powered publishing job for years. Carrie was building up a pile of book packages by the door to take over to her friend soon. She was looking forward to tea, cake and a catch up with Gretchen.

'Oh. God. It's you.' The words were out of her mouth

before she could control them, and Carrie stared almost uncomprehendingly at Rory McCrae, who stood on her doorstep, glowering dark clouds behind him in the sky over the loch, holding a bunch of pink roses.

'Not quite the greeting I was hoping for, but... yeah. It's me. Hi.'

'Hi.' Carrie didn't know what else to say. It had been a couple of months since Rory had left, and she'd started to accept that whatever the moment between them had been, it had passed. They'd had one amazing night, and then he'd left, and never messaged, texted or called. Not even once. That seemed a pretty clear message to Carrie.

'Hi.' Rory held out the roses to her. 'These are for you.'

Thunder rumbled in the distance, and Carrie looked warily at the sky. It looked like it was about to hurl it down at any moment.

'Thanks.' She took them, refusing to ask him in. If it rained – or hailed – then Rory would just have to get wet. She put the roses on top of the pile of Gretchen's book packages by the door. 'So, you're back.'

'I just got back last night.'

'How was the mission?' She crossed her arms over her chest, remembering suddenly what she was wearing. Surely there were people out there who managed luckily to look amazing when their errant one-night stands knocked on their doors unexpectedly. *Sadly, you're not one of them*, she thought to herself. Carrie didn't think she could have looked worse. The only saving grace was, she supposed, that she was wearing shorts and had just shaved her legs the day before, chiefly because her leg hairs had been so long that she thought she might be nearing the stage where she could weave them into permanent socks.

'Successful. It wasn't a mission – I was training people, remember?' Rory smiled a little.

Carrie felt herself softening at his smile. It always had the same effect on her. She frowned, and looked away. She wasn't happy with him for ignoring her all this time, and no amount of sexy smiling on his part was going to help that. 'Good,' she said, shortly. There was a silence, and she raised an eyebrow at him. 'So?'

The thunder rumbled again, louder, and lightning flashed, lighting up the now-bare trees at the edge of the loch.

'It's going to hammer it down in a minute. Can I come in?' he asked, looking cautiously at the sky.

'No. You'll be all right where you are.' She gave him a level stare. *You could have come in if you'd sent me some messages,* she thought. *Tough.*

'Oh. Umm. Yeah. Well, I wanted to let you know I'm planning to reopen the restaurant from this Friday. I just need a couple of days to get up and running again. So I wanted to see if you were happy to come back, or...?' He trailed off, looking unsure.

'*That*'s what you came to ask me?' Carrie was irritated. 'At the very least, you could start with an apology.'

'What do I need to apologise for?' Rory looked guarded. 'You knew I was going to be away. I paid you what we agreed.'

'Pay? You *paid* me?' Carrie raised her voice. 'That's not what I mean, and you know it!' She felt herself getting really angry now. How could Rory be so tone-deaf about this? Surely he knew what she was talking about.

'Carrie. We had an amazing night together. But you knew I was leaving the next day,' he repeated. 'What else did you want me to do? I didn't plan for us to sleep together, but it happened, and it was... amazing. I thought you were cool about it.'

'I was... I am *cool* about it,' Carrie spat, realising that she sounded the opposite of cool about anything just then, and hating herself a little for sounding as harsh as she did. But she had a right to be annoyed. 'What I'm not cool about is you completely ignoring me for two months afterwards. It would have been basic politeness to check in every now and again and say hi, and if you didn't want to see me again, then it would have been polite to say that too.'

It started raining. Big, fat drops that hit Rory's head and his coat with hard splashes.

'Oh.' Rory looked chagrined. 'Shit. I'm so sorry, Carrie. I thought that I would be able to stay in touch a bit, but when I got to the place we were based, there was no WiFi, no signal, nothing. All telecoms were useless. It's how it is, sometimes.'

'And you didn't know that ahead of time? I feel like you would have been told that in some kind of... briefing.' She waved her hands in the air, impatiently.

'Well, yes, I did know that it might be possible. It was all very quick, like I told you. They gave me the outline of what they wanted me to do, and often this kind of work means you'll be pretty incommunicado. But I hoped I'd get some opportunity to keep in touch. But when I got there, I found out they'd upped the security level of the training. Telecoms blackout.'

'I fail to believe that you couldn't have sent me just the shortest of texts. You might have been dead for all I knew.'

'Carrie. I would have if I could, I promise.' Rory stepped forward and reached for her hand. The rain intensified, and water started running down his face. He wiped it out of his eye.

She pulled her hand away, and an expression of pain settled into his eyes.

'No. You really hurt me,' she said. 'I... I don't sleep around. What we did was... it was special to me. And then you just totally ignored me. Do you know how that feels?'

'I'm sorry. I do know. Or, I know what it's like to feel betrayed and lost. I'm sorry,' he repeated, his brow furrowing. 'I didn't want to do that to you. Believe me, if I could have stayed in touch, I would have. That night was special to me too.'

'It didn't feel it was,' Carrie shot back. 'I... you really hurt me, Rory,' she repeated, not knowing what else to say. 'So, I'm not sure if I can come back to the restaurant. It would be weird.'

'Carrie, please. I don't want you to stop working with me. I need you there.' Rory looked supremely uncomfortable. 'Look, can I come in and talk? It's kind of... exposed, out here.'

Carrie looked up and down the pathway that led past Gretchen's cottage and along Queen's Point. It was deserted, though she could see Angus duck into his front door to get out of the rain. 'There's nobody here,' she said. 'You can say whatever you've got to say to me where you are.' She put her hands on her hips, deliberately misunderstanding what he meant. 'Give me one good reason why I should come back to the restaurant, apart from the fact I need the money. But you know what? I can get another job. I don't need...' she waved one hand towards him, '... all this complication.'

'Okay. Fine.' Rory took in a deep breath and let it out again. 'If you don't want to work at the restaurant anymore, I understand. I can find someone to replace you, not that they'll be as good, probably. Or anyone that I'll enjoy having around as much as I do you,' he added, pushing his now-sodden hair out of his eyes. 'But, listen. I want to explain.'

'Explain, then. Not that I can see there's much to say. We slept together and you ignored me. For whatever reason.' Carrie still wished she wasn't wearing a T-shirt that said I LOVE BEAR HUGS; she peeled off her rubber gloves and dropped them to one side of the door. Those, at least, she could take off.

'I'm sorry I didn't contact you at all, after that night. I'm not lying about the comms blackout; I mean, when I got to where I was going, there was literally nothing. Other than send a carrier pigeon, I was stuck. And as soon as I realised that, I regretted not at least sending you a text when I was at the airport. Because I did care about what happened. It was incredibly special to me.' Rory sighed and continued. 'I was stupid. After you left, that morning, I was... I didn't know what to think.

Making love to you made me feel vulnerable again. And I panicked, because the last time I let myself be open to someone, she broke my heart. And I swore I'd never put myself in that situation again.'

Unexpectedly, Rory began to cry.

Carrie's eyes widened in surprise: this, she hadn't expected. 'Oh. Rory, I...' She stepped over the threshold of the door. Awkwardly, she touched his face. 'Don't cry.'

'I'm sorry.' He wiped the tears away, which merged with the rain on his face. 'I've actually... I've actually been doing a lot of soul-searching, while I was away. When I wasn't working. It was horrible, being away from you. And being away from home. I hated it. For the first time, I hated my navy work, and I never used to. It was always an adventure. It always made me feel alive.' He took a deep breath. 'But I realised, when I was away, that there was something – someone – that made me feel more alive than defusing bombs did.' He chuckled, wiping away another tear. 'Wow. That was a ridiculous sentence to say out loud, wasn't it?'

'No. Not at all. Well...' Carrie took a minute, and smiled for the first time. 'Kind of.'

'Well, I mean it,' Rory continued. 'I saw that I had true feelings for you, Carrie. And it scared the hell out of me. More than I've ever been scared by anything. And I've done some pretty scary things in my time.'

Thunder banged loudly overhead; the storm had arrived in full. Lightning flashed dramatically.

'Oh.' Carrie didn't quite know what to say. If she was honest with herself, she had deep feelings for Rory too, but she'd been trying to ignore them. What use was it, having feelings for someone who had disappeared from her life and was, to all intents and purposes, ignoring her? 'I don't know what to say to that. I... I have feelings for you too. That's why I'm so upset that I didn't hear from you.'

'I need to explain some stuff. Can I come in now?' Rory pleaded. He looked so pathetic.

Carrie's heart went out to him then. 'Of course, you can.' She stepped aside. 'I'm sorry. I should have invited you in already.'

'Don't be sorry. I was an idiot.' He stepped inside the doorway. 'And I should have done this when you opened the door, instead of trying to argue a stupid point. I'm sorry that I am a bit soaked through, though.'

Rory took her face in both of his hands and kissed her, his lips meeting hers softly. His touch was as electric as she remembered, and Carrie was taken aback for a moment at the suddenness of his lips on hers. Yet, just as instantly, she was taken back into the hot, sweet current of energy that existed between them: it was a constant, ongoing, harmonious connection that just felt right and whole and deeply satisfying, while making her want more.

'I missed you,' she breathed, as his lips grew more intense on hers. 'I missed you so much.'

'I missed you too,' Rory murmured, as he took her in his strong arms. 'And I never want to leave you, ever again.'

THIRTY-FOUR

'I need to tell you some things.' Rory broke away from their kiss, clearing his throat and laughing softly. 'Before we get into any... serious kissing. Not that I don't want to, of course. It's almost all I've thought about for two months. God alone knows how I managed to deliver that training, I was so distracted.' He ran his hand through his dripping black, tousled hair and sighed. 'I've never known anyone like you, Carrie. You... you do something to me.'

'You have a very... strong effect on me too,' she admitted. 'Look, can I just go and change? These are my cleaning clothes. I don't exactly look my best.'

'You look perfect to me.' Rory looked surprised. 'To be fair, I'm literally soaked through. I hadn't even noticed what you were wearing.' He frowned for a moment, looking at her T-shirt. 'That shirt is cute as hell, though. Makes me want you even more.' He let out a long, deep breath that sounded halfway like a growl. 'It's not helping me focus right now.'

'This?' Carrie looked down at the cartoon bears. 'Are you serious? This is the most unsexy outfit anyone has ever worn, in the history of the world.'

'You could wear a bin bag and I'd still want you. I'd still think you were the sexiest woman alive.' Rory rubbed his face with both hands. 'It's actually torture looking at you right now and not... doing much more, if I'm honest.'

'Well, I'm not sure I believe you, but okay,' Carrie half laughed. 'Come in,' she said, pointing to the lounge. 'Let me get you a towel, at least.'

Rory walked through, and she shut the front door, nipping into the bathroom to get a fluffy pink bath towel and following him into the lounge. He perched nervously on the edge of the pink chaise longue, taking the towel when she handed it to him. He stripped off his coat and the long-sleeved sweater he wore underneath and towelled himself off.

Carrie tried not to gape at his ripped, muscular torso and the black hair on his chest.

'Okay, so, come on. What is it that you have to say?' She cleared her throat, sitting on the white sofa, facing him, glad she'd hoovered already and tidied up the lounge. It was a very girly, cosy room, and Carrie reflected for a moment that Rory looked slightly incongruous in it: bare chested in a pink towel and jeans and work boots against the pink chair, the floral wallpaper and the vintage fireplace.

'I need to explain something to you,' Rory sighed. 'I hope it's going to clarify why I might have been a little... off with you, here and there. And explain what I mentioned just now.' He put the towel on the chaise next to him.

'You had your heart broken,' Carrie interjected. 'I'm sorry about that. It's hard. Not that I've ever... well, not in that way, anyway. Not a man,' she added. 'Losing my sister broke my heart. Forever. I don't think I'll ever get over it.'

'I know, and I'm so sorry. I should have thought about what you were going through before I... you know.' Rory shook his head. 'I was thoughtless. I shouldn't have slept with you, maybe. You were probably too vulnerable, and...'

'I wasn't. I mean, yes, I'm going through some stuff, but I was more than ready for that night,' Carrie replied, honestly. 'It was one of the best nights of my life. Definitely the best... you know.' She blushed and looked away.

'I'm very glad to hear it,' he said in a low voice, giving her a long look under his thick black eyelashes that made her quiver with pleasure. 'But I have to get this out.'

'Okay.' Carrie looked down at her hands. It was an effort not to go over to where he sat and wrap her arms around his chest.

'Right. So, the last relationship I had was when I was in the navy. Her name was Sarah. In the beginning it was amazing. I fell hard for her, like I hadn't ever done before, or since. Well, not until now,' he added, giving Carrie a small smile. 'I would have moved heaven and earth for her. I wanted to marry her, have babies, everything. Even though I knew that my life didn't really allow for that kind of set-up.

'Anyway, we were seeing each other pretty much long distance. I'd be away for months at a time, but then we'd have a few amazing weeks together, and it was hard when I was away, but I also loved my job and I was able to lose myself in it, you know?'

Carrie nodded.

'Well, I went home on leave about two years into our rela-tionship. She was acting weirdly. Like, wouldn't look me in the eye. She was disappearing in the evenings, refusing to explain where she was going. In the end, we had a big barny and I found out that she'd been seeing someone else. A friend of mine, in fact.' He let out a long breath. 'She'd been seeing him behind my back for a year.'

'Oh. I'm sorry to hear that.' Carrie frowned. 'That's tough.'

'Yes, it was. But long-distance relationships are an affair waiting to happen. No,' Rory checked himself and shook his head, 'that's the wrong way to put it.' He sighed. 'See, after I found out, I was... very angry. I did some things that I regret, and that I've apologised to her for.'

'What things?' Carrie asked, cautiously.

'When she told me what she'd done, I lost the plot and kicked a hole in one of the inside doors. Then I...' he looked ashamed, '... I don't like saying this.'

'What?'

'I pulled it off its hinges.'

'The whole door?' Carrie was aware that she probably looked horrified, but she tried to control her expression.

He nodded. 'I was so angry. But you've got to understand that I had a lot of unprocessed rage from my childhood. Sure, I was upset about what had happened, but it wasn't really her I was angry at. It was my father. I'd been suppressing a lot of anger for a long time, and it came out. That's a whole other story.'

'So, what happened?' Carrie folded her arms over her chest. 'Even if you did have unhealed trauma, you didn't have a right to frighten her like that. I bet she was terrified.'

'She was. I know, and I've spent a lot of time working through that anger. I apologised profusely. She and I have made our peace now.'

'That's good to know, at least,' Carrie said, watching him. 'Do you still have anger issues?'

'No. My therapist has helped a lot in dealing with my past. Remember I said I was seeing one?'

Carrie nodded.

'Well, my dad was an alcoholic. He could be violent. Had a violent temper.' Rory took a deep breath. 'When I did... that, on that day, I took a step outside myself and I saw him. That was me, kicking that door, pulling it off its hinges, but it was something I learnt from my dad. And it horrified me.' His voice shook. 'In retrospect, I don't blame Sarah for finding someone else. Long distance is hard, and I was so unavailable. Sometimes I'd be on a job and I wouldn't speak to her for a couple of weeks or more. I wasn't the ideal boyfriend. Very far from it,' he sighed. 'The thing was that I thought I was ready for marriage and babies, but I wasn't. Not really. I loved Sarah, but all that grown-up stuff scared me rigid. Which was part of why I always preferred to be away, doing this crazy job that literally required me to be permanently having an adventure and not living a normal life. I realised that, when I was away this time. What that life really is. And, yeah, initially I was terrified after we slept together, because all these feelings erupted in me, and I didn't want to have my heart broken again – or to unleash that kind of emotion that broke everything before. And then, when I'd been away a couple of weeks, for the first time, I missed all the normal things. I missed the restaurant. My house. And I missed you. And I knew you were who I wanted, and that I should stop being a total idiot and come back to you the first opportunity I had.'

'I missed you too,' she said, feeling herself blush at the intimacy of Rory's words.

'I needed to tell you that. I needed to get it out.' Rory heaved a huge sigh. 'It's in the past, and I'm a different person now. But I needed you to understand.'

'I understand.' Carrie got up and went over to him. 'I know that we all carry wounds, and they can make us do things we regret,' she said, kneeling in front of the chaise longue and taking Rory's hands in hers. 'Believe me, I know. But I also know that we can decide to move on, when we're ready. Our pasts don't have to define us.' She leaned forwards, and kissed him gently.

He responded, kissing her back. 'Oh, Carrie. I've been such an idiot. Can you forgive me?' he asked, again kissing her gently, his hand stroking her hair. 'I want you so badly. Not just for one night. For every night, if you'll have me.'

'I will,' she breathed, melting into his arms. 'There's nowhere else I'd rather be than with you.'

THIRTY-FIVE

The sun shone brightly on the trees and the flowers in the little graveyard, and Carrie shaded her eyes from the light. She was glad it wasn't raining. It seemed right and fitting for the laying of Claire's memorial stone in the grounds of the little chapel on the hill that overlooked Loch Cameron. Carrie had asked that the ceremony take place outside rather than inside the chapel, as she thought Claire would have preferred it.

'And though Claire's ashes have been scattered in the loch itself, we are placing this stone here today to provide a special place to remember her,' the vicar said, as the group gathered around the stone that Carrie had had inscribed with Claire's name, her dates of birth and death, and a short message: LOVED AND MISSED ALWAYS.

'May our heavenly father bless her and keep her. Into your hands, O merciful Saviour, we commend Claire. Acknowledge, we pray, a sheep of your own fold, a lamb of your own flock. Enfold her in the arms of your mercy, in the blessed rest of ever-lasting peace and in the glorious company of the saints in light. Amen.'

The vicar nodded to Carrie, who stepped forward in the

ring of friends that had gathered for the ceremony. Rory had been holding her hand tightly, but he squeezed it and let her go. Graham stood on Carrie's other side, and there were quite a few villagers there too, who had come to pay their respects to a girl none of them remembered – or, only remembered as a child, so many years ago – but had nonetheless turned up to support Carrie. Angus was there, as was Dotty, with a lace hankie already wiping away tears. Next to her, June and Dr Dan stood respectfully, as did Bess and Sally, wearing matching black suits and ties. Most of the choir had gathered there as well, and though Gretchen hadn't been able to make the walk up the steep steps to the chapel she had sent Carrie a beautiful bouquet of flowers with a note that said: *Gone but never forgotten. Much love, G xxx.*

Carrie cleared her throat. 'Claire was the best sister I could ever have asked for. And I know that she was also the best fiancée, the best friend and, sometimes, the worst smart aleck,' she began, smiling, and appreciating the group chuckling. 'But that just meant she was clever, she was funny, and she was my world.'

Carrie's voice thickened for a moment as the emotion started to well up inside her. Rory stepped forward and took her arm, but she nodded.

'It's okay. I'm okay,' she murmured, and then raised her voice so that everyone could hear her. 'I don't want to say much. You all know that I came to Loch Cameron to try to get over losing Claire. I don't think I ever will, but I did realise some things while I was here. And some of you – all of you, in your different ways – helped me deal with the loss.' Here she met June's eyes, who nodded, in her kind but firm way.

'So, I want to say thank you. Because I don't think I'd be standing here today without you all. And your cups of tea and coffee, and cake, and the choir, and your wisdom. All of it. Thank you.' Carrie bowed her head for a moment. As she looked up, she caught Angus's eye, who winked at her and mouthed, 'Proud of you.'

She smiled back at her neighbour. 'So, in a minute, I've asked the choir to sing, but first I just wanted to say this. It's something I found online, and it resonated with me. I tweaked it a bit.

> 'Claire, may your love be reflected in all who
>   knew you, and may you continue to live on
>   through the lives of those you leave behind.
> Your legacy is the memory of a kind heart and a
>   protective nature.
> Your legacy is our memories of you.
> Your legacy is all the times you gave of yourself
>   to us: hugs, time, favours, actions, conversa-
>   tions. Laughs.'

Carrie nodded to Graham, who stepped forward.

> 'And so, into the freedom of wind and sunshine
> We let you go
> Into the dance of the moon and planets
> We let you go
> Into the wind's breath and the hands of the stars
> We let you go
> And into the sadness and smiles of our memories
> We let you go
> Go safely, go with love in your heart, and may
>   you forever be at peace.
> I love you, sweetheart. I'll love you forever.
> Amen.'

'Amen,' the group repeated.

Carrie nodded at the choir, who started singing "Ave

Maria". Despite Claire not being particularly religious, she loved it as a piece of music.

'Well done,' Rory whispered, as he gathered her into his arms.

Carrie let out a sigh of relief: she'd done it, and she hadn't cried. Now, she could cry, and dissolve in his arms. Because it was safe to do that.

'I love you,' she whispered.

'I love you too. Always,' he murmured back, kissing the top of her head. He continued to hold her as they stood on the hill, listening to the choir.

I love you, Claire, she thought. *I always will.*

For once, there was no answer. But Carrie knew that her sister had heard her, and that she understood.

And, despite her sadness, she was also, finally, happy.

EPILOGUE

SIX MONTHS LATER

Carrie tugged nervously at her nurse's tunic, waiting for June to finish settling herself at the piano. The rest of the choir milled around her, taking their places at the end of the hospital reception area, gossiping and fidgeting with their outfits. Angus looked surprisingly smart in a tailored black suit and tartan tie, his long hair slicked back in a ponytail. Dotty looked as glamorous as ever with her silver hair arranged in a neat chignon, and wore a pink twinset and pearls. June, always stylish, today wore a billowing paisley gown in peacock colours with kimono-style sleeves and a heavy gold necklace which glowed beautifully against her dark brown skin.

Carrie felt drab, compared to everyone else, but she was the only one in the choir who actually worked at the hospital. The concert for the patients was just a part of Carrie's day today, but she had put on some red lipstick and brushed her hair so that she looked presentable. The week before she'd also finally made it to the only hairdresser's in the village and had her bob cut back in, and her deep red colour redone, so that she looked like herself again.

Before the rest of the choir had arrived, Carrie, Dr Dan and some of other nurses had moved the usual chairs from the end of the waiting area and turned them around, so that patients could sit and watch the concert. Many patients had been brought down in wheelchairs, and some of them sat attached to drips and breathing equipment with the nursing staff on hand, sometimes sitting next to a patient to help them if it was needed.

Rory sat in the first row, and she gave him a shy wave. He mouthed, 'You got this,' and grinned. Her heart fluttered just like it did every time she saw him. It had been six months since they'd started seeing each other and it had been the happiest six months of Carrie's life.

Not just because of Rory, however. Carrie had started her nursing degree three months before, and Dr Dan had managed to arrange it so that she could do her first placement training at St Bernadette's. She had tons to study, and she was exhausted from being on her feet all day when she was at work, but she was absolutely loving it too.

For the first time, Carrie felt as though she had a purpose. She was needed, and she could help people. She had helped so many patients already, from helping them put on their slippers to taking them to the toilet when they needed an arm; to monitoring their heart rate and watching the other nurses, who taught her how to put in cannulas, check blood pressure and a million other tasks.

She had stopped working at the restaurant with Rory, and he had found another kitchen assistant – Tom, a twenty-year-old young man who was going to catering college and was determined that he was going to have his own restaurant by the time he was twenty-five. Rory said Tom was a handful, but he was enjoying the challenge of having someone to train who was passionate about food.

Graham sat next to Rory. They'd actually become friends, the three of them, in the last couple of months. Graham had come up to Loch Cameron a few times and had dinner with them both, and Graham and Rory had got on very well. They'd also all gone up to the little chapel where Claire's memorial stone was laid and taken flowers a few times since her service, with Carrie and Graham exchanging stories about Claire, making Rory laugh with her witticisms.

June played the opening chords of 'Alone'. As the first bars of the song started, and Carrie lifted her voice with that of the others in the first verse, she felt her heart lift, and her whole body fill with happiness as if it was filled with bubbles. Finally, her cup was full, just like June had said it would be, and she had stepped out of the grief and darkness that she had been mired in when she'd arrived in Loch Cameron.

She had also started seeing a therapist at the hospital. It was early days, but she had stopped hearing Claire's voice in her head as often. In a way, she missed it. She knew it had been her brain's way of trying to keep a link to her sister, the person she had loved so much. The person she would always love. And that was okay. It was okay to want to hang on to loved ones when we lost them.

What would Claire say, if she was here? Carrie wondered. What would she think of Carrie becoming a nurse, or of Rory? She knew the answer. Claire would be proud of her. Carrie imagined her sitting in the back row of the chairs, smiling. She could almost see her now.

As she broke into the dramatic chorus of 'Alone', Carrie remembered the song that had been on the radio when the crash happened. She hadn't been able to listen to it since that day; it was too triggering. But, just this morning, when she'd been getting ready for work, the song had come on the radio. It was like a sign, or a message of some kind.

And when you need me in the dead of night, I'm just a minute away... ooh, ooh

Carrie had stood there, listening, all the way through. She

had cried, but it wasn't bad. She would probably always cry, listening to that song. But, at least now, she *could* listen to it.

Maybe it was a message from Claire. *When you need me, I'll be there.* Carrie liked the idea. She knew she would never not feel connected to Claire, even though Claire wasn't around anymore. Because she *was* around. She was part of Carrie's DNA. And she lived on in Carrie's memory, forever.

She was still emotional, when she thought about Claire, which was often. There wasn't a day that passed when she didn't think about her sister, and she hoped there never would be. She wanted to remember Claire.

But as she pushed her voice to reach the long, high notes of 'Alone', she poured all of her emotion into the song, and, again, she felt some of the loss leave her, as if she was setting it free. This was what singing could do for her. She would never forget Claire, but she could start to free some of the aching pain of loss that clung to her heart like mud.

For now, Carrie could concentrate on her new job, helping others, and her role with the choir. There were new songs to sing, and a new life to live. And that was okay. That was more than okay, in fact, because if Carrie had learnt anything from her time in Loch Cameron, it was that life continued, and life could change for the better.

She smiled as she sang, and the song filled the room.

A LETTER FROM KENNEDY

Hello,

Thanks so much for reading *The Diary from the Cottage by the Loch*. If you enjoyed it, I'd be delighted if you left a review – reviews are so important to get books noticed by new readers! If you did enjoy it, and want to keep up to date with all my latest releases, just sign up at the following link. Your email address will never be shared and you can unsubscribe at any time.

www.bookouture.com/kennedy-kerr

In this book, Carrie loses her sister in a freak accident; a tragic event that, sadly, happens to many people the world over. As ever with my books, I wanted to take a character from a life-changing event and give her a place of safety and refuge and an opportunity to heal. Loch Cameron is one of those places I think we all dream of sometimes: a place where we can breathe, and a place where we can hide if we want to – but also a place where the community is ready to envelop us in its arms when we're ready.

I did also indulge my unashamed love of power ballads and especially Bonnie Tyler in this book. Music is a great healer, and there is so much to be gained by listening to, singing along to and dancing to emotive songs like her big hits. Of course, whatever works for you, but I love a big chorus, an even bigger guitar solo and as much dry ice (in the video) as can be had without a threat to public health.

If you've lost someone close to you, I know how that goes, and I know we never stop missing those bright and beautiful loved ones. But we can remember them and love them still.

I love hearing from my readers – you can get in touch on my Facebook page, through Twitter, or through Instagram.

Much love to you all,

Kennedy

facebook.com/kennedykerrauthor

twitter.com/kennedykerr5

instagram.com/kennedykerrauthor

AUTHOR'S NOTE

I have fictionalised Rory being called back to provide some specialist training, with apologies to the navy for any incorrectness. My thanks goes to A, an ex-navy diver, who in real life did do all sorts of Boy's Own Adventures things, including defusing bombs underwater whilst in service. My thanks to him for explaining what his job entailed and giving me "providing specialist training" as a reason that Rory could conceivably be required to go back into active service after having retired from the navy.

I am also indebted to David Green from the Department of Geography at King's College London who wrote a very interesting blog about postmistresses on the Postal Museum blog. He notes that, in contrast to postmen and sorters, many of whom had to retire early because of ill health, postmistresses often worked well into their sixties and seventies.

Eliza Adamson was reputed to have been the oldest postmistress in Britain when she died in May 1898, having served for fifty-eight years in the small fishing village of Auchmithie, on the east coast of Scotland. Eliza Adamson's age and length of service were noteworthy but not exceptional. Mrs Limond, who was born in 1815, was the subpostmistress of Minishant, a village in Ayrshire, for fifty-three years. She was described as: 'tall and erect, lithe and nimble, with memory and eyesight unimpaired, her handwriting, for legibility and steadiness, resembling that of a lady of nineteen rather than of ninety.'

When they retired, postmistresses and subpostmistresses

had worked on average for more than twenty-five years and, like Eliza Adamson and Mrs Limond, nearly one in six had performed the role for forty years or more. Many of the hundreds of postmistresses and sub-postmistresses employed in the Post Office could be found in small market towns and remote rural areas. They often inherited their role from their parents or took over from their husbands, but in many cases, were also appointed in their own right. Their longevity and their role which they, and often their families before them, had performed for many years meant they were familiar and highly respected figures in their communities.

Though David's article is more specifically about post-mistresses in Victorian Britain, I did use it to inform Great-Aunt Maud's diaries.

I have quoted a little from the Church of England funeral worship texts in Claire's remembrance service, as well as from a suggested memorial speech found at Roxanne Angelique's Ceremonies website. Roxanne is an Independent Civil Celebrant based in Essex in the UK. I loved her personalised approach to providing funeral ceremonies.

Printed in Great Britain
by Amazon